HIDDEN KNIGHTS

KNIGHTS OF THE REALM, BOOK 3

JENNIFER ANNE DAVIS

Published by Reign Publishing

Cover Design by KimG-Design
Editing by Cynthia Shepp

ISBN (paperback): 978-1-7344947-2-3
ISBN (ebook): 978-1-7323661-9-0

Library of Congress Control Number: 1-8530521571

OTHER BOOKS BY JENNIFER ANNE DAVIS

True Reign:

The Key

Red

War

Reign of Secrets:

Cage of Deceit

Cage of Darkness

Cage of Destiny

Oath of Deception

Oath of Destruction

The Order of the Krigers:

Rise

Burning Shadows

Conquering Fate

Knights of the Realm:

Realm of Knights

Shadow Knights

Hidden Knights

Single Titles:

The Voice

Kingdom Of Marsden

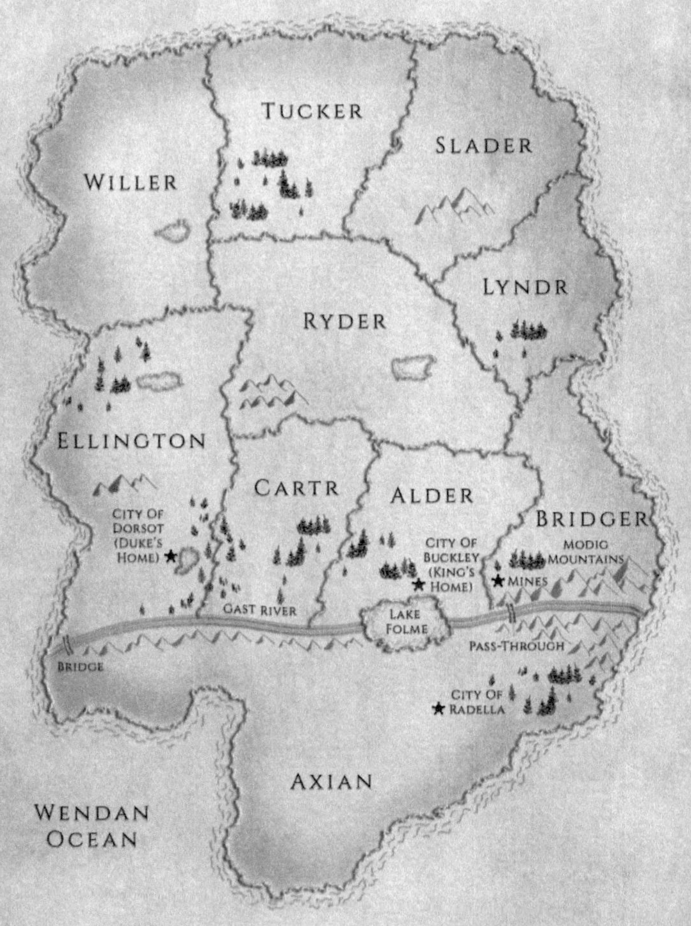

S tunned, Reid stood there, not sure what to say or do. Finn nudged her hand, trying to get her to pet his head again. However, she couldn't spare a thought for the dog because this woman—Anna—was her mother. Reid was certain of it.

"Why don't you come inside so we can discuss the matter?" Anna said.

Duke Ellington shifted his weight from foot to foot while watching his daughter, not bothering to offer any explanation. Had he known Anna—*Brianna*—was alive this entire time? Or was he just as stunned as Reid was? She had so many questions, but she didn't know where to start.

"Reid?" Duke Ellington said.

"Give her a moment," Anna whispered. "She appears to be in shock."

Reid did not want or need a minute to compose herself. And this woman had no right to presume to know what was best for Reid. Fury started to rise as a plethora of emotions warred with one another.

"Duke Ellington," Dexter said, his loud voice cutting through the quiet evening. "Would you be so kind as to show us to our rooms? It has been a long, trying two days. Once we've had a chance to settle in, we can talk."

The duke nodded before heading into the manor.

Colbert ordered a couple of stable hands to take the horses to the barn.

Finn barked and sprinted inside.

Dexter placed his large hand on Reid's back, ushering her up the steps and through the front door. They went straight to the staircase, then up to the second floor. Reid walked of her own accord, not even aware she was moving. Anger, happiness, fear, and more anger consumed her. How could her mother be alive?

"Ackley, you can have this room," Duke Ellington said. "And Gordon can take the room across from him." He turned to face Reid and Dexter. "Are you two married?"

Reid opened her mouth, planning to tell her father that the king's announcement of Henrick's death had interrupted the wedding ceremony. She still couldn't believe Eldon had tried to assassinate Ackley, blaming the Knights for Henrick's death. She rubbed her temples, a headache forming.

"Yes," Dexter said, surprising Reid. "We'll be staying in the same room."

Duke Ellington nodded, then opened another door. "You two are in here. You have one hour. Then I want to discuss what happened over supper."

Reid entered the room, not even sparing a glance at her father. After removing her heavy cape and tossing it on a chair in the corner, she observed the single bed, nightstand, two armoires, and wash basin. Everything had a subtle elegance to it.

The door clicked shut. Dexter unclasped his cape, folding it and setting it aside before stretching out on the bed. Stubble covered his usually impeccable chin.

Reid crawled onto the bed, sitting beside him. "Why did you tell my father we're married?" Duke Ellington would discover the truth soon enough.

His eyes intense, Dexter scrutinized her, making her stomach flutter. "I don't want you in a room alone right now." He reached out, taking hold of her hand. "We need to stick together. I'm not sure who we can trust."

Everything was a mess. Her own mother, the leader of the Knights, had been lying to Reid this entire time.

"You looked like you were about to attack Anna, so I got you out of there. Talk to me. What are you thinking?"

What was she thinking? Flopping onto her back so she could stare at the ceiling instead of the man beside her, she tried organizing her jumbled thoughts. Only, she couldn't. There were too many warring for attention. "My mother's not dead." Anna had been alive and well all these years. "I think my father knew." There wasn't any other conclusion—not since he'd gone to see the leader of the Knights, and he was here with Anna.

"Did Duke Ellington ever hint at or give any indication she might be alive?"

"No. Never." A tear slid from the corner of Reid's eye. Her mother had abandoned them. Why? To serve a cause? To lead the Knights? Was being a woman in northern Marsden so deplorable she'd had to leave her husband and five young daughters? Reid punched the bed. Anger and hurt mixed together, making her frustrated and confused.

"Maybe you need to talk to your parents," Dexter said.

"Allow them to explain before you draw your own conclusions." He rolled onto his side, facing her.

Reid felt him watching her. She kept her eyes focused on the ceiling, trying not to cry. It didn't work. The tears started falling. "I'm hurt." An ache bloomed in her chest.

"I'd be hurt, too." He reached out, wiping her tears away.

She rolled onto her side to face him, studying the man she'd feared only a few weeks ago.

His right hand cupped her left cheek. "Have you considered the possibility that Ackley first came to Ellington to seek you out for a specific reason?"

The room went unnaturally quiet. "What do you mean?"

"Maybe he didn't stumble upon you as you'd thought. Maybe your mother sent him to recruit you as a Knight." Dexter's hand slid over Reid's shoulder and down her arm, taking hold of her fingers.

She hadn't considered that.

"Reid." Dexter licked his lips, his eyes darkening as intensity shone through.

Her breath caught, and she leaned forward.

"I hardly think now's the time to be cuddling in bed," Ackley said as he sauntered into the room, not even bothering to knock.

Reid flew upright. "What are you doing in here?"

Gordon entered behind Ackley, shutting the door. "We need to talk." Gordon scanned the room, looking everywhere but at Reid.

Dexter sat up, propping himself against the headboard. "While I do agree we need to talk, I wanted a couple of minutes alone with Reid."

"Just a couple?" Ackley smirked as he leaned against the wash basin, folding his arms.

"Reid just discovered her mother is alive," Dexter stated. "I hardly think now is the time for snide comments. Wouldn't you agree, cousin?" He cocked his head, watching Ackley.

Ackley glanced between Dexter and Reid. "You know you're not married yet, don't you?"

"Shut it, Ackley," Gordon murmured. "We need to talk while we have the chance." He paced at the end of the bed. "We have to get the Melenia soldiers out of Marsden. Then I can set things right."

"What do you mean by that?" Reid asked, folding her legs under her.

Gordon stopped pacing, eyeing her.

"He thinks we can control Eldon," Ackley explained. "That we can convince Eldon to want the same things we do. Well, in case you haven't realized it yet Gordon, we no longer hold any loyalty to our half-brother. After he killed our father, he went and killed his own."

Reid glanced at Dexter, who seemed to be handling the loss of his father remarkably well. It was probably too soon for him to have processed everything that had happened over the past forty-eight hours. She'd been so shocked by her mother being alive that she hadn't even asked Dexter how he was doing.

Someone knocked on the door. "Everyone in there?" Colbert said from the hallway.

Ackley opened the door. "We're plotting my brother's demise."

"As interesting as that sounds," Colbert replied, "supper is ready. I've been asked to escort everyone to the dining room." He peered inside, studying Reid. "Are you okay?"

She nodded. "I'm fine." Then to Dexter, she whispered, "Do you need a moment alone with your brother?" She wasn't sure if anyone had informed Colbert of his father's passing.

"I do need to talk to him," Dexter said. "But I'm famished. We'll talk after we eat." He stood, pulling Reid up with him.

When Reid stepped into the hallway, Finn jumped on her, knocking her against the wall. She laughed as he licked her chin.

"Don't let him jump on you," Colbert said before ordering Finn to heel.

"I don't mind." Reid straightened her tunic.

"I didn't ask you if you minded." Colbert shook his head. "I don't want him jumping on people."

Markis exited one of the rooms, joining them in the hallway. "Where's Gytha?"

"She's still at the palace," Dexter answered.

Markis rubbed the nape of his neck. "Who accompanied your group here?"

"No one," Dexter replied. "We're the only ones who made it out."

"I'm sure Gytha will be fine," Markis said as he made his way down the steps, everyone following him. "I'm going to do a perimeter run." He exited the manor.

Reid also worried about Nara. Thankfully, the princess was a fighter and could defend herself. However, with Henrick's death, Reid didn't know what state of mind Nara would be in.

The group made their way toward the dining room. At the threshold, Reid froze, unable to cross. She stepped to the side, leaning against the wall as Ackley, Gordon, and Colbert entered. Sucking in a deep breath, she blew it out, trying to calm her racing heart. Her parents were in there.

"Are you okay?" Dexter asked, his deep voice rumbling through her.

She nodded, unable to speak. What would she say to her mother? Where would she begin the conversation? *How are you alive?* And what about Reid's father? He was the one person she depended on and loved the most. How could he have lied to her for all these years?

Leaning down, Dexter slid his fingers around hers, clutching her hand. "You don't have to speak to your parents right now," he whispered. "Just go in there, eat, and listen to what they have to say. After supper, we'll figure this out." He pulled her away from the wall.

She untangled her hand from Dexter's. If Reid's father had lied to her and she knew him well, how could she trust this man whom she barely knew? What was to prevent Dexter from lying to her?

"If you'd rather head back to our bedchamber, go ahead. I'll bring your food up later." He took a step toward the dining room, waiting for her decision.

Everyone was in there, expecting Reid to walk through the door and join them for supper. If she hid in her room, she'd only be putting off the inevitable. At some point, she'd have to talk to them. Better to just get it over with. "No. I'll face my parents." She imagined invisible armor surrounding her. Later, when she was alone, she'd try to figure out how she felt about this.

"You've got bigger balls than I do," Dexter murmured. "I'm not sure I could do what you're about to."

She glared. "Now you tell me?"

He chuckled. "Let's go." Taking hold of Reid's hand, he tugged her into the dining room before coming to an abrupt halt. Reid bumped into him. "I was hoping you'd be here."

Reid peered around Dexter's massive shoulders to see who he was speaking to. She blinked, trying to banish the ghost of Prince Henrick, who stood next to Colbert, looking alive and well.

Dexter released Reid's hand, rushing straight to his father and hugging him. "I wasn't sure if you were faking your illness or not."

"Sorry, son." Henrick hugged him back. "I couldn't risk anyone knowing."

Fury built inside Reid. "Is no one dead who's supposed to be dead?" she snapped, sick of the lying and deceit.

"Why doesn't everyone take a seat?" Anna said.

Reid swallowed the ten nasty retorts hovering on the tip of her tongue. She needed to do as Dexter said and hear her parents out. Afterward, she could process everything and decide how to proceed. Rolling her shoulders back, she went over to an empty chair and sat. Ackley plopped on the chair next to her.

"Move," Dexter ordered.

Ackley chuckled. "There's a chair on her other side, cousin."

Dexter mumbled something unintelligible, then sat on the chair to Reid's left. Gordon sat on Dexter's other side, her grandparents at either end of the table. Anna, Duke Ellington, Colbert, and Henrick settled across from Reid. It felt like a lifetime since she'd been here. So much had changed.

"What about Mother?" Dexter asked, addressing his father.

Glad for the distraction, Reid surreptitiously observed Anna, who seemed oblivious to the tension radiating through the room as she carefully spooned potatoes on her plate. Her aloofness made Reid want to scream.

"Your mother and I never discussed it," Henrick answered. "I couldn't risk anyone overhearing that conversation. She believed I was poisoned until the day of your wedding when Seb dressed as a Melenia soldier and snuck a dead body into the palace. Once the body was in my bed, I managed to get out through the secret passageways. Your mother agreed to remain behind in order to maintain the ruse."

"Do I even want to know where the dead body came from?" Dexter asked, raising a single eyebrow.

"A farmer a few miles out died from a heart attack."

Reid scrutinized Dexter, trying to determine if he was upset with his father for leaving his mother behind. What if something happened to her?

Ackley handed Reid a bowl of potatoes. Taking it, she scooped a helping on her plate before pushing the bowl toward Dexter.

Dexter folded his arms, leaning back in his chair. "What's the plan?"

"There will be plenty of time to discuss it later," Anna said. "For now, let's enjoy supper."

Reid cocked her head. "Enjoy supper?" Was her mother delusional? "How are we supposed to *enjoy supper* when a foreign army is in Marsden, our people are in danger, and those we love and care for are stuck in the palace and we have no idea if they're all right?"

Dexter slid his hand onto Reid's thigh, squeezing it gently. "I agree with Reid," he said, surprising her. "We need to strategize. Everything else can wait."

"Very well," Anna said, setting her fork down. "I thought we'd have a nice meal, but if you wish to discuss what I have planned, we can do that."

Dexter bristled. It was Reid's turn to slide her hand onto his thigh, gripping it so he'd maintain his composure. When she felt the hard muscles in his leg and the heat radiating from his body, she flushed. They were in the middle of a crisis, and she was thinking about the muscles in Dexter's leg. Reid needed to get her priorities straight. Not only that, but her father sat across from her. She could feel him watching her. When she went to remove her hand, Dexter grabbed it, holding it in place.

"Before we get to your plan," Dexter said, addressing Anna, "please explain how you're alive."

"Agreed," Gordon said, not bothering to eat.

Anna glanced at Reid. "Delivering my fifth child was difficult. The midwife who came to help with the delivery thought I'd died since there was so much blood. After she left, I told Tatum I couldn't stay in Ellington any longer. I had to use the opportunity given to me—it was the perfect cover. Tatum agreed, so he announced my death. He had my body transported to Axian, where I was to be buried."

Anna's response lacked emotion, remorse, or reason. Dexter clenched Reid's hand. She remained quiet, not sure what to ask since her thoughts were jumbled.

"Once you returned to Axian, what did you do?" Dexter inquired.

Anna's focus zeroed in on Dexter. There was something about her eyes that made Reid squirm. It almost seemed as if malice or contempt filled them.

"Please," Reid said. "I'd like to know." And she wanted Anna's attention off Dexter.

Anna glanced at her parents, the duke and duchess of Axian, before answering. "The Axian family has been in charge of the Knights for generations. Normally, the eldest son inherited the dukedom while the second-born son took over the Knights. Since there was no way for me to inherit the title and land, I decided to take control of the Knights."

Shock rolled through Reid. Her mother had chosen running the Knights over raising her five children? Tears filled her eyes.

"Your mother wasn't happy with us," Duke Ellington

explained to Reid. "When she almost died, I realized I had to set her free. That's why I helped her get to Axian. After that, I had no contact with her. All these years, I hoped she was alive and well. I assumed she was running the Knights, but I never knew for sure."

Reid didn't want to hear another word from either of her parents right now. She was about to stand when Ackley reached across her to grab a bowl of vegetables.

"Stay," he whispered. "I know you're upset, but we have more important things to deal with right now." He spooned a serving of green beans onto his plate.

Of course he was right. Reid couldn't let her family drama distract her from saving the kingdom.

"You abandoned your five daughters," Dexter said. Laced with fury, his deep voice cut across the room.

"For a greater cause," Anna replied, as if it should be obvious. "The Knights were in need of a leader."

"Who was in charge of it before you?" Reid inquired. "Grandfather's brother?" She realized Duke Gregor had to have a brother since she'd met Victor, her second cousin. Where was he now? What had happened to him?

"As fun as this family reunion is," Ackley drawled, "we have more pressing matters to discuss." He tapped his finger on the table, impatient as always.

"I agree," Anna replied. "We need to focus on what's important."

How could this heartless woman be Reid's mother? She'd always assumed a mother was nurturing, kind, and protected her children. Anna didn't seem to possess any of those traits.

"A group of Marsden soldiers will travel to the palace," Anna stated. "Once they arrive, they will attack the Melenia soldiers, causing the chaos we need."

"Chaos for what?" Colbert asked.

"For the Knights to kill the king."

Ackley pursed his lips. "And once the king is eliminated?"

"Now that Prince Henrick is dead," Anna stated, "Dexter and Reid will rule."

Reid rubbed her throbbing head, wondering why no one was arguing with Anna's asinine plan. They couldn't sacrifice soldiers to create a distraction in order to murder the king. This was madness.

"You're assuming the Marsden soldiers will kill enough of the Melenia soldiers that they won't be a threat any longer, I take it?" Colbert asked.

"Yes."

They couldn't possibly be considering Anna's plan, could they? Reid had thought Ackley, Gordon, Colbert, and Dexter were smarter than that.

The queen's warning came back to her—in order to circumvent someone's plans, Reid had to know what his or her end goal was. Anna's appeared to be killing the king, which was what Reid hoped to accomplish as well. So what was she missing? Something didn't feel right.

"Gordon will return to the City of Buckley, where the majority of his soldiers are stationed." Anna folded her hands, leaning her elbows on the table as she continued to explain. "He will then lead them to the City of Radella."

Reid narrowed her eyes. Anna wanted Gordon to lead the fight, effectively ensuring his demise. Which happened to be rather convenient since Gordon was the only person who could contest the throne since Ackley's title had been stripped.

"Very well," Gordon replied. "I'll leave tomorrow." He stood, then exited the room.

"I hope you keep him on as the commander of your army,"

Henrick said to Dexter. "You'll need someone like him at the helm."

Reid glanced at Henrick. "You intend to remain dead?" Even after they finished this, he didn't want to return to his family?

"Yes." Henrick took a sip of his water. "I think it's time someone younger inherits the throne. Dexter is ready. He should be king."

While Reid agreed, there was one major problem—she didn't want to be queen. "Ackley, you have no objections to this plan? You're okay with Dexter inheriting the throne?"

"I'm on board on one condition."

"Which is?" Anna asked.

"I'm the one who kills Eldon."

CHAPTER TWO

"**W**hy must you always be so difficult?" Anna asked Ackley.

He simply smiled.

"You can be the one to kill Eldon so long as you don't hesitate because he's your brother. It needs to be a clean, quick kill."

"Consider it done." He shoved his chair back, extending his legs and crossing them at the ankles.

Dexter stood. "If you'll excuse us. It has been a long day." He held his hand out to Reid.

She slid her hand into his and rose. They headed for the door.

"Are you retiring for the night?" Ackley asked, his voice holding a hint of mischief. He laced his fingers behind his head, peering at them.

"We are." Dexter started walking faster.

"Well, now. If I remember correctly, you two aren't actually married." Ackley smiled at Reid.

"You told me you were," Duke Ellington huffed.

Reid froze at the doorway. "We were in the middle of the ceremony when Eldon announced Prince Henrick's death and the Melenia army stormed the palace."

"So you're not wed?" Anna asked.

"No," Reid answered.

"We can't move forward with our plans until you are," Anna stated, briefly glancing at the ceiling as she tried to mask her irritation. In that moment, she reminded Reid of Kamden.

"Tell me, Reid, do you still want to marry my son?" Henrick inquired.

"Why are you asking her this now?" Dexter demanded, his hand tightening around Reid's. "We've already discussed why we should marry. You and I have already agreed. There is no need to rehash it."

Shaking his head, Henrick said, "That was before. Everything is different now since you will take up the mantle as king. It is a huge responsibility. Reid should have a choice. She needs to be a willing participant. Quite simply, I'm not convinced Reid wants to be queen."

She didn't want to be queen. The mere thought overwhelmed her. She had no idea what her responsibilities would be in such a position.

"We can train her," Anna insisted.

"I'm sorry," Dexter said, addressing Anna. "But if anyone is going to help Reid navigate her duties, it will be my mother, Princess Nara. You're dead. As such, you have no say in Reid's life." He looked at Reid. "I'm sorry if I've overstepped my place," he murmured so only she could hear.

"Thank you all for your concern," Reid said, addressing those present. "However, I intend to stand by Dexter's side. If that means I will be the queen of Marsden, then so be it." Turning, she glided out of the room, Dexter behind her.

She supposed she would have to get used to standing up for herself if she were to be queen. Thoughts of Harlow formed. What would happen to Harlow once Eldon was dead? The conversation Reid had with the queen still haunted her. Harlow had said not everyone supported the removal of the king. Did that include her?

When Dexter and Reid entered their bedchamber, Dexter started pacing.

"What's the matter?" she asked, pulling off her boots and tossing them on the floor.

"I can't stay in this manor." He tilted his head, cracking his neck. "Not with Anna here. I don't trust her."

Reid was about to respond—to say the feeling was mutual—when someone knocked on the door. Dexter opened it.

"Reid," Duke Ellington said, peering around Dexter. "I'll show you to your room."

Knowing she couldn't share a room with Dexter, she grabbed her boots and followed her father to the other end of the hallway.

After ushering her inside an empty bedchamber, Duke Ellington closed the door. He lit two candles. "We need to talk."

Tears threatened. "How could you lie to my sisters and me for all these years?" They all believed their mother was dead. Reid couldn't even count the number of nights she'd spent crying over her mother's death.

"There was no other way. I needed to oversee the county of Ellington, and Anna had to control the Knights."

The Knights did a stellar job moving undetected throughout the kingdom of Marsden. They even managed to sneak into Axian to train. Surely Anna could have found a way to visit her family on occasion. "Aren't you mad at her for abandoning us?"

"Raising five daughters alone hasn't been easy," Duke Ellington admitted. "But what other choice did I have?" He went over to the window, pulling the curtains shut.

"There were plenty of other options besides telling us Mother was dead." She shook her head.

"We've all made sacrifices to get here."

"What does that mean?" A cold chill slid over Reid's skin.

"Everything we've done has been to get us to this point—to get rid of the Winstons. This is finally our chance."

"The Winstons?" Reid asked. "Dexter is a Winston. When we marry, I will be a Winston, too."

He nodded absently. "I meant to make positive changes throughout Marsden, so things are fair and equal."

Suddenly, Reid wasn't so sure. She needed time alone to dissect everything that had happened.

"It's been a long day. Get some sleep. We'll talk more in the morning." He exited the room, closing the door behind him.

Although exhausted, Reid wasn't tired. Not bothering to change, she stretched out on the bed, staring at the ceiling. The events of the past few days inundated her—her almost wedding to Dexter, Eldon issuing the kill order on all the Knights, and the Melenia soldiers invading Marsden to do Eldon's bidding. She closed her eyes. Images of Gytha turning to face the oncoming soldiers so Reid could escape with Dexter, Ackley, and Gordon tormented her. At least Gytha was a formidable fighter capable of taking on two soldiers at once. Reid had to have faith the warrior woman had found her way out of the underground tunnels.

The thought of Nara stuck in the palace and grieving over Henrick still bothered Reid. Would the king feel threatened by her? Would he do anything to harm her? Or would he leave

Nara alone? And what about Gordon's wife, Dana? Was she in danger?

Reid sighed, thinking about the people in her life, starting with her mother. What did Anna hope to accomplish? Did she simply want to remove the king from power? Reid got the feeling that part of Anna's plan had always been for Reid to be queen. Did Anna hope to influence laws and policies through her daughter?

And what about Ackley and Gordon? Why were the two brothers going along with Anna's plan? Reid had spent enough time with them to know neither would approve of it. Gordon was the commander of the Marsden army. He didn't have to take orders from Anna. The mere idea of taking a contingent of men to attack and dispose of the Melenia soldiers didn't make sense. A large scale attack seemed like a better idea.

A queasy feeling overcame Reid. It could be something she ate or the events of the past few days. An unexplained desire to flee the manor assaulted her. Jumping off the bed, she hurried to the door. She reached for the handle. It wouldn't budge. Why had her father locked the door? Running her hands through her hair, she tried to think logically. Duke Ellington probably wanted to make sure Dexter didn't try to sneak into Reid's bedchamber at night. That had to be the reason. There was no need to panic. She closed her eyes, took a deep breath, and reopened them, trying to remain calm.

What if there was a fire? How would she get out? She jiggled the handle, trying to force the lock to pop open. When it didn't, she banged on the door.

"Reid?" Ackley said from out in the hallway.

"I'm in here. The door is locked."

"Hang on." There was a clicking sound, the handle moved,

and the door swung open. "Why didn't you pick the lock?" he asked as he slipped inside, closing the door behind him.

"I don't know how." She'd never learned.

"Lucky for you I was passing by."

"What's in the bag?" she asked. And why was he wearing black pants and a plain black shirt?

"I'm pretending to accompany Gordon to the City of Buckley."

"Where are you really going?"

He winked. "To Ellington. I intend to get my mother and Idina. I don't want them up there all alone while the king prepares for war."

"What about the Knights' plan to stop him?"

"It'll never work."

"Then why did you agree to go along with it?"

Ackley set his bag down, then leaned against the dresser. "I've known Anna for several years. I've learned not to argue with her. She always gets her way."

Reid sat on the end of the bed. "Your plan is to leave with Gordon tomorrow morning?"

He nodded.

"And you're going to my home?"

"I am."

"Then I'm going with you." She stood, intent on packing her belongings. It took a moment to realize she didn't have a single personal item with her.

"It's safer for you here."

"You shouldn't travel alone. Someone needs to watch your back. And...I can't stay in this manor." Not only did it feel like the walls were closing in on Reid, but she also wasn't ready to face her mother again. She needed some time and space to process. A trip home would do just that.

Ackley regarded her for a long minute. "Okay."

Relief filled Reid. She'd been afraid he'd argue against it.

"But seeing as how your father locked you in here, I'm not sure he's going to let you leave the manor."

She realized her mother wouldn't either—especially not alone with Ackley and Gordon. Not only that, but Dexter would be furious if she ran off without discussing it with him. She'd been in such a hurry to leave that she hadn't stopped to consider his feelings. "I can't go without talking to Dexter."

Ackley smirked. "You need to ask your fiancé's permission to leave with me?"

"No." Reid sighed. "I can't leave without telling him where I'm going and what I'm doing." She didn't need to ask him if she could go.

Dexter stepped into the room. "What's going on?" he demanded, glancing between Ackley and Reid.

Colbert, Markis, and Gordon also filed in.

"I was just about to come find you," Reid said.

Dexter closed the door before turning to face her. "You were? Because the last time you left, you ran off without telling me."

"That was different."

"How?" He took a step closer.

"That was…before." Before they were friends. Before she felt a connection to him.

"What's going on?" Colbert asked.

"I'm going north to retrieve my mother and sister before Eldon sends someone after them," Ackley said. "Reid can't stand being here, so she's coming with me."

"North where?" Dexter asked.

"To Ellington," Reid replied. "While we're there, I want to

organize my father's soldiers. Anna's plan is never going to work."

"That's an excellent idea," Dexter said. "I'll accompany you."

Ackley tilted his head back, mumbling something at the ceiling. "Fine. But we travel fast and light. I'm worried about Idina."

"While Gordon has a reason to leave, I'm not sure Anna is going to let anyone else go," Colbert pointed out. "She seems to think she's in charge and calling the shots."

"I'll figure something out," Ackley said. "Just go along with whatever I say at breakfast tomorrow."

"I want Colbert to remain here," Dexter said. "That way, he can keep tabs on Anna. And if something ends up happening to me, there will still be a living heir."

Everyone agreed.

"I'm going to bed," Ackley said, pushing off the dresser and retrieving his bag. "We have a long week ahead of us. I suggest everyone else return to their bedchambers to pack for the journey."

Everyone exited Reid's room. When Dexter turned to close the door, he paused. "What's the matter?"

"My father locked me in here." She wasn't sure she could handle being in there all night, knowing someone could lock her in again.

"Yet, Ackley still managed to find a way in."

Reid shrugged, not wanting to talk about Ackley.

Dexter sighed. "Would you like me to stay with you?"

What did he mean by that?

"I'll take the floor," he clarified.

Reid didn't want to seem like a child, afraid of sleeping alone. However, the thought of him there subdued the uneasiness she felt. Unable to verbally admit how much she needed a companion, Reid simply nodded.

Dexter stepped back into the room, shutting the door behind him. "Is it okay if I lock it from the inside so no one can get in? I'll sleep better that way."

She hated the idea of the door being locked at all. However, she understood his concern. "What if someone locks it from the outside again?"

"Either I'll pick the lock or knock the door down."

Smiling, Reid crawled under the covers, leaving her clothes on.

After snuffing out the candles, Dexter situated himself on the floor.

Since the bedchamber didn't have a fireplace, the room's temperature wasn't all that comfortable. "Dexter?" Reid whispered.

"Yeah?"

"Ummm..." She wasn't sure how to say what she wanted to. "It *is* rather cold."

"Yes, it is." The floor creaked as Dexter tried to get comfortable.

Instead of tossing him a blanket, Reid scooted over. "Will you join me? I could use your body heat." And she needed his strong presence beside her. The room was so dark she couldn't even see her own hand in front of her face. And, if she were being completely honest, she wanted Dexter next to her.

"I'm not sure that's a smart idea with your parents in the manor." His voice sounded husky.

"I don't care."

The floor creaked again. There was a rustling sound. "Are you sure?"

"Yes."

The bed dipped as Dexter climbed on it, sprawling next to her.

Reid rolled onto her side to face him, although she couldn't see him in the darkness. "Are you on top of the covers?"

"I am." He swallowed.

"You don't want to get under them?"

He was quiet for a minute before answering. "It's not that I don't *want* to..."

"I'm fully clothed." It wasn't like she was wearing a thin nightdress. She even had on socks. "It's freezing, and it's only going to get colder."

"If I get under these blankets, I can't guarantee I'll keep my hands to myself."

The thought of him wanting her—of him even thinking about her that way—made Reid's heart race. "The whole point of you being in bed with me is for us to stay warm. We've slept side by side before." And they *were* getting married. What was the harm in sleeping in the same bed?

Dexter slid under the covers. His hand slowly inched over Reid's torso, pulling her toward him. The last time she'd laid with him, she'd been facing away from him. Face to face was entirely different. She could feel his breath on her lips. It felt too intimate.

"This is definitely much warmer," he murmured. "And more comfortable."

She couldn't form a coherent response, so she nodded. Which, of course, he couldn't see.

"Are you okay?" he asked.

No, she was not okay. Her heart was beating too fast, her breathing too rapid, and now she was too hot. "Umm..."

"I don't want to make you uncomfortable," he whispered, sending a shiver down her spine.

"I'm going to face the other direction." So she wouldn't be tempted to do something stupid—like kiss him. She rolled over. His arm remained draped over her hip, his hand now on her stomach.

"Goodnight, Reid." He kissed the back of her head. "Sweet dreams."

Closing her eyes, she listened to Dexter's breathing as it evened out. Before she knew it, she fell into a deep sleep.

Peeling her eyelids open, Reid blinked at the sunlight streaming in through the window.

Dexter laid on his side with his head propped on his hand. "Sorry. I didn't mean to wake you."

She rubbed her eyes, then stretched.

Dexter raised his eyebrows. "I think I could get used to this."

"What?" she asked, sitting up.

Shaking his head, he slid out of bed. "Let's go eat breakfast so we can leave."

Reid liked the sound of that. After getting out of bed, she pulled on her boots while Dexter opened the door. Anna stood there with her arms crossed, her face expressionless.

"Morning," Dexter said, blocking the doorway. "Is there something you need?"

"I want a moment alone with Reid."

"Don't we all?" Dexter murmured. "We were just heading downstairs for breakfast."

"Excellent. You go to the dining room. I will escort Reid there in a few minutes."

"Give me a moment." He stepped back, closing the door in Anna's face. "Do you want to talk to her?"

Reid wasn't prepared to have any sort of in-depth conversation with her mother. Too much anger and hurt filled her to be able to speak calmly.

Dexter came over to Reid, placing his large hands on her shoulders. "How about she comes in here to talk to you while I remain outside in the hallway? If you need me, all you have to do is raise your voice and I'll come in."

While Reid appreciated the gesture, she didn't want to rely on others. "You can go to breakfast. I'll be along shortly."

Instead of questioning her or arguing, Dexter simply inclined his head and exited the room, leaving the door open.

Not wanting to talk to Anna inside the bedchamber, Reid stepped into the hallway. "You wanted to see me?" At least out here, Reid had an escape route.

"When we spoke at the Knights' headquarters, we discussed your relationship with Prince Dexter."

"We did?" Reid felt a swell of uneasiness.

Anna stepped closer. "I told you not to get involved with him."

"No. You told me to gain his trust so I could figure out what he was doing at night." As soon as the words were out, Reid realized she'd made an error. While she *had* discovered Dexter was meeting with a group of revolutionaries, she hadn't informed the Knights about it.

"And?" Anna asked. "What have you learned?"

"Nothing that will help our cause." Reid laced her hands together, trying to appear calm and in control.

"What, exactly, is our cause?" Anna moved even closer, until their toes almost touched.

Reid often wondered that very same thing. "I thought the Knights were protectors of the Marsden people."

"We are. Which is why I'm telling you not to get emotional on me."

"What's that supposed to mean?"

"It means that while I need you to marry Dexter, I don't want you to fall in love with him."

How could Reid's mother be so cold?

"Don't look at me like that," Anna snapped. "This is business. We can't let our feelings get in the way. If you allow Dexter to ensnare you, it will be your demise. Don't be so weak as to let a man lead you astray. Stay firm to your beliefs. If you play this right, you will be ruling over Dexter instead of him over you. Then, when you establish your reign, we can eliminate him. As the queen of Marsden, you will not need a man by your side." Her mother's eyes flashed with triumph.

Reid recalled the conversation she'd had with Dexter a few weeks ago. He'd said he didn't want to fall in love because he didn't want another person to have control over him. While Reid might not have experienced love before, she knew enough to understand that ruling over or controlling another person wasn't what it entailed. She had too much respect for Dexter to manipulate him. He was his own person, and she would not impose herself upon him.

As far as eliminating him? She couldn't believe her mother had concocted this entire plan to put Reid on the throne. She didn't know anything about this woman—nor did she want to. "Maybe it was a blessing you left us when I was only a baby. I'm not sure you are qualified to raise children." With that, she hurried away from Anna, striding along the hallway to the staircase. She practically fell down the steps in her haste to escape.

At the bottom, a strong hand wrapped around her wrist, yanking her into an empty room. The person pulled her against his body, a hand covering her mouth.

"It's me," Ackley whispered. "Don't say anything. I'll explain more later. When we meet in the dining room, don't reveal our destination is Ellington. If anyone asks, we are going to the City of Buckley. Idina and Leigh are there. Understand?"

Reid nodded.

Ackley pushed her back into the hallway. Alone again, she wondered what that had been about. Were Idina and Leigh in danger from the Knights? Reid made her way to the dining room. She hadn't even had breakfast, yet the day was already off to a terrible start.

Entering the dining room, she found her grandparents, Constance and Gregor, speaking quietly with one another. "Good morning." She took a seat.

Conversation immediately ceased.

Constance fiddled with her spoon. "I want to apologize," she said to Reid. "I'm sorry we lied about your mother. That we didn't tell you she was alive."

Reid forced a smile. "I understand why you did it." After all, they'd only just met her. Plus, Dexter had been with her. Perhaps if she'd been alone, they would have told her the truth.

Constance stood, running her hands down the front of her dress. "I was just about to take your grandfather out to the lake for a bit. He likes to watch the ducks. Would you care to join us?"

Didn't they know their kingdom was on the verge of war? How could they be so calm? "Thank you for the invite. However, after I eat, I have some things to take care of."

"If you change your mind," Gregor said, "you know where we'll be."

Constance came up behind him, using the handles on the back of his chair to maneuver him out from under the table. The wheels on the chair appeared large enough to traverse over the gravel path outside. However, Reid wondered if he could get upstairs. Gregor's bedchamber must be on the first floor. Constance rolled him out of the dining room.

Reid surveyed the offered fare, taking a bowl of oatmeal. Colbert, Dexter, Ackley, Gordon, and Markis entered the room. They sat around the table, but no one talked as they grabbed fruit and bread off the platters. A moment later, Tatum entered, followed by Anna. Just being in the same room as her mother put Reid on edge. She didn't trust the woman.

Gordon cleared his throat, gaining everyone's attention. "After breakfast, I'm leaving."

"I don't want my brother traveling alone," Ackley said. "I'm going with him."

Anna put her slice of toast down, observing Ackley. "I thought you wanted to be the one to kill Eldon?"

"I do. When Gordon and his soldiers are close enough to the City of Radella, I'll check in with you. I can infiltrate the palace then."

"In order to guarantee our success," Anna said, "other men will be in place as well."

"I think that's a wise plan," Ackley replied.

"I don't think it's safe for Reid or myself to remain here," Dexter said. "Eldon will be searching for us. It seems logical he would have his men check Reid's grandparents' manor."

"I agree," Anna said. "I want Reid to come with me. I will see to her safety."

Reid wondered if her mother intended to return to the Knights' headquarters. "What of Grandfather and Grandmother?" she asked. Would they be safe from Eldon?

"They will remain here," Anna replied. "It would look suspicious if they weren't home where they belong."

"Father, where do you plan to go?" Reid asked. Did he intend to remain in Axian or return to Ellington?

"I am staying with your mother."

Anna stiffened. "I have no need for you here. You may go home."

"My home is where you are," he replied. "Now that everything is changing, you don't have to pretend to be dead any longer." Hope shone in his eyes.

Anna had her hair pulled back into a braid, not a single strand out of place. Her crisp tunic had no wrinkles in sight. "I have work to do here. I intend to have my family's land, title, and rights restored. My daughter will sit on the throne. I am in charge of the Knights."

"Ackley can take over the Knights," Duke Ellington suggested.

At that, Anna raised her brows. "Ackley?"

Duke Ellington nodded. "He is more than capable."

Ackley leaned back in his chair, watching Reid's parents argue.

"The Winston family has taken enough from me. I am in charge of the Knights. That will not change." For the first time since Reid had met Anna, the woman's voice shook slightly, as if filled with intense fury.

"Brianna, be reasonable," Tatum said.

Anna twisted to face him. "I am not the Brianna from eighteen years ago. That girl is dead. I am a grown woman, and you are not my keeper."

Duke Ellington's brows drew together in confusion. "Don't you want to be a part of your family now that you can? You have five beautiful daughters."

"I am no longer your wife," she hissed. "It is time for you to go." She stood, then stalked from the room.

Ackley whistled. "She never ceases to amaze me."

Ignoring that snide comment, Reid focused on her father. "Are you all right?"

Absently, Duke Ellington nodded, his eyes vacant.

"Dexter and I will escort you home. Then we can join the others at the City of Buckley."

"Yes," the duke replied. "I think it is time for me to go home." The lines around his eyes deepened.

Reid had the urge to punch her mother for treating her father so rudely. However, Anna's behavior didn't surprise her. Anna was obviously an independent woman who had no desire to be tied to another person—not a husband and certainly not her daughters.

"I'll take Colbert to another location," Markis said. "I have a few ideas of safe places we can go."

Reid rubbed her forehead. "And what of Princess Nara and Captain Gytha? Do we assume they're all right? Or do we send someone to help them?"

The corners of Dexter's lips rose. "We assume they're fine."

Henrick entered the room, carrying a bag.

"Are you going somewhere?" Colbert asked.

"I can't stay here." He patted Dexter on the back. "I also don't think it's wise for me to travel with either of my sons."

"Where do you plan to go?" Reid asked.

"There's a place for me," he said. "But since I'm dead, no one can know where."

"What about Nara?" she asked.

"We've already said our goodbyes."

Why were so many people disappointing Reid today? How

could Henrick walk away from his wife? His marriage? His kids?

Abruptly, Dexter stood and hugged his father, bidding him farewell. Colbert did the same. Neither tried to convince Henrick to stay.

CHAPTER THREE

They set out after breakfast. Ackley and Gordon rode in front, Duke Ellington in the middle, and Reid and Dexter brought up the rear. Dexter insisted they stay off the main roads in case Eldon had soldiers searching for them.

They traveled all day, barely speaking. Nervous and on edge, Reid kept scanning the nearby areas, on the lookout for threats—or a wagon with a broken wheel, like the assassins had used the last time to try to lure Reid and Dexter in. When it became too dark to safely navigate, they stopped. Since Dexter didn't want to risk a fire, they ate the bread and cheese they'd brought with them. Afterward, they stretched out on the hard ground and slept.

Ackley woke them before the sun crested the horizon. After another day of traversing over rolling green hills, they stopped just before suppertime.

"You don't want to ride for a few more hours?" Reid asked.

"There's a town up ahead," Dexter explained as he dismounted. "If we skirt around it, it'll take us an extra day to reach the Gast River." He wiped his brow on his sleeve. "I'll go ahead and scout the town to see if there are any Melenia or Marsden soldiers. I can't imagine there are, but I want to be sure."

"I'll go with you," Ackley said.

Dexter nodded. "Gordon, you remain here with the duke and Reid. We'll be back in two hours."

Reid dismounted, watching Ackley and Dexter walk in the direction of the town. Taking hers and Dexter's horses, she led them over to the stream so they could drink. After feeding and rubbing them down, Reid sat, leaning against a tree.

Gordon announced he wanted to scout out the area to be sure no one was nearby. After he left, Duke Ellington sat across from his daughter.

"It's pretty here," he said.

They'd stopped in a valley. A stream cut through it with tall maple trees on either side. Clouds filled the sky, hinting at rain.

"Can I ask you something?"

Duke Ellington nodded.

Reid picked up a stick, twirling it between her fingers. "Did you know Anna was in charge of the Knights?"

He sighed. "Before agreeing to send her to Axian, I made her tell me why she wanted to go. She told me about the organization, and explained how her father needed her."

"A few weeks back, when you went to see if she'd help us, how'd you know where to find her?"

"I didn't. Shortly after I arrived in Axian for your wedding, I visited Gregor and Constance. I told them I wanted to see Brianna. After I explained how there were rumors of a foreign army in Marsden, I said it was imperative I speak with her. I told them I'd return to the manor in a couple of weeks, which is what I did."

"You don't know where the Knights' headquarters is located?" Reid tossed the stick on the ground, then wiped her hands on her pants.

"No." The wind ruffled his gray hair.

Now for the question Reid had been pondering over since she'd left the manor. "Why do you think Anna doesn't want a relationship with us?" And how could she have treated them so coldly?

"I wish I could answer that for you. However, I fear I must admit to not knowing or understanding your mother as well as I thought I did." He stood and faced the stream, his back to Reid. His fingers curled in, making two fists. "I take it back—that woman isn't your mother. She may have given birth to you, but that's it."

Reid wholeheartedly agreed. "I'm sorry she was so rude." Considering Duke Ellington could expose Anna's secret to the kingdom, Reid thought the woman would have been nicer to him. Not only that, but didn't she feel *anything* for the man she'd had five children with?

"Because of her, I have never been with another woman." He slid his hands in his pockets, shoulders slumped.

Reid had forgotten the promise he'd made Anna on her deathbed—that he'd never remarry. Now, Reid realized he couldn't have. Not legally.

"I thought she'd finish running the Knights and come back to me one day. I stayed true to her all these years."

Sadness filled Reid. Her father had sacrificed companionship on the slim chance he'd be reunited with his first love—a woman who had never and would never return that love. And when they'd finally been reunited, it hadn't ended up as her father hoped it would. Anna had been cold, uncaring, and ambivalent to his feelings.

Boots crunched on dirt as Gordon emerged from the trees. "I didn't see anyone nearby," he said, sitting beside Reid. "You two okay?"

Reid nodded, lost in thought. There had to be a way to oust the Melenia army, dethrone Eldon, and crown Dexter king, all while ensuring minimal loss of life. And Reid needed to make sure Anna didn't double cross them. As much as Reid didn't want to admit it, she saw the way Anna had looked at Dexter and Colbert—as if they were filth beneath her feet. Reid didn't trust her mother for one second. She had a feeling once she was crowned queen, Anna would find a way to kill both Dexter and Colbert.

While Reid continued to ponder how to rid the kingdom of the Melenia soldiers and Eldon, Gordon spoke with Duke Ellington about the number of soldiers in Ellington, where they were stationed, and how to call them to arms quickly.

About an hour later, Dexter and Ackley returned.

"We didn't see any evidence of Melenia soldiers," Dexter announced.

"Although, there are a few Axian soldiers," Ackley said as he plopped on the ground.

"You don't think they'd report your whereabouts to the king, do you?" Reid asked.

"No, I don't." Dexter sat next to her. "They are loyal to me. It's safe for us to travel through the town, but I want to make sure we don't attract any attention. If the king sends someone here, I don't want any of the citizens to mention they saw us traveling north."

Reid nodded in understanding. She knew she'd have to pretend to be a man when they reached Ellington. It made no difference to her if she had to don the persona a little earlier than expected. If someone was on the lookout for three men and one woman, they wouldn't think twice when seeing their traveling party—especially since there were five of them.

"What about rallying your men?" Gordon asked Dexter. "How many do you have spread throughout the county?"

"In each of the major towns, I have fifty men stationed."

"Are the majority in the City of Radella?" Gordon rubbed his jaw.

"They are," Dexter replied. "And to answer your previous question, when Captain Gytha put the military compound on lockdown, a few things happened. Not only did we evacuate the city, but half my soldiers also left as well. They are supposed to meet at Camp Lival about five miles outside the city. The rest of my men are awaiting orders in the compound."

Hopefully, since the military compound resembled every other building in the city, Eldon would have no idea the soldiers were there.

"I've been meaning to ask," Duke Ellington said. "Your father mentioned a man named Seb. Was he referring to Sebastian Rutter?"

Dexter nodded. "The one and only."

"Do you know him?" Reid recalled Seb had only agreed to make the weapons for Dexter after he'd learned the prince was marrying her. Seb had also been the commander under King Broc.

"Funny you should ask," the duke said. "Seb's nephew is Becket."

Shock rolled through Reid. "Ainsley's husband?"

"Yes. Seb's sister, Sara, married a wealthy landholder who resided in Ellington before trade and travel ceased with Axian."

Reid couldn't believe her eldest sister was married to Seb's nephew. She whacked Dexter's arm. "Did you know?"

"I knew Seb's sister had moved to Ellington and married

well. During negotiations, I used your father's name to persuade Seb to work with me. But I had no idea how intimately he was connected to your family."

"As entertaining as this is," Ackley said, "I'd like to get through the town before dark, so we have time to set up camp." He jumped to his feet.

Reid clambered to hers, too. "I'm worried Anna is planning more than she told us." Reid went over to her horse, untying it from the tree.

"Oh, I'm certain she is," Ackley said as he tightened the girth straps on his horse. "That's why it's imperative I reach the City of Buckley to speak to the Knights in the army."

"Do you think they'll side with you over her? After all, Anna is their leader."

"I've been working with them for years. They'll listen to me."

Reid hoped he was right. She mounted her horse. "How'd you become a Knight?" Since Anna seemed to hate the Winston family, why had she recruited Ackley?

"That's a long story."

"I'd like to hear it."

"Tell you what—let's make it through town without incident. When we set up camp for the night, I will bestow my story upon you." He waved his hand in a grand flourish.

Reid laughed. "Deal."

As they rode through the stream, Gordon continued to scan the land. "Five riders traveling together will gain unwanted attention."

"I agree," Dexter replied. "That's why we're going to split up. I'll go with you and the duke. Ackley will stay with Reid."

"We'll head to the east end," Ackley said. "Once we cross through, we'll maintain a northerly course until we reunite."

"Excellent. We'll go to the west. I don't want anyone to know we're here. Be as discreet as possible."

Ackley nodded in acknowledgment.

The duke dropped back beside Reid. "Are you armed?"

She patted the daggers strapped to her arms and thighs, hidden underneath her clothing.

"Good. Stick close to Ackley and be careful."

"I will." While she didn't like the idea of separating, she understood the necessity of it.

"Lady Reid," Ackley drawled. "Follow me." He steered his horse to the right, veering off the path.

"Silly Ackley," she said as she joined him. "You should know I'd much prefer you following me."

Chuckling, he moved his horse over so she could ride alongside him.

Glancing over her shoulder, she watched as the others headed in the opposite direction.

"They'll be fine," Ackley assured her.

"I know."

At the top of the rise, the town came into view. It appeared roughly a mile or so away. Still riding side by side, Ackley started humming a tune Reid wasn't familiar with.

"Here you go." Ackley handed Reid a black hat.

She put it on, shoving her hair underneath it.

At the first set of buildings, the dirt road turned to cobblestone. Reid thought the City of Radella had been the only place afforded such luxury, but apparently not. Were all the cities and towns in Axian equally equipped? The structures they passed were two or three stories, made from bricks and stones—not the wooden buildings she was accustomed to back home. Only a few people milled about. The deeper Reid and Ackley traveled into the town, the more crowded the streets became. Most citizens seemed to be walking, even those with horses.

"Let's dismount," Ackley said, pulling his horse to a halt.

Reid climbed off her horse. "Should I put my cape on?" It would help hide the fact she was a woman.

"No. The hat will suffice." He scanned the area. "It's not like at home. People don't need to believe you're a man. We just don't want one of the king's men to realize it's you if spotted." He gestured to the side, so Reid headed that way.

In order to not attract unwanted attention, they meandered along the street, peering into various store windows. Ackley even smiled at a few people, as if he knew who they were. Almost everyone they encountered seemed to be from the merchant class. Their well-made clothes lacked the holes and patches Reid was used to seeing in northern Marsden.

The sweet smell of cakes baking wafted in the air. Reid breathed in deeply, then smiled. When she reached the bakery, she stopped to look in the window.

"Do you want to get something?" Ackley asked.

"No." Since the sun had already set, the sky was starting to darken. Seeing inside the bakery was good enough for her. A handful of tables dominated the left side. People sat around them, eating and talking. A counter covered with breads, cakes, and muffins stretched along the right side. Behind the counter, a woman took orders, exchanging the baked goods for money. Reid loved to see a woman working while people treated her with respect.

As she turned to leave, an eerie sensation prickled her skin. Remaining rooted in place, she tried to find the source of her unease. Ackley remained beside her, also staring through the window. Reid focused on the reflection in the glass. On the other side of the street, a man passed by for the second time.

There was something familiar about the way he carried himself.

"Well, I lost that bet." Ackley scoffed. "I could have sworn he was following Dexter, not you." He sighed. "Dexter is never going to let me hear the end of this."

"Is that Victor?" Reid hissed.

"It is. I assume Anna sent him to keep an eye on you. While I have nothing against the man, he's not someone I'd willingly spend time with."

"What are we going to do?"

"Nothing." He moved to the left, and Reid followed. "For now, at least."

Reid adjusted her grip on her horse's reins, trying to act casual as she strolled through the town with a Knight. "Should we say something to him?" Pretending she didn't know Victor was there was hard. Maybe it would be better to just acknowledge him.

"No. We'll allow him to follow us. Let him see us heading north, just like we told Anna we would." He smiled.

They finally exited the town. "What do you think he's going to do now?" Reid asked as she mounted her horse, stealthily peeking behind her as she did so. She didn't see Victor.

"Well," Ackley said, climbing on his horse. "I imagine he will follow from a distance. With the horses, it's not hard to track us."

When the cobblestones ended, the road returned to dirt. Reid kept glancing to the left, hoping to see Dexter, her father, and Gordon riding toward them. After about thirty minutes, three figures emerged. When they cut across the field directly toward them, relief filled her.

"You were right," Ackley said to Dexter when he neared. "It's Reid."

"Thought so," Dexter replied, steering his horse alongside her.

"I thought maybe Anna had sent Victor to murder you in your sleep." Ackley shrugged, acting as if discussing Dexter's death was no big deal.

Dexter glanced sidelong at Ackley. "As much as you'd enjoy that, Anna won't try to have me killed until her daughter is securely on the throne."

"Can we please stop talking about Dexter being assassinated?" Reid asked, exasperated.

"The issue will need to be dealt with," Duke Ellington chided her. "At some point, we will need to discuss it so we can come up with a plan to stop her."

The number of insurmountable tasks kept piling up. Trying not to let her thoughts overwhelm her, she focused on the scenery. On this side of the town, the land was flat. Field after field full of agriculture dotted the landscape. "Where are we making camp?" She didn't like the idea of being out in the open—especially with Victor following them.

"There's a cave up ahead," Dexter replied. "We'll stay in there. That way, we can have a fire tonight."

"In that case..." Ackley pulled his horse to the side. "I'm going hunting. I'll catch up with you in an hour or so." A wicked smile spread across his face.

"When you say hunting, you do mean animals, right?" Reid asked jokingly.

"I can't promise anything." With that, he nudged his horse and veered to the right.

Shaking his head with amusement, Dexter led the way between two plots of land.

"I'm not sure where Ackley plans to find animals to hunt,"

Gordon muttered. He was probably upset he didn't get to go with his brother.

"I want everyone to ride single file behind me," Dexter ordered. "There's a crevice up ahead. Since the sun has set, it's getting harder to see."

Everyone did as instructed. He led the way off the road, traveling slightly northwest.

"How are we going to cross this crevice?" Reid asked. The last time she'd traversed a great divide had been the Gast River. The bridge she and Harlan strode over had been so high up that she'd had to crawl on her hands and knees. She couldn't imagine doing something like that on a horse.

"We can take the road that zigzags down the side of it, make our way along the rocky bottom, and then go up a steep incline. The journey will take all day because we'll have to walk."

She didn't remember encountering this obstacle when she was here with Harlan last time. "Is there another way?"

Dexter peered over his shoulder, twisting his lips. "There is."

She wanted to smack him for making her panic like that.

Chuckling, he said, "The crevice only extends another mile east. Skirting around it will be faster, safer, and easier. However, we're going a little way down into the crevice tonight —to where the cave is located. That's why I'm in such a hurry to get there before it's too dark."

After another mile, the ground abruptly turned rocky. Dexter halted everyone. Looking past him, Reid saw a narrow crevice, only a quarter of a mile wide, cut into the ground. On the other side, the agricultural plots resumed. The fissure blended in so well with the ground she never would have spotted it had Dexter not pointed it out.

"There's a narrow path along here somewhere," Dexter mumbled as he dismounted. Walking parallel to the crevice, he peered over the side, searching for the path. After a hundred feet, he found it. "I'll go first. Lead your horse down slowly."

Reid had flashbacks of descending the mountain from the Knights' headquarters. It had been so steep her horse had slipped.

"Reid?" Duke Ellington said. "Are you okay?"

"I'm fine," she lied.

"Then why do you look so scared?" her father asked.

She narrowed her eyes, not wanting Dexter to think her weak. "I'm wondering if the cave is safe for us to stay in."

Dexter placed his hand on her shoulder, squeezing it. "The cave is perfectly safe. I promise." His eyes flashed with mischief and his lips twitched, as if he were on the verge of laughter. There was something he wasn't telling her.

"What?" she asked curiously, half afraid to know.

"You'll see. Let's go."

Carefully leading his horse, Dexter went first, followed by Duke Ellington.

"Your turn," Gordon said. "I'm waiting here for Ackley."

Rolling her shoulders, she approached the edge. The *path*, as Dexter had the nerve to call it, was simply an etched-out portion of the cliff. While the agricultural plots had been variations of green, the sides of the crevice were a deep red. Trees littered the bottom.

Taking a deep breath, she began the descent, guiding her horse behind her. Thankfully, the dirt path was sticky, making it easy to hike down. She kept a firm hold on the reins, wanting to make sure her horse didn't spook. After twenty feet, she came to what she assumed was the cave. It appeared as if someone had taken a spoon and carved a chunk out of the earth.

The ground was the same dark red dirt as the path, the sides a harder variation.

Dexter and Duke Ellington stood next to a wooden fence, which extended from one end to the other.

"There's hay for the horses in here," Dexter said, opening a gate in the fence.

Reid led her horse inside, where she quickly removed his saddle. "How'd the fence get here?" she asked when she rejoined Dexter.

"I've used this place enough times that I had the fence built," Dexter explained.

"Where are we going to sleep?" There didn't appear to be enough room for five people to lie down. And she didn't like being so close to the edge.

"Funny you should ask," Dexter muttered.

"No, there is nothing funny about that question," Reid said, folding her arms. "In fact, nothing good ever starts with *funny you should ask.*"

Duke Ellington chuckled. "I can tell you two are going to have a wonderful marriage."

Reid eyed her father, trying to determine what he meant. Was that a good or a bad thing?

"You know how you asked about being safe?" Dexter said, his voice suddenly placating.

Reid tapped her foot. She knew she wasn't going to like whatever it was he had to say.

"We're safe because there's another cave. It's...hidden." He waved the duke and Reid over to the side.

When Reid got closer, she could see a dark tunnel.

"It's through here." Dexter ducked inside.

"Go on," Duke Ellington said.

Reid stepped into the tunnel. The ground felt...squishy. Was the red clay damper here? After ten feet, the ground turned solid again. She found herself in a similarly situated cave, though this one didn't have a fence. In the middle, several rocks formed a circle filled with wood. Dexter knelt, fumbling with a couple of rocks and dry leaves. He seemed to be trying to get a fire started.

Reid and Duke Ellington sat near the mouth of the cave, staring at the crevice before them. The stars dotted the sky as night descended.

Once the fire finally took, Dexter sat beside Reid. After another twenty minutes, Ackley and Gordon joined them.

Dexter jumped to his feet. He went over to the tunnel, then pulled something toward him. It looked like several tree branches had been tied together, making a ten-foot-long plank. "It's a bridge," he explained. "You asked how this place is safe, and this is how. If anyone tries to get from the first cave into this one, he'll fall to his death."

Horrified, Reid stood. "You mean to tell me that I walked across those flimsy branches?"

Dexter placed the *bridge* against the side of the cave. "It's perfectly sturdy."

"Sturdy?" It had been squishy. She could have fallen to her death.

Ackley chuckled. "As entertaining as this is, I have three skinned rabbits I'd like to cook." He knelt by the fire, arranging the carcasses on a stick above the flames. "And, as promised, I have a story to tell."

CHAPTER FOUR

ckley sat next to the fire. "You asked me how I became a Knight."

"I did." Reid positioned herself beside him. Since Anna hated the Winstons and blamed them for her family's demise, Reid couldn't understand why her mother would have wanted Ackley to be a Knight.

Duke Ellington, Gordon, and Dexter also sat around the fire, no one saying a word.

Ackley stared into the flames, not looking at anyone as he delved into the past. "When I was eight years old, I loved to sneak around the castle. I'd eavesdrop on my father and his men during important meetings. I knew all the hiding places. That was about the time I noticed a woman who also appeared to be hiding in the shadows, listening in on conversations. I knew she didn't work at the castle, so I asked Mum about it. But Mum didn't know who the woman was." He twisted the stick the rabbits were hanging on, so they cooked evenly. "I decided to hide and wait for her. A few days later, I crouched behind a door. When she passed, I confronted her. I demanded to know who she was and what she was doing there. She smiled kindly, then said she could use someone with my unique skills. She told me she needed my help to protect the kingdom. Since I was only eight and didn't know any better, I said yes."

Reid swallowed, trying to process the information. Her mother, Anna, had been in northern Marsden, spying on the royal family? And she'd recruited Ackley to be a Knight when he was only eight?

"Over the next couple of years, I was Anna's eyes and ears in the castle. Every three to four months, we'd meet in the city. I'd give her a full report, mostly focusing on who was visiting and why." He turned the stick again. "One day, Anna asked about my father. She said something about my mother not being true to him, and she asked if Eldon was even my legitimate brother. It was all my twelve-year-old brain needed to start snooping into my family's past, searching for things that may or may not have been there. I had no idea Anna was manipulating me. It wasn't until I turned fifteen that I even thought to question her motives."

"Why then?" Reid asked, wondering what had changed.

"That's when I went to the Knights' headquarters to train. While there, I snooped." He smiled wryly. "I figured I should put the things Anna taught me into action. One night, I picked the lock to her desk. I found an old, worn letter addressed to my father. The writer expressed her love for him, along with her dissatisfaction with his upcoming wedding to a foreigner. It was signed by Anna. When I returned home, I discussed it with Idina. We both agreed Anna had to be using me for something—we just couldn't figure out what. Then Anna kept telling me things about Eldon...things that made me question what he was doing and why."

Ackley rubbed his face. "As the years went by, Anna managed to convince me that Eldon was a power-hungry, self-serving, conniving man. I even found evidence Eldon had killed our father. And I believed it all."

"What are you saying?" Reid whispered.

"Something just didn't add up." Ackley stared directly at her. "Did you know Hudson was poisoned the same way as Broc?"

Reid shook her head.

"All these years, I thought my father had killed my grandfather. Then I believed my brother had killed my father. But that's not the case. I think Anna killed them both."

Reid wasn't so sure about that. Henrick had explained how erratic Hudson was being before their father's death. "Maybe you're looking for something that isn't there?" she suggested.

He shook his head. "I don't know. I need to talk to Idina. She always sees and understands things quicker than I do."

Grease sizzled in the fire, and Ackley removed the cooked rabbits.

"Reid once said something about being a pawn," Dexter mumbled, his deep voice echoing in the space. He glanced up, meeting her eyes. "I fear we have all been pawns."

Gordon rubbed his face. "I think we should alter our plans. Instead of splitting up, we'll all go to Ellington. Once we've fetched Mum and Idina, we'll travel to the City of Buckley to get Ackley's fellow Knights and my soldiers. Then, we'll retake Marsden."

"I think that's a wise idea," Duke Ellington said.

Reid didn't think it would be that easy. Especially if Eldon wasn't the mastermind. If Anna had devised some elaborate plot, they'd have to deal with her. The problem was that Anna had years to perfect her plan.

Setting out early the next morning, the group rode fast in order to reach the Gast River as soon as possible. If they wanted to thwart the king's plans, they didn't have a lot of time.

"Do you think Victor is still tracking us?" Reid asked, glancing over her shoulder. There was nothing but flat fields for miles. If her second cousin were pursuing her, she should be able to see him.

"He won't be a problem," Ackley replied with a grin.

"What did you do?" she demanded.

"When I went hunting, I backtracked, found him, and slipped him something."

"Did you kill him?" Reid asked, horrified.

"No." He sighed. "I knew you wouldn't want me to. I simply gave him a sleeping tonic to ensure we could get far ahead of him before he woke."

"It's not hard to figure out where we're going," Dexter pointed out. "I'm sure he can catch up."

Reid eyed Ackley. He was acting far too confident. "What else did you do?"

He winked. "I may have given him a little something extra."

"What?" Reid and Dexter asked at the same time.

Ackley rolled his eyes. "Nothing that will harm him. Just something that'll throw off his vision for the next week or so."

Reid wondered if Ackley traveled with these tonics or if he'd managed to acquire them that quickly. She decided she was better off not knowing. "Remind me to never get on your bad side."

"Oh, my dear Reid, I only have a bad side." He smiled wickedly.

Two days later, the Gast River came into view. They'd been traveling west in order to cross the bridge directly into Ellington—it was the same one Reid and Harlan had used what seemed like a lifetime ago.

Once Duke Ellington, Ackley, and Gordon had each crossed the bridge, Reid steered her horse onto it.

"Are you good?" Dexter asked from behind her, still safely on solid ground.

"Yes." A mixture of trepidation and relief filled her. Uncertain of how much weight the bridge could hold, they'd decided to cross one person and horse at a time. As scared as she was to be on the wooden bridge with rushing water beneath it, the thought of being back in Ellington was enough to propel her onward.

The river below drowned out the creaking bridge. Her horse whinnied, so she murmured a few soothing words to him, hoping he heard her.

"Welcome home," Duke Ellington said when Reid joined him.

She breathed in the crisp air. As good as it felt to be in her homeland, it came at a price. Pulling her hat out of the saddlebag, she put it on, concealing her hair. Now was not the time to attract unwanted attention by gallivanting around Ellington as a woman. While here, she needed to blend in. Once Eldon and the Melenia army were dealt with, she could work on turning Marsden into the kingdom she wished it to be.

With little fanfare, they made their way north. Each mile they traversed, the landscape dulled, the green rolling hills turning brown. The towns and homes they passed were all wooden structures in dire need of repair. The farms were scarce. In many places, the land was rocky and barren. The air turned cool.

Even though Dexter didn't comment on the scenery, Reid felt him stiffen when they passed a home with a lopsided roof, its doors hanging off their hinges, and children running around with holes in their clothes. She wanted to assure him it wasn't her father's fault—that he was doing his best. It was the infertile land, the harsh weather, the heavy taxes, and the restrictive laws.

"How about we go into the next town?" Ackley suggested.

"We're only a day away from my castle," Duke Ellington said. "There's no need to stop." They had enough food and water.

"I want to hear what people are saying," Ackley explained. "Has word reached them that a foreign army is here? Do people have any idea things are amiss?"

While Reid thought it was a good idea, they could glean that information from the town closest to her home.

"Ackley's right," Dexter said.

Reid narrowed her eyes. Dexter was agreeing with Ackley? That was a first.

"If we wait until we reach the City of Dorsot," Dexter said, "people will already know we're there. They might be more reserved with their tongues." He nudged his horse, riding alongside Ackley, both speaking in hushed whispers.

Gordon positioned his horse next to Reid. "If you don't want to go into town," he murmured, "I can wait on the outskirts with you."

"Why do you think I don't want to go?"

He shrugged. "In town, you will have to play a role you

thought you'd no longer have to. Axian was your freedom. This is your cage. I can see it on your face."

Her cheeks warmed at his astute observation—he'd always been good at reading her. However, he was only partially right. Her hesitation also stemmed from Dexter. She didn't want him to see how uneducated her people were, the rampant poverty, or the poor living conditions. Most of all, she didn't want him to see her bend to society's laws.

Facing Gordon, she forced a smile. "This cage is one of your father's making. One whose bars I intend to break."

Gordon snorted. "Normally, I'd argue with you, but I won't. You've accomplished more than I thought possible. If you say you're going to change things, I believe you will."

He tended to side with the old ways, believing a woman's place was beneath a man's—in more ways than one. "I know you weren't in Axian long, but you must admit it is a beautiful county. Women work, own property, and are treated equally. It's prosperous—and everything I want northern Marsden to be."

He scratched the back of his head. "I guess."

"You guess?" she said a little louder than necessary.

Dexter glanced over his shoulder, eyebrows raised.

Reid shook her head, indicating everything was fine. As Dexter turned around, he paused, then looked at Gordon. Brow creased, he turned his lips downward before facing forward again. Reid wondered what had caught his attention.

The road turned to the right, then the town came into view. Nestled next to the forest, the buildings were mostly two-story structures, some leaning precariously to the side.

After tying their horses up, they headed into the first tavern they came across.

Dexter wiped his brow. "Is this one of your smaller towns?"

As Reid's eyes adjusted to the darkness inside, she headed to a table in the center of the room, hoping they'd be able to hear more conversation from that location. Taking a seat, she cleared her throat and lowered her voice. "No. This is one of our larger ones."

"Why aren't the streets paved? Why aren't there any stone buildings?"

The notion of a town not having those luxuries seemed like a foreign concept to Dexter. Reid tried her hardest not to smile at his naïveté. "We don't have those amenities here."

When the bartender came over, Gordon ordered a round of drinks.

The man wiped his hands on his apron, eyeing Reid. "Where'd you say you're from?"

"We didn't," Reid replied, her voice not as deep as it should have been. Not using her male voice for so many weeks had gotten her out of practice.

The man opened his mouth to argue when Ackley slapped his shoulder. "Don't mind my brother. He can be a pain in the arse. We're hoping he finally gets some hair on that dainty chest of his. I'm tired of watching out for him all the time."

The bartender nodded. "I have a younger brother. He's a pain. Make sure you don't let him drink too much." With that, he turned and lumbered away.

Dexter scanned the room. "Women are honestly not allowed to be in here?" It sounded like the mere thought was ludicrous to him.

"A woman is only allowed out in public with the proper protection—meaning a man at her side." Ackley leaned back in his chair, smiling at the absurdity of it.

"If Reid is allowed to be here so long as she's with us, then why the disguise?" Dexter whispered.

"Because even though it's allowed, it is frowned upon. Women should be home tending to the children, not at a tavern drinking." Ackley winked.

"And women aren't allowed to wear pants," Gordon reminded him. "It's against the law."

The bartender returned, passing each a mug filled to the brim.

Dexter took a drink. When he set his mug down, he studied Reid. "You are starting to make more sense to me."

Ackley laughed. "There is no making sense of Reid."

Reid whacked him. He only laughed harder.

Reid's castle came into view. She hadn't realized how much she missed this place until seeing it again. Tears filled her eyes. It was like a warm blanket offering comfort after a chilly day. This was home. Gray clouds covered the sky, promising rain.

Royce stepped out of the stables, blinking. "Lady Reid?"

"The one and only." She dismounted, handing the reins of her horse to her longtime friend. "How are things around here?"

He glanced at the others before answering. "The same as always."

"I'm sure you remember Prince Ackley and Prince Gordon."

Royce nodded.

"And this is Prince Dexter, my fiancé."

Duke Ellington dismounted. "Everything under control?"

"It is the same as when you left, sir." Royce reached forward, taking the reins to the duke's horse and eyeing the three princes.

"Good. I've returned home with my daughter and Prince

Dexter. Make no mention of the other princes. Do not allow anyone inside the castle without my permission. Understood?"

Royce nodded. "Your squad of soldiers is still nearby."

"Let them know I'm home. Inform no one else unless they ask."

"Knox's father fell ill, and Knox has taken up the watchman's duties. He comes by every morning to see if you've returned."

Ackley barked out a laugh. He climbed off his horse before taking it into the stables. "He'd probably pee his pants if he saw me again."

Dexter also dismounted. "Do I even want to know what that's about?"

"No." Gordon also got off his horse, leading it into the stables. "With Ackley, it's best to not know."

"Reid, I want you to go see Knox first thing tomorrow. Inform him that I've returned."

"Will do, and I'll take Dexter with me so I can show him the town."

Once they took care of the horses, they entered the castle.

"Kamden," Reid called. "I'm home!"

Kamden came running around the corner, throwing her arms around Reid and almost knocking her over. "I've missed you."

"I've missed you, too." Reid laughed. It felt good to hug her sister.

Kamden released her, scrunching her nose. "What are you wearing?"

"We traveled here from Axian. Please don't start on my clothes."

Kamden pursed her lips. "You're going to be a princess, yet you're dressed like a commoner."

Dexter stepped forward. "Lady Kamden, I presume?"

A slow, seductive smile spread across Kamden's face. "Yes," she purred. "And who might you be?"

Reid folded her arms, not liking her sister's interest in Dexter.

He took Kamden's hand, brushing his lips over her knuckles. "It is an honor to meet my new sister-in-law."

Kamden's cheeks turned scarlet. Reid was secretly glad she wasn't the only family member with that trait.

"Not yet," Ackley said, patting Dexter on the back. "But nice try. You two still get separate rooms."

"Ackley?" a familiar voice said.

Then Reid felt her. A force to be reckoned with. Idina stepped around the corner, observing their party with shrewd eyes. "I thought I heard your voice." She smiled.

Ackley wrapped his sister in a hug. "It's good to see you. How's Mum?"

"Better." She released Ackley, then hugged Gordon. "I didn't expect you to show up here."

"Can we see Mother?" Gordon asked.

Idina nodded. "She's in one of the guest rooms." She led Gordon and Ackley upstairs.

"We don't have any servants in the castle," Kamden said. "When Leigh and Idina arrived, Father sent the cook away."

Reid laughed. "Don't tell me you've taken over the duties of feeding everyone?"

Kamden flipped her hair over her shoulder. "I have. And I must admit, I'm quite good at it. If you'd like to have a seat in the sitting room, I'll make us some tea."

"Thank you," Duke Ellington said, kissing his daughter's cheek. "However, I am going to speak with my soldiers." He headed toward the kitchen where the back door was located.

"I'll take you up on that offer," Reid said. "First, though, I'm going to bathe."

Kamden nodded. "It'll take about twenty minutes to prepare anyway."

"Come," Reid said to Dexter. "I'll show you to your room." She led him upstairs to a guest bedchamber. "You can stay in here." She pushed open the door, but remained in the hallway.

He nodded.

"Down there," she pointed to her right, "is the bathing chamber. It's not nearly as fancy as the ones at your palace."

"Do you want to bathe first or should I?" His deep voice rumbled through her.

In the dim hallway, she had the sudden desire to brush her lips against his. However, there were too many people nearby to be so bold. "I'll go first," she replied, her voice breathy. "That way I can have a few moments alone with my sister before you join us, and she inundates you with questions."

Instead of smiling as she thought he would, he reached out, plucking the hat from her head. His eyes flashed with intensity. Reid held still, afraid to move.

"Try not to be in there too long. I only have so much self-control." And with that, he went into his room, closing the door behind him.

Reid let out a long breath. Maybe she should have put him farther away from her own bedchamber.

After a quick bath, Reid dressed in pants and a tunic. She supposed she could have borrowed one of Kamden's dresses, but she didn't see the need to worry about what she wore since they were staying in the castle for the rest of the evening.

Reid entered the sitting room, finding Kamden perched on one of the sofas.

Smiling at her sister, Reid poured herself a cup of steaming tea before sitting next to her.

"Father looks exhausted," Kamden observed.

"He's been through a lot." Reid realized her sister had no idea their mother was alive. Setting her cup on the low table, she twisted to face her. "There's something you need to know." She wasn't sure how to reveal the truth in a way that wouldn't be shocking. Best to just come out with it. "Kamden, when I was in Axian, I met—"

"There you are," Ackley said as he sauntered into the room. "I remember one of our first conversations took place in this very room." He slid his hands in his pockets. "This is where you tried to convince me that you were a man. Only, you'd stuffed your pants with a stocking, which had fallen to the side." He chuckled.

She wanted to ask him if Anna had told him that she was a woman or if he'd figured it out on his own.

"Lady Kamden, I don't mean to be rude, but I must steal your sister for a moment."

Rising, Reid followed Ackley to her father's study.

He closed the door. "I need you to send your sister away." He left no room for argument.

"You don't trust her?"

"It's not safe for her to be near us right now."

Reid hadn't considered coming here would put Kamden in harm's way.

"I've already spoken to your father on the matter. Royce is going to escort Kamden to your sister's house. Which one is the closest?"

"Bailey." Her sister's home was less than a day from the

castle.

"Tell Kamden to pack. She leaves in fifteen minutes."

"Even though she knows Idina and Leigh are here?"

He went over to the window, gazing outside. "Yes. It'll be safer. It's only a matter of time before Victor or someone else shows up looking for you."

The thought of Victor or anyone interrogating Kamden didn't sit well with Reid.

"I know it's hard," Ackley murmured. "I know you want to spend time with her. But sometimes, because of the position we are in, the power we wield, we have to do things we may not want to for the betterment of others."

"I understand." Reid had already been doing that her entire life.

On her way back to the sitting room, Reid heard Kamden giggling. When she stepped into the room, she found Dexter—with wet hair—sitting across from Kamden. He was telling her some hunting story. Reid hadn't even known he hunted.

She cleared her throat, capturing their attention. "Sorry to interrupt. Kamden, I need you to go pack. You're going to Bailey's house. Now."

Eyes wide, Kamden stood. "Is everything all right?"

"Yes." Reid forced a smile. "This is simply a precautionary measure. Nothing to worry about."

"If I leave, who will cook for you and your guests?"

"We're not staying here long."

"Then why send me away?"

"War is brewing. I need you somewhere safe."

Kamden nodded. "I always enjoy going to Bailey's. While my niece may be a terror, the watchman's son more than makes up for any inconvenience."

Reid pursed her lips, deciding not to reply. Father would

never allow Kamden to marry a commoner. Shaking her head, she watched Kamden hurry from the room.

Dexter managed to start a fire in the hearth. The wood crackled as it took. "It's wise to send your sister away." He sat back on the sofa.

"You're agreeing with Ackley again? You must be ill." She took a seat next to him.

Running a hand through his damp hair, he grinned. "So this is where you grew up."

"It is." Suddenly nervous at the idea of revealing so much of her life to this man, she became tongue-tied, not sure what to say.

"I think we should stay here until we have a formal plan in place. Once we know what we're doing, then we can travel to the City of Buckley."

"Should I send word to any of my other sisters to tell them to be on guard?" While they'd all married well, none were in positions of importance.

"No." He stretched his arms along the back of the sofa. "They should be safe. The king is after the dukes. Anna is after the king."

Kamden came down the stairs, pausing at the entrance to the sitting room. "I'm packed." She sighed. "It looks like it's going to pour. I hate riding in the rain."

"Then I suggest you hurry," Reid said. Since they didn't own a carriage, Kamden had no choice but to ride.

Duke Ellington came up behind Kamden. "Change of plans. Instead of Royce, I'll be escorting Kamden. Along the way, I plan to send messages to my men, readying them for war."

"Are you ordering them to convene here?" Dexter asked.

"I am. Expect the first wave to arrive tomorrow."

CHAPTER FIVE

After bidding her father and sister goodbye, Reid entered the great hall. Ackley and Dexter were sitting at the long table, each with a drink in hand.

"Where's everyone?" Reid asked, sitting alongside Dexter.

Ackley chuckled.

"What?" Reid asked, not sure she wanted to know.

"Gordon is attempting to cook us something to eat while Mother and Idina hover over him, driving him nuts."

"That's why we're out here," Dexter said. "Too many cooks in the kitchen."

"Do they even know how to cook?"

Dexter slid his cup to Reid. She took a sip, then gave it back.

"Gordon is like me," Ackley replied. "He can cook if necessary. A skill we both learned from our time traveling in the army. Idina and my mum can't even make tea."

"Huh." Reid turned to face Dexter. "What about you?"

He raised his eyebrows. "Are you asking if I can cook?"

"I am." She needed to learn more about this man who would be her husband.

"I can. Like Ackley, it's a skill I learned in the army. What about you?"

Reid shook her head. She was useless in the kitchen.

Idina stormed into the room with a stack of bowls. "Apparently, we are eating like commoners in a tavern." She tossed the bowls on the table with a loud *thud* before spinning on her heels, exiting the room with a dramatic flair.

A moment later, Gordon entered, carrying a cooking pot. "We're going to serve ourselves," he explained. "Idina couldn't handle carrying bowls filled with soup from the kitchen to here." He quickly glanced over his shoulder, making sure his sister didn't overhear him.

"Lady Reid," Leigh said as she came into the room. "You look well." The queen mother wore a dark blue dress, her hair resting in soft waves down her back. Reid had never seen Leigh with her hair down before.

"As do you." Reid inadvertently peered at Leigh's neck, trying to see if the woman had healed from Eldon attempting to strangle her. With her hair down, Reid couldn't tell.

Idina returned carrying a handful of spoons, which she flung on the table. "I'm not serving anyone." She plopped down next to Ackley.

"It's okay, sister," Ackley said. He leaned forward to pick up a bowl. "I can serve you. My head isn't so far up my arse that I can't help out."

Idina whacked him. "My place is in a war room, not a kitchen."

At that, Dexter raised his eyebrows. "Do tell."

"I'm exceptionally good at puzzles and games of that

nature. I love helping my brothers and breaking codes. Working in the kitchen, serving others…not so much."

Ackley slid a bowl full of soup in front of her. "Can I serve anyone else?"

"Since you're offering," Leigh said as she sat next to Idina, "I'd be honored for my son to serve me."

With a flourish, Ackley slid another bowl in front of his mother. He then proceeded to serve everyone else at the table before serving himself.

Idina noticed her mother wasn't eating. "I'm sorry." She shook her head. "Prince Dexter, you have not been formally introduced to my mother."

"Since we're all family," Leigh replied, "let's do away with the titles, shall we?"

Dexter nodded. "Sounds like a good idea to me. It's nice to finally meet my aunt."

Leigh smiled. "You look like your father."

Reid took a bite of her soup. It was rather bland. However, it was better than what they'd been eating over the past week.

"What's going on in the City of Buckley?" Gordon asked his sister.

"Our soldiers are in the barracks at the castle," Idina answered. "Everyone's accounted for except the hundred soldiers Eldon took with him."

"Does anyone in northern Marsden know what's going on in the south? We went into a tavern to try to hear the local gossip, but there wasn't any." Gordon slurped a spoonful of soup.

"No one is aware of the events in Axian. People believe the king is there for the wedding, nothing more."

"I met with the Melenia officers. There are five hundred

Melenia soldiers in Axian. We should be able to overpower them so long as my men remain loyal to me."

"And that will be the tricky part," Idina mused. "Yesterday, a letter came for Duchess Ellington. Since I know there isn't a duchess here and the letter bore the king's seal, I opened it." She reached into the folds of her dress and produced the letter, tossing it on the table. "It states the wedding was delayed due to the death of Prince Henrick. It then goes on to say the king requests the duchess to travel with a guard of one hundred men to the wedding. Once she arrives, the wedding will take place."

The spoon slipped from Leigh's fingers, clanking on the table. "Prince Henrick is dead?"

Idina pursed her lips. "Sorry, Mother. I withheld that information yesterday."

"My father is..." Dexter trailed off.

He was probably going to say his father wasn't dead, but he thought better of it. In order for Henrick's plan to work, no one could know he was alive.

"My father is at peace now," Dexter said, focusing on his soup as he spoke.

"If you'll excuse me," Leigh said, her voice weak. "I'm retiring for the night." She stood, then hurried from the room.

"That was awkward," Ackley mumbled once his mother was gone.

"I didn't think she'd still have feelings for my father," Dexter replied.

Reid hadn't either. However, it made sense since Henrick still cared about Leigh, even though he was married to Nara.

"Why do you suppose Eldon sent this letter?" Idina asked.

Dexter plucked the letter off the table, examining it. "I recognize the handwriting. When the king sent word he'd be coming, we evacuated all servants and replaced them with soldiers. I assigned Stewart as my father's deputy. Stewart wrote this—I'm certain of it."

"I know my brother," Idina said. "He wouldn't waste his time writing letters to the duchesses. He'd make a scribe do it for him. If Stewart was around, he'd use him."

Reid leaned forward on her arms. "So…the king instructed Stewart to write to all the duchesses and invite them to the City of Radella for the wedding. Is it not well known my father is a widow?" Reid swallowed, realizing her father *wasn't* a widow. He was still married. And her mother was technically the duchess of Ellington.

"You're assuming each duchess in Marsden received an identical letter?" Idina inquired.

"Yes."

"To answer your question," Dexter said to Reid, "most know your father is a widow. I think Stewart sent the letter to Duchess Ellington, feigning ignorance on the chance you came here to hide, or someone here would know where you are."

"Which means Stewart thought we needed to know about this," Reid mused, tapping the letter.

"The question is then, why does the king want the duchesses and a hundred soldiers per duchess to travel to Axian?" Idina smiled, as if she already knew the answer, but was waiting to see if anyone else guessed it.

Ackley cursed. "He plans to either strip the dukes and duchesses of their titles or kill them."

"Precisely," Idina replied. "Thankfully, we have people watching the ports. I've received word there are several Melenia ships off the coast of northern Marsden. The king has no idea they are there. I believe Melenia intends to invade once the army and all dukes and duchess are south."

"I agree," Gordon said. "When I talked with the Melenia officers before I left, they told me they wanted Marsden's resources. I got the distinct impression they plan to stab Eldon in the back the first chance they get."

Idina's smile grew. "I've been investigating the land across the ocean to the east of us. It is known as the Mainland. Melenia is but one kingdom of many there. Years ago, my father was engaged to marry a princess from Melenia. King Broc wished to unite the two kingdoms and open trade. However, my grandfather died, so the marriage contract was severed. Melenia has been upset with us ever since."

"While this is all very interesting," Ackley said around a yawn, "I'm tired and would like you to get to the point—if there is one."

"I have a point." Idina scooted forward on her chair, leaning on the table. "It just so happens war is brewing on the Mainland. There is a kingdom there called Russek. Its king has been showing signs of wanting to take over the neighboring kingdoms. So I wrote him a letter informing him a substantial portion of the Melenia army is hundreds of miles away. If he wants to invade Melenia, now is the time."

"Idina!" Ackley said. "That is devious. Even for you." He rubbed his chin.

"When the Melenia soldiers here receive word their kingdom is being invaded, they'll rush back home and leave us the hell alone." She folded her hands together. "What? Why are you all staring at me like that?"

"You're mad," Gordon mumbled.

"I think she's a genius," Ackley countered.

"I'm glad you're my cousin," Dexter said admiringly, "and not my enemy."

"What if word doesn't come in time?" Reid asked.

"If any of the ships dock, I'll tell them myself," Gordon said. "I can lie and say we received word from Melenia requesting aid immediately."

Reid supposed that would work. "As far as the duchesses go, we should send each a letter."

"Why?" Ackley asked, twirling a spoon between his fingers.

Reid stood and started pacing, a crazy idea forming in her mind. "I think I know how we can stop Eldon."

"Do tell." He set the spoon down, folding his arms.

She thumbed the ring on her finger. The ring of a duke. It gave her the power to call on the other dukes. "Since the dukes are absent, and are most likely being held hostage, I am going to call on each duchess." When everyone continued to stare at her with blank faces, not understanding, she extrapolated. "I'm going to invoke the power of the ring to insist each duchess raise her county's army."

"That's ballsy," Ackley mumbled. "I like it." His eyes flashed with excitement.

"You want the duchesses, the women, to call up their armies?" Gordon sounded skeptical.

"I do." The more Reid thought about it, the more she liked the idea of women banning together to save the kingdom.

Gordon scratched the side of his face. "The duchesses won't know how to raise their armies, let alone how to lead their soldiers. That's a man's job."

Dexter chuckled. "It's a good thing my captain, Gytha, isn't present to hear you insult her like that."

"Weren't you just in Axian?" Reid tapped her foot.

Gordon nodded.

"And while there, didn't you see that women are perfectly capable of working, managing land, and being soldiers in the army?"

Gordon chewed on his bottom lip. "But the duchesses were raised very differently and won't know what to do."

"I know you believe that," Idina chimed in, "but I bet that's not the case. I think all the duchesses know exactly what to do. If their husbands didn't tell them, then they probably heard and saw enough to figure it out on their own. And once they raise their armies, the captains will lead the soldiers to the City of Buckley. From there, Gordon and Dexter will take over."

Ackley slapped the table. "Eldon's going to crap in his pants when he learns the women are conspiring against him. I love it."

"I suggest you get started on those letters," Idina said to Reid, her face alight with hope. "It's time the women of Marsden rally to save this kingdom."

"So this is your private bedchamber," Dexter mused as he entered Reid's room.

"It is." Reid knelt and picked up the discarded chess set, putting it back on the bookshelf. Rising, she found herself suddenly nervous to have Dexter in her bedchamber.

With his hands clasped behind his back, he walked around the room, examining the knickknacks on her dresser, the books on her shelves, and the weapons discarded around the room. "I'll admit, it's not what I pictured."

Sitting on the edge of her bed, she asked, "What did you envision my room would look like?"

He shrugged. "I thought it would be lighter and brighter." Large gray stones, not wood like the palace, made up her walls, which gave the room a darker feel. Thunder boomed and the rain picked up, pattering against the windows. Dexter went over to the hearth, then stoked the dying fire back to life. "What do you usually do in the evenings around here?"

"Read or play a game." Often times, she played chess or cards with her father.

He stood, resuming his inspection. "Have you read all these books?"

She nodded. "Some twice." Or even three times.

He stopped at her desk, surveying the knives, daggers, and swords strewn over the surface. Dexter picked up a small knife, feeling the weight of it in his palm. He set it down before examining a few of the other weapons.

Reid remained sitting on the edge of her bed, watching him.

"Do you have a favorite?" he asked.

"For throwing, I prefer the ones with the black hilts." Their weight was balanced, the handles small, making them easier for her to throw.

"And for fighting?"

"My twin swords."

"Where are they?"

"In the scabbard on the dresser." It had been far too long since she'd held them in her hands.

"I prefer my longsword." He turned and leaned against the edge of her desk, folding his arms and studying her. "Where do you practice?"

They didn't have a training yard on the premises. "In town." Thunder boomed again, making Reid shiver.

Dexter pushed off the desk and came over to the bed, sitting on the edge about two feet away from her. "I'd like to see it."

Reid wanted to show Dexter what her life here had been like—the good and the bad. He needed to understand why she wanted to implement the changes she did.

"I'm heading to bed," Ackley said, startling Reid. He was leaning against the frame of the open door. "You still have the first watch?"

"I do." Dexter stood.

"I'll show you to the tower. It'll allow you an unobstructed view of the land surrounding the castle. Though, in this storm, it'll be difficult to see far." Pushing off the doorframe, he left.

"I wish your father and sister weren't riding in this weather." Dexter headed to the window, glancing out.

There were plenty of homes along the way for them to stay at. "My father is used to traveling in storms like this." On the other hand, Kamden was probably complaining incessantly.

"You coming?" Ackley called from down the hallway.

"I better go. I'll see you in the morning." Dexter exited Reid's room, closing the door behind him.

She had the distinct impression something was on his mind. However, she had no idea what could be bothering him.

Reid woke up, the gray light of dawn filtering in through her window. The fire in the hearth blazed, which meant someone had been in her bedchamber. While she appreciated waking to a toasty room, the thought of someone being in there while she slept made her uncomfortable.

Sliding out of bed, she went over to the window, peering outside. Until now, she hadn't realized how much she missed this view. Thick fog coated the land like a blanket, the gray sky promising more rain. The ground was muddy, the air crisp. Breathing in, Reid savored it all.

Someone knocked. "Come in," Reid called.

"I was hoping you'd be awake," Idina said as she stepped

into the room. "Kamden told me you like black tea." She held a mug in her hands.

Reid eyed her. "I thought you refused to serve others."

Idina shoved the mug at Reid. "Just take it."

"What do you want?" Reid took the steaming mug, wrapping her hands around it.

"Why do you think I want something?"

Instead of answering, Reid held up the mug as if that were proof.

"Fine." Idina sighed. "Since I've been staying here, Kamden and I became friends. I don't think it's fair to keep her cooped up in Ellington. She deserves to see more of the kingdom. I'd like for her to come with me to the castle as my personal friend. I'd like to show her around. Introduce her to eligible men."

Reid tried not to let it bother her that Idina and Kamden had become close. She should be happy two people she cared about were also friends. "Don't you think you should be asking my father's permission?" After all, he was still the duke and in charge of Kamden.

"You're going to be the queen. It will be up to you to decide who resides at court."

"Just so you know, I plan to reside in the City of Radella." Not only was the palace Dexter's home, but it was also far more welcoming than the castle in the City of Buckley.

"Can we come with you?" Idina pushed her red hair behind her ears. "I hear Axian is far more accommodating than here."

"I don't see why not. I'm going to need some women I trust around." And it would be nice to have Idina and Kamden nearby. A log shifted in the fireplace. "Do you know who made sure my fire was burning?" It unnerved Reid that someone had been in her room, and she'd had no idea.

Idina placed her hands on her hips. "I had Gordon tend to it before he went on watch about an hour ago. But don't worry, I came in here with him. He was the perfect gentleman."

"I should hope so seeing as how he's married and his wife is pregnant." Reid took a sip of her tea.

"Don't remind me." Idina shivered even though the room was toasty. "I do have another question."

"What is it?" Reid asked, curious as to what Idina could possibly want.

"Once we're settled in the City of Radella, will you teach me to fight?"

"You're assuming we'll win," Reid muttered. If only she were that confident.

"We will."

"How can you be so sure?"

"The alternative isn't acceptable."

Reid chuckled. "I happen to agree with you." She eyed her friend. "You want to learn to fight?" While Reid had no doubt Idina could do it, the request surprised her. The woman had always been so good at organizing covert operations and seeing patterns that Reid wasn't sure why Idina would want to learn to fight.

"I'd like to be able to defend myself."

Reid understood the value in that. "Why wait? We can start your training now." Quite frankly, it surprised her that Idina's brothers hadn't taught her already. It was a skill every princess should know. Especially when war loomed on the horizon.

"Thank you."

"How's your mother?" Reid hadn't seen Leigh since supper last night.

"She's fine. Although, I haven't told her anything about our plans to assassinate Eldon. She knows we plan to remove him from power—which she agrees with given his erratic behavior."

That made Reid remember something. "Henrick said Hudson behaved similarly around the time his father died." Could there be a connection between the two? Some sort of illness? Or drug perhaps?

"Eldon can't stand the fact Mum confronted him. Even though she is his mother, he holds little respect for women. So while his behavior seems erratic, it is in line with how he's always been. My father loved his wine, women, and doing whatever he wanted. Even though Eldon is not his biological child, they are remarkably similar. And Father doted on Eldon."

Reid took another sip of her tea before setting her mug on the dresser. "Are you okay with us assassinating your brother? We could just…put him in the dungeon?" There were ways to eliminate him from power without killing him.

"I've studied enough to know we have little choice in the matter. While I don't want my brother to be murdered, someone has to stop him. He intends to destroy Marsden and harm thousands of people. I can't let him do that. If killing him saves all those lives, spares this kingdom, and brings peace, it is a small price to pay."

"I agree." Even though the thought of intentionally killing Eldon made Reid's stomach queasy. "I have a question for you."

Idina plopped on Reid's bed. "What is it?"

"How do you feel about Dexter being king?" Would Idina rather one of her brothers hold the position? Would there be problems in the future? Bitterness? Resentment?

She shrugged. "I don't personally know Dexter that well, but my research has told me that he is qualified to rule this kingdom. I fear Gordon is too focused on the army to be able to handle the citizens and dukes. Ackley is, well, Ackley. He could never stay in one place. It would be too confining, and it would destroy him."

Reid still hadn't asked Dexter if he wanted to be king. So far, he'd been willing to accept the responsibility his father had shoved on him, but that didn't mean he wanted it.

"What do you plan to do with Harlow?" Idina asked, plucking at a string on the blanket.

"I hadn't thought about it."

"Make sure you do. She is young and from a powerful county. You'll need her father, Duke Bridger, on board. You can't assassinate Harlow's husband without offering her family some sort of retribution."

Why hadn't Reid thought about Harlow being from Bridger before? Duke Bridger controlled the mines—the mines Melenia was after. Reid filed the information away in case it came in handy later.

"What is it you want out of this deal?" Reid asked.

"Other than not being forced to marry some useless lord, I don't know what I want. I've never been given the choice. Traveling with you to the City of Radella, seeing the kingdom, and having some freedom is more than I could ever ask for. I also think bringing your sister along will be good for her. She has only ever considered marrying. I want her to see there are other options out there. She is capable of so much more."

Reid happened to wholeheartedly agree with Idina.

CHAPTER SIX

"Will your mother be okay by herself?" Reid asked. Since there weren't any servants in the castle, Leigh would be completely alone.

"She'll be fine," Ackley said. "And Royce is nearby in the stables if she needs anything."

They left, Dexter and Reid riding side by side while Gordon, Ackley, and Idina rode behind them. Reid steered her horse toward town, a nervous energy filling her. Ackley had been there before, so he knew what he was getting himself into. Dexter, on the other hand, would probably think the place small and rundown compared to what he was used to in Axian. Regardless, this was where she'd spent countless days, and she couldn't wait to share that part of her life with him.

When they reached the outskirts of town, Reid led the way to one of the three main streets where most of the businesses were located. At the apothecary's, she dismounted, tying her horse to the post outside. Everyone followed suit.

Without waiting for her companions, Reid pushed the door open, rushing into the store.

Harlan sat at the table, grinding leaves in a small bowl. He glanced up. "Reid?" A huge smile spread across his face.

She ran around the table, throwing her arms around him as he tried to stand.

"It's good to see you." He chuckled at her enthusiasm. Holding her at arm's length, he scanned her from head to toe. "You look about the same. How's Axian?"

"Interesting." Not knowing if anyone was in the back section of the shop, she kept her answer short, not wanting to go into details until she was sure they were alone.

Harlan stiffened as he peered over her shoulder, releasing her.

Dexter closed the door, turning to face Harlan and Reid while Ackley, Idina, and Gordon remained outside.

Grabbing Harlan's arm, Reid dragged him around the side of the table. "I'd like for you to meet Dexter, my fiancé." As a safety precaution, she chose not to use his formal title or last name.

Harlan wiped his hands on his pants before shaking Dexter's hand.

"Nice to meet you," Dexter replied, his voice oddly stiff and formal, as if he were nervous.

"What about you?" Reid asked, nudging Harlan. "Are you married?" He'd told Reid he was engaged to the apothecary's eldest daughter, Sophie, but he hadn't said when they were supposed to marry. Reid had hoped to make it back in time for the wedding.

"I am." Harlan sat back on the chair, then resumed crushing the leaves in his bowl. "It's good to see you. I've been worried."

"We're not sure how long we'll be in town," Dexter said. "But I would be honored if you'd come to Duke Ellington's later today. I'd like to have a drink to celebrate your wedding."

Harlan paused before peering at Dexter.

The prince cleared his throat. "I'd like to get to know Reid's friends."

Harlan nodded. "I'll come by after work." He set his bowl down. "If you don't mind, I'd like a moment alone with Reid."

Dexter nodded, then stepped outside.

"I'm glad he isn't the hovering type." Harlan rubbed his face. "Are you okay? I mean, really okay?"

"I am." Reid perched on the edge of the table.

Harlan reached out, taking her hand. "You two aren't married yet?"

She shook her head.

"Why are you in Ellington?"

"It's a long story. I'll explain later."

"Is he…treating you right?"

Reid squeezed Harlan's hand. She was about to say Dexter had been nothing but kind to her. However, that wasn't true, and she didn't want to lie to her friend. "We've grown to care for one another, and I consider him a friend."

Relief shone on his face. "That's good enough for me."

"Will your wife be joining you this evening?" Over the years, Reid had seen the apothecary's daughter a few times. However, she'd never spoken to the young woman.

"No. It'll just be me. That way we can talk."

Reid stood. "I've missed you." While she'd made friends in Axian, no one knew her as well as Harlan.

"It's not the same around here without you."

After one last hug, she bid him goodbye and exited the store.

"It's about time," Ackley said. "Now where to?" He

surveyed the street. "Shall we find that obnoxious, over-controlling friend of yours?"

"Do you mean Knox?" she asked.

He smiled. "Why do you think I call him obnoxious? It's the only way I can remember his name."

Rolling her eyes, Reid said, "Leave him alone. He means well."

"I'm sure he does." Ackley led the way to the watchtower, the fighting yard located adjacent to it. That was where Reid had seen Ackley for the first time.

Since the fenced-in training yard was empty, Reid instructed her friends to wait there. Entering the watchtower, she found Knox sitting at a desk. "Now isn't this an interesting sight?" she said by way of greeting.

"I'll be damned," he said, jumping to his feet. "I didn't think I'd see you back here any time soon." He slapped her on the shoulder, almost knocking her over. "Got tired of that entitled prick of a prince in Axian?"

"Not exactly."

He folded his arms. "What are you doing here?"

It struck Reid as odd no one knew the king was on the verge of overthrowing the dukes and taking complete control of Marsden. Taking a deep breath, she shoved those thoughts aside and focused on Knox. "I'm here to spar with my friend."

He nodded as if expecting that. Through the years, how many times had she come here to spar with him? Too many to count.

Reaching under his desk, he pulled out his sword. "Listen, Reid, I want to apologize."

"No need." She knew his personality. Knox would always see her as someone weaker than him who should be protected. It had been ingrained in him since childhood. Harlan was one of the few people who saw her for the person she was on the inside.

"I should have stayed with you instead of going home. When you needed me, I wasn't there for you. I'm sorry." He ducked his head.

She'd never heard him apologize before. "You're forgiven." Ironically, Harlan—the least skilled of her friends when it came to fighting—was the only one who had stayed with her. "Now, are we going to just stand here and gossip? Or are we going to get to work?"

Smiling, he sheathed his sword in the scabbard strapped to his waist. He opened the door, ushering Reid outside. When Knox saw Ackley and Gordon, he stopped. "What are they doing here?" he muttered.

"I'm not sure why my father hasn't told you anything, but the king is trying to take over the kingdom."

"In case you haven't heard, the king is in charge of the kingdom."

She shook her head. "He's either going to overthrow the dukes or kill them so he has complete control."

"And you think you're going to stop him?"

"Not quite. We're just here to regroup. Come on."

When they reached the training yard, Reid quickly introduced Knox to everyone. "He's the one who taught me to fight." She patted him on the shoulder.

"That explains why your skills are lacking," Ackley drawled.

Reid was going to whack Ackley on the back of his head. However, Dexter beat her to it.

"When will I learn to defend myself?" Idina asked.

"I can show you some basics," Knox offered.

"Not a chance in hell," Ackley said.

Reid wondered if Ackley's objection was due to Knox's lack of skill or the fact he was an unmarried man.

"I'll work with you," Gordon said. He led Idina across the muddy training yard, off to the side and out of everyone's way. Gordon proceeded to show Idina what to do if someone came at her with a knife. It surprised Reid that neither Gordon nor Ackley had thought to show Idina some basic self-defense moves before now. They must never have thought it necessary.

"I'll take the big guy," Ackley said, pointing at Dexter with a wicked gleam in his eye.

That left Reid with Knox for a partner. She pulled her swords free from their scabbards, reveling in the sounds the blades made as she unsheathed them. It had been far too long.

"You look nervous," Knox commented with a low chuckle.

"I'm rusty." She swung her arms, trying to loosen up. Knox never went easy on her.

"Are you gonna complain about it?"

"The only one complaining is you."

A smile spread across his face. "I forgot how much I enjoy your banter."

She adjusted her hands on the hilts of her swords, preparing for his attack.

Knox removed his shirt, tossing it on the fence.

"Is that necessary?" she asked. While it had stopped raining, heavy clouds still covered the sky, making the air chilly.

He shrugged. "I always fight without a shirt."

She'd assumed that since he was now aware of her womanhood, he'd keep his shirt on for proprietary reasons.

"What? Am I too distracting?" He winked.

"You wish." Instead of letting Knox strike first, she swung her right sword, knowing he'd shut up and block it.

And just like that, they fell into their old routine. Reid had feared she'd be slower since she hadn't used her swords in so long. However, the movements came back to her as naturally as breathing. If anything, Knox felt a little sluggish to her. "Maybe you're the one who hasn't practiced," she teased.

"I've maintained my daily drills," he said, a huff to his voice she wasn't familiar with. "It's you who has improved."

"I'm not sure how that's possible since I haven't been training regularly." She spun, missing his attack. Since his sword was heavy and his momentum was going forward, she easily came up behind him, one sword at his throat, the other at his stomach. "I win."

He nodded in acknowledgment. She'd never—*never*—won the first round against him.

"You're fighting with more confidence," Knox said. "As if you know you're going to win and are toying with me."

She shrugged. "Shall we have another bout?"

"Of course. Can't let you beat me once and have it go to your head." He attacked faster than usual, his intent to beat her clear.

Reid raised both swords, blocking his strike. When she lifted her right leg to kick him, he twisted, knocking her off balance. She landed in the mud. Clamoring to her feet, she faced him again. "Have you always held back when going against me?"

"I have." He circled her like a predator. "It seems I don't have to anymore. I still wish you'd fight without your cap and shirt on though for different reasons now."

Instead of taking offense, she laughed, knowing he was just trying to throw her off. He swung his sword low, luring her in. Blocking with her left sword, she held her right at the ready, assuming he planned to punch her. When his right arm flew at her torso, she hit it with her sword and twisted, trying to get in closer to disarm him. He swept her legs out from under her, and she landed in the mud.

Knox reached down. She took hold of his hand, and he pulled her to her feet.

Reid caught sight of Dexter and Ackley sparring without weapons. Each man had a different body shape and fighting style. Yet, they were well matched. Where Dexter was all power, muscle, and brute strength, Ackley exhibited lean, cat-like precision.

"Done?" Knox asked, pulling her attention from Dexter and Ackley's match.

"No," she replied. "One more round to determine the winner." Her arms shook slightly, but she wouldn't let Knox know her muscles were tired. At least he had a sheen of sweat across his torso, revealing some exhaustion on his part.

She flicked a chunk of mud off her hair, thankful most of it was caked to the back of her head so she could still see.

"Hang on," Knox said as he squatted to tie his boot.

Reid removed her cap, tossing it off to the side. She didn't like the shadow it cast over her face on this cloudy day. And, if she were being honest with herself, she'd gotten used to not wearing it.

"Look at you." Knox righted himself, pointing his sword at her. "I've never seen you remove a single article of clothing before."

"It's a cap. That's hardly clothing." They started circling one another. She knew he was getting ready to attack—could see it in the way he shifted his fingers on the sword's hilt as he widened his stance.

She raised her swords, barely blocking his strike in time. He grinned, and she knew he was planning something. She jumped backward, out of striking range, narrowly missing his front kick. Instead of giving him a moment to regroup, she came at him with a series of attacks, trying to force him to make an error so she could have the upper hand. If she were going to have any hope of winning, she needed to disarm him. A plan formed. She pretended she could barely hold her swords up. He fell for it, trying to attack higher in order to wear her out faster. The second he went higher, she lashed out. Both swords on his wrist, she applied just enough pressure that he dropped his weapon.

She stood, chest heaving, both swords now pointed at his torso. "Concede?" She grinned.

He nodded. "I was holding back."

"What do you mean?" She sheathed her swords, feeling a blister already forming on her right hand.

"Since I now know you're a woman," he said, "I went easier on you."

Eyes narrowing, she took a step closer to him. "I've fought you countless times over the years. You didn't go easier on me." If anything, he'd been harder and more intense.

"But you're a woman. You're not as strong as a man."

Without intending to, she punched him, the hit landing on his cheek.

He cursed. "What was that for?"

Her hand hurt like hell. Cradling it to her chest, she tried not to scream. She should have punched him in the stomach, then she wouldn't have hurt her knuckles.

Ackley, Dexter, Gordon, and Idina all gaped at her with wide eyes.

Embarrassed she'd lost her temper, Reid muttered, "He deserved it," before climbing over the fence and exiting the sparring area.

Grabbing her cap, she returned to where they'd left the horses. She wished Knox would have flown feet over head and landed on his back. That would have been more satisfying than the weak punch she'd delivered, barely making a mark while injuring her own hand in the process.

"Reid," Dexter called from behind her.

Instead of facing him, she untied her horse, pretending she hadn't heard him.

He caught up to her, grabbing her hand. "Are you all right?" He examined her knuckles.

"I'm fine." She pulled her hand free, then mounted. "Where are the others?"

"They're going to head back to the castle in a moment." He climbed on his horse. "I was hoping you'd show me more of the town."

"I'm just going to go home, too."

He steered his horse in front of hers, blocking the path. "I'd like to spend some time alone with you."

Reid adjusted the sheathes on either side of her legs. There was one place she wanted to visit before they left. "I'll take you somewhere I spent countless hours throughout the years." She led the way out of town, to the east, bypassing the castle and heading to the narrow pathway hidden between the trees. Since no one had been there recently, leaves covered the path, and the rain made it slightly muddy. At the top of the rise, she steered her horse toward the lake. Pausing at the shore, she scanned the area. Although it hadn't changed a bit, it seemed smaller than before.

After tying her horse to a tree, she removed her boots and socks, wadding into the frigid water.

"This is your favorite place?" Dexter asked, removing his footgear as well.

"It is."

He stood beside her. "It's nice you have someplace so close to your home."

She closed her eyes, breathing in the smell of the pine trees. "Do you have a favorite spot?"

When he chuckled, she peered at him.

"I have a new favorite spot now." He moved to stand before her.

"You like my lake?"

He shook his head. "The sparring area."

"At your military compound back home?"

"No, the one we were just at."

"Why?" It was nothing compared to his sparring area. That place had grass instead of mud, and it was a lot bigger.

A dubious smile spread across Dexter's face. He took a step closer to Reid, his hands settling on her hips. "Seeing you with those twin swords will be something I never forget."

He'd seen her fight before. She didn't know why today was any different.

"There's something about you wielding a sword in each hand that has me all riled up." His fingers dug into her hips, and he leaned his forehead against hers. "If I had known that was your weapon of choice, I would have gotten you twin swords back home."

She had no idea what to say. His presence was intoxicating, and she couldn't think clearly.

His lips moved to her left ear. "I'm not sure which was sexier...you making Knox yield or watching the fire in you flare to life, which led to that delightful punch."

Her face flamed red. While she knew how to punch, had done so numerous times during sparring matches, she'd never done so out of anger before.

Dexter chuckled, the sound deep and throaty. He unlatched the belt holding her sheaths, tossing it on the ground.

"What are you doing?" she squeaked, her heart pounding.

He plucked the cap from her head, chucking it behind her. "You're covered with mud."

She rolled her eyes.

"And I'm still picturing you with those swords." He fingered the edge of her tunic, then pulled it over her head, leaving her in only a thin undershirt. His hands slid around her, then he delicately pressed his lips to her neck.

She gasped, not expecting him to be so gentle. Then she felt him tilt backward, pulling her with him. She squealed as they fell into the water. When he released her, she stood, the water coming up to her waist.

"I didn't expect it to be so cold," he said, laughing. He removed his wet tunic, tossing it on the shore. Then he removed his undershirt.

All thoughts left Reid as she watched him ball up his shirt, tossing it alongside his tunic.

"Thought we'd rinse the mud off."

Reaching up, she felt mud still caked on the back of her head. She ducked under the water, trying to get it off. When she resurfaced, Dexter was swimming about twenty feet away. Since it was hard to swim with pants on, she removed them, knowing he couldn't see her under the water. She chucked them on the shoreline.

"You shouldn't have done that," Dexter said, treading water fifteen feet away.

"Why is that?" Her body started shaking from the frigid water.

"Because that might have snapped the last of my self-control."

Had he gotten closer to her? Or was she moving in his direction?

"Seeing you wield those swords was…well, it was the sexiest thing I've ever experienced. But knowing you're here, in the water with me, with no pants on? I can't guarantee I'll be able to keep my hands to myself."

"But you've been around women fighting your entire life. Gytha is probably your best fighter." So why would he find Reid sparring with Knox sexy?

Dexter was only five feet away now. His dark eyes focused on Reid, making her want to melt into the water.

"Have you ever considered Knox attractive while he's fighting?"

"No." Knox was Knox. Reid had never found him remotely enticing.

"Because you don't have feelings for Knox."

Reid swallowed, understanding Dexter was admitting he had feelings for her. She didn't know how to respond.

He swam right in front of her, then stood, the water coming up to his shoulders. Too far out to touch the bottom, Reid continued to tread water, watching the man before her.

"Gytha is one of my captains. She is a soldier and a friend. You, Reid Ellington, are…" He grabbed her waist, pulling her toward him. When her legs slid around his torso, his hands clasped her back, holding her body against his. "You are unexpected." His lips enveloped hers.

Reid found herself wanting more. She curled her fingers around his neck, pulling him to her.

"Marry me," he murmured against her lips.

"I've already said yes." Her legs tightened around him, and she tangled her hands in his wet hair.

"No. I'm not asking Lady Reid Ellington to marry Prince

Dexter Winston." He pulled back slightly, his eyes searching hers. "I'm asking you, Reid, to marry me, Dexter. Titles, land, and all that aside, I want you to want to marry me—the person." His eyes seemed uncertain, vulnerable even.

A droplet of water slid down the side of his face. Reid brushed it aside. "You're saying even if you didn't have to marry me, you'd want to?"

"I thought that was obvious."

Her breath caught as she saw the desire emanating from him. She realized he was still waiting for her answer. "I don't know how it happened, or when, but, at some point, I started to care for you."

"I don't want you to *care* for me."

Reid covered his lips with her palm, silencing him. "I'm not done." He playfully bit her finger, so she fastened her grip behind his neck again. "I've been afraid to fully trust and love another person." The fact her father had lied about her mother's death only exemplified that point. "I'm inexperienced with relationships, love, kissing." Taking a deep breath, she decided to just come out and say it as plainly as she could so he would understand. "While I've been attracted to your... body...from the beginning, it wasn't until I got to know you that I started to fall in love with you." She placed her right hand on his bare chest, trying to explain. "At first, I didn't understand it because I'd never been in love before. I'd been so careful to keep my secrets close, to never feel anything for another man and blow my cover. So when I started to see the type of person you are—passionate about your army, devoted to your family, protective of your county—I realized I'd already fallen for you without even realizing it."

He leaned his forehead against hers, trapping her hand between them as he gazed into her eyes. "Is that a yes?"

"Yes. I'll marry you." She couldn't believe she'd gone from an unwilling participant to wanting and desiring the man before her.

He pressed his lips gently against hers. Then he deepened the kiss. One of his hands slid beneath her thin undershirt, pressing against her back.

"You're so cold you're shaking," he mumbled against her lips.

The feel of Dexter consumed her so much she hadn't thought about being cold. However, now that he'd said something, she realized she was trembling.

"Let's resume this next to a fire," he said as he released her.

A few things came to mind—one of those being that Ackley knew about this place. The last thing she wanted was for him to show up and see her and Dexter having a private moment. The second thing she feared was if Dexter started kissing her like that again, she wouldn't have the self-control to stop him. She swam to the shore. "As tempting as that sounds, I think we need to head back before the others start worrying about us."

Dexter got out of the lake, shaking his head and spraying water everywhere.

Reid stood on the shore with her arms covering her chest, trying to figure out how to get her tunic. The thin white material of her undershirt left little to the imagination, so she didn't want to move her arms.

Dexter reached down and picked up her dry tunic, handing it to her. Turning her back to him, she quickly put it on.

"Too bad our wedding ceremony was interrupted," he said, attempting to put his wet shirt back on.

"Why is that?" She ran her hands through her hair, trying to remove the tangles.

"Because then we'd be married already, and we could share a bed tonight. Because then I could take you as often as I like."

She recalled the conversation they'd had the night of their engagement announcement. That felt like a lifetime ago. "I thought you commissioned separate bedchambers." She tried to keep the smile from her voice.

He took a step closer, and she took one back.

"Besides," she shrugged, "who's to say I'm going to let you have your way with me whenever you want?"

Dexter's eyes gleamed as he stared Reid down, making her want to melt. He still hadn't managed to get his shirt on. And she was standing there without pants. Leaning down, he whispered, "You're right. *You* can have your way with *me* whenever you like. And the separate bedchambers on either side of our *joined* bedchamber is only to prevent others from hearing us."

Her legs almost gave out. It took every ounce of her self-control to remain upright. "We'll see." She smiled sweetly, issuing the challenge.

"Yes," he purred in her ear, "we will see." With that, he stepped away, leaving Reid suddenly cold.

Her wet pants didn't want to cooperate. Nevertheless, Reid forced them on. When she finished, she joined Dexter by the horses.

"Is there someone nearby who can marry us?" he asked.

"You mean in the City of Dorsot?" Reid mounted her horse.

"Yes. I want to marry you. Now."

She nodded. There was a man who could perform the ceremony. "I'd like for my father and sisters to be present for it."

"We'll still have a large ceremony for our family, the dukes, and the leaders of the kingdom," he said as he mounted.

"However, I'd like a small, intimate ceremony with just us. Especially before we tackle the events before us."

"You know you don't have to marry me to make sure I'm taken care of in the event something happens to you. You understand I'll be fine no matter what, right?" Which wasn't true. If something happened to him, she'd be devastated.

"I wish to marry you because it's something I want. And I rarely get to make my own decisions or do what I want. So I'm being selfish. If you're not ready, I understand."

"It's not that. I just don't want you to feel like you have to marry me to protect me."

"I don't."

They headed away from the lake, weaving between the trees. As they made their way back to the duke's castle, Reid mulled over the idea of marrying Dexter now. It would be nice to get married in Ellington. Harlan could attend the wedding. And their wedding night would be private.

The castle came into view. Off to the side, Reid saw soldiers had already started to gather there. "Okay."

Dexter eyed her sidelong. "Okay?"

"I'd like to marry here in Ellington."

"You would?"

"Yes."

He smiled, sitting up straighter on his horse. "It's settled then. I'll speak to the marriage binder to make the arrangements."

"And I'll find a dress to wear and...prepare a room for us to share." Her face warmed just thinking about it.

CHAPTER SEVEN

W hen Reid and Dexter returned to the castle, they found everyone in the great hall studying a worn map.

"It doesn't matter," Idina said. "It won't take Anna long to figure out we're not following her plan."

"I'll tell her it is her plan, just altered a bit." Ackley folded his arms.

"We need a place where we can battle the Melenia soldiers," Gordon said, tapping the map. "I assume Dexter can recommend a location that will cause the least amount of damage to property."

"I'll think on the matter," Dexter replied. "Perhaps some place north of the City of Radella. We'd need to lure the soldiers in the city there, but I'm sure it can be done."

"And Anna," Ackley reminded everyone. "We can't forget about her and her personal agenda."

"I think we need a break," Leigh said. "After supper, we'll revisit this. Hopefully, there will be some new ideas."

Gordon rolled up the map. "Reid, I took this from your father's office. I hope he won't mind."

"It's yours to use." She sat at the table.

"I'm going outside to start organizing the men," he responded. "Once you and Idina are done writing those letters to the duchesses, I'll have someone deliver them."

"Is that your way of telling me to get the letters written?" she asked. She'd never written a formal letter before. However, with Idina's help, she should be fine.

"The sooner, the better. It'll take the duchesses some time to organize their soldiers and travel to the City of Buckley."

"Is that where you want everyone to convene?"

"Yes," he answered. "All the supplies we need are there."

"I want to be there when they arrive." Reid needed to speak to the duchesses to ensure they understood the importance of banning together.

"I suggest we split into two groups," Idina said. "Half of us will go with the first wave of Ellington soldiers, the second half will wait until the rest show up and travel with the remaining ones."

"Good idea," Dexter said, hovering behind Reid. "Um..." When he cleared his throat, everyone turned to him. "I asked Reid to marry me."

Idina smirked. "Yes, we are all aware you two are going to marry."

"I mean now."

"Now?" Idina asked, her voice incredulous.

"I want to marry Reid now," Dexter reiterated.

Ackley chuckled.

Reid glared.

Leaning on the table, Ackley's chuckle escalated into a full-on belly laugh.

"What's so funny?" Reid demanded.

Shaking his head, Ackley went over to the cabinet off to the side. He pulled out a jug of her father's alcohol, along with several cups.

Royce entered. "Harlan's here. He said he was invited?"

Ackley waved him in. Harlan stepped around Royce, joining them in the great hall.

"You came just in time," Ackley said. "We're about to make a toast to Dexter and Reid."

"I fear this is my doing," Leigh said with a sigh. "I must have dropped him on his head when he was an infant."

"Mother," Ackley said. "My friend," he handed Dexter a cup, "is eager to enter into marital relations with Reid." He winked.

Reid plopped her head onto the table, hiding her face with her arms. Could Ackley be any more embarrassing?

"What?" Ackley said. "Stop looking at me like that. You all know it's true."

"Yes, but that doesn't mean you have to say it out loud," Idina chided. "Regardless of the reason, I think it's a wise move."

"Come on, Reid," Ackley goaded. "Head up. You agreed to it, so you must be equally eager to share his bed."

She grabbed the cup someone had set in front of her, drained it in four gulps, then chucked it at Ackley. He ducked, the cup narrowly missing his head before banging against the wall and crashing to the floor.

Leigh clapped twice, effectively silencing everyone. "Ackley, leave Reid alone. Reid, go get out of your wet clothes—I'm cold just looking at you. Idina, help Reid get the letters written." She scanned the room. "Gordon, organize the army. Ackley, help your brother. Dexter, entertain Harlan. We will meet back here for supper in one hour." On her way toward the exit, she came to an abrupt halt. "Apparently, I will be cooking supper. Maybe one of the soldiers can help." She tapped her finger on her chin. "Well, what's everyone waiting for? Do as you were told. Now."

Reid jumped up. Hurrying from the great hall, she then ran up the stairs two at a time. Inside her bedchamber, she peeled off her wet clothing. After dressing in dry pants and a tunic, she opened her door to find Idina there.

"Do you have paper and ink in here?"

"No." Reid led Idina to the duke's office. Sitting in her father's chair, Reid pulled open the top drawer, taking out several sheets of paper. She felt so small in her father's chair. She'd never sat in it before.

"Do you know what to say?" Idina asked as she perched on the chair across from Reid.

Taking the quill, she dipped it in ink. "I know exactly what to say."

Reid poured her heart into the letters. She explained how she'd been raised, how she'd pretended to be a man so her father wouldn't lose his land and title, how she'd been sent to Axian where she learned another way of life, how the king had brought an army here from Melenia, and how they—the women of the kingdom—had the power to save it. She not only called on the power the ring invoked, but she also called on each duchess, each woman, personally, encouraging her to raise her army to fight the king and the invading foreign army. When she finished, she dipped her ring in ink, pressing it to each letter to verify she possessed the ring and had the authority to call upon them. Then she closed the letters with her father's wax seal.

"Give these to Gordon. See that each one makes it to the correct duchess."

With a nod, Idina took the letters.

"Make sure the soldiers remain along the northern coastline watching Melenia's ships. If we're sending our troops south, we don't want to be caught unaware in the north."

"I'll speak to Gordon on the matter."

After Idina left, Reid exited her father's office and headed to the great hall. She found Dexter and Harlan at the table, each with a drink in hand.

"Everything all right?" Reid inquired.

"Yes." Dexter patted Harlan on the back. "I'm just trying to get to know your friend."

"Spill it," Reid said, taking a seat across from them. "Don't look at me like you don't know what I'm talking about, Harlan. Tell me what's wrong." She'd grown up with him. She knew something was bothering him by his hunched shoulders and the way he kept glancing at Dexter while chewing on his bottom lip.

He shrugged. "I'm worried about how you're faring in Axian."

"I've been trying to assure him you're fine." Dexter rubbed the nape of his neck. "Probably would have been more convincing if I left out the assassination attempt."

"You know," Harlan said as he twisted his cup in his hands, "I almost went to Axian to save you. But then I realized you didn't need me—or anyone else—to do that."

Reid reached across the table, taking Harlan's hand. "I should have written to let you know I was doing okay. I'm sorry." She'd taken the time to write her father, and she should have done the same with Harlan and her sisters. However, she'd never been good with correspondence of that nature.

He finished off his drink. "I'll be honest, Reid. I didn't expect you to *want* to marry Prince Dexter."

To Reid, Dexter said, "I filled Harlan in on everything." Then, to Harlan, "Please, there's no need for titles and formalities."

Harlan nodded. "When I saw Reid earlier at the apothecary's shop, I was worried Axian would have changed her. But she's still Reid. And for that, I'm glad."

Dexter drummed his fingers on the table. "How well versed are you with antidotes to commonly used poisons?"

"Very," Harlan answered. "Since there's only one apothecary in town, and I'll be taking over for him, my education is extensive."

"I think you should come with us."

"Why?" Harlan's brows drew together in confusion.

"Since you know how to make different antidotes, you might come in handy. Anna does love her poisons."

"Who's Anna?" he asked.

"I didn't tell him that part," Dexter said to Reid. "I figured you'd want to handle that one when you're ready."

"Yes, I would." And she was nowhere near ready to talk about her mother with Harlan or anyone else for that matter. "I understand having Harlan with us might be vital, but have you asked him if he wants to come?"

"No. I only just thought of bringing him along now." Dexter took a drink.

Reid looked expectantly at Harlan. "Do you want to come to the City of Buckley?"

"You know I hate to travel. But yes, I'll come to help. If anything happened to you, I'd never forgive myself."

"Will the apothecary be okay if you leave for a bit?" Reid asked.

"He has to be. If you don't pull this off, Marsden might cease to exist."

"And your wife?" Would Sophie be okay with him leaving?

"She will be fine for a couple of weeks without me." He stared down at his empty cup.

"How's married life?" she asked. Harlan had always been a private person, rarely sharing the details of his home life.

"We're still getting to know one another as husband and wife." He stood. "Speaking of Sophie, I should get home. She will be wondering where I am."

"Before you go, I have a question," Dexter said. "Will you do me the honor of standing in for my brother when Reid and I marry?"

Harlan faced Reid. "Do you truly want to marry Dexter?"

"Yes."

"Not to save the kingdom, your land, or your father, I mean. Do you love Dexter and want to marry him?"

"I do."

He nodded before addressing Dexter. "Then yes, I will stand in for your brother. Reid deserves the best. I'm glad she has found someone she wants to share her life with."

"Thank you," Dexter replied humbly.

Harlan headed toward the exit. "Oh...there's one more thing." He pivoted toward Dexter. "If you harm Reid in any way, you won't have to worry about Anna, Eldon, or anyone else. You'll need to worry about me. Every bite you take, every breath you breathe, could be your last. I'll use a poison you know nothing about, and you'll never ever see it coming." With that, he left.

"I like him," Dexter said.

Reid snorted. Harlan usually didn't threaten people, and he was rarely so direct—especially with someone like Dexter.

However, she understood why he'd done it. It warmed her heart. "He's my best friend."

"I know. And I'm jealous of that. I hope to steal the title from him one of these days."

Leigh entered the room. "I enlisted two men to cook for us. Since they're soldiers, I'm not sure what they plan to make, but they assured me I didn't need to worry." She sat next to Reid. "It appears we have a wedding to plan."

"There's nothing to plan other than getting the town's marriage binder," Reid said.

"Since I can't help with the army, I intend to help with the wedding." Leigh abruptly stood. "I have an idea. I'll be back." She hurried from the room.

"It's strange for me to be around her," Dexter mumbled.

Reid had forgotten Dexter's father, Henrick, had been in love with Leigh before Nara. "I'm sorry. If it's easier, we can get married without anyone else present."

"No. She's my aunt, and Gordon, Ackley, and Idina are my cousins. I'd like to have a couple of witnesses. It'll be fine. It's just...odd. But I honestly can't complain. Not when you just discovered your mother is still alive."

Ackley sauntered into the room. "Thought I'd find you two love birds in here." He sat next to Reid, across from Dexter. Running his hands through his hair, he let out a sigh. "A letter just arrived."

"From whom?" Reid asked.

"Colbert."

"Who delivered it?" Dexter asked, a hint of panic in his voice.

"A young guy. He's outside if you want to question him."

"What does the letter say?"

"Gordon has it if you want to read it. It's just an update.

Basically, it says the dukes have been stripped of their titles and are being held in the dungeon. Colbert believes once the duchesses arrive, the dukes and duchesses will be killed."

So nothing they hadn't expected.

"I'd like to speak with the messenger." Dexter stood. "Will you take me to him?"

Ackley agreed, and the two men exited the room.

Dexter had to be worried about his brother. Reid had wanted to ask if there was anything in the letter about Nara, but she knew not to. The warrior princess could take care of herself. Same with Gytha. Dexter had enough to worry about without reminding him of those he cared for who were stuck in the palace with Eldon.

It was hard to reconcile the fact Eldon and Dexter were half-brothers. How could two people who shared blood be so different? Of course, all Reid had to do was look at her own mother. Anna was cold, shrewd, and the opposite of what a mother should be in every way.

The following morning, Reid exited the castle and headed to where the soldiers had gathered. Men loaded supplies onto carts. Off to the side, several others sparred. Since she hadn't seen Dexter, Ackley, or Gordon at breakfast, she assumed they were out here somewhere.

She entered the only erected tent, which served as Gordon's command center. "You're alone," she said as she entered. "I thought Dexter and Ackley would be with you."

He set his quill on the low table, observing her. "I suspect they're sparring."

She sat across from him. "Why is that?"

"I know my brother," he replied. "And Dexter is a challenge to him. He fights, moves, and thinks differently."

Scanning the maps and correspondence strewn on the table, she asked, "How are things going?"

He rubbed his face. "I'm trying to figure out how to lure Eldon out of the City of Radella in order to preserve the city. I don't want to turn it into a battlefield."

"Any ideas?" Dexter had marked a spot on the map where he wanted the battle to take place. It was about five miles north of the city.

"Not yet. Whenever I think about my brother, I get so angry and confused. How could he kill our father? That's when I remember Hudson wasn't his father, Henrick was. And that's how he could have done it."

Reid wasn't convinced Eldon had killed Hudson. She suspected her mother had something to do with it. However, that didn't change anything. Eldon intended to murder the dukes and duchesses in order to have total and complete control of Marsden. He'd also invited a foreign army into the kingdom. And, most importantly, Eldon wasn't the rightful heir—Henrick was. Of course, Henrick was dead. Sort of. Which made Dexter the rightful heir.

"I intend to leave first thing tomorrow morning with my mother and Idina," Gordon said. "We'll be accompanied by half of your father's men. I hope other counties' soldiers start arriving at the City of Buckley about the same time as we do." He pinched the bridge of his nose.

"What else is bothering you?"

"I hope Dana is okay."

Dana. His pregnant wife. Reid didn't know what to say because she had no idea what Eldon planned to do with the woman.

"You and Dexter seem to get along." He picked his quill up.

Reid nodded.

"Are you certain you want to marry him? You don't have to. You can still offer Ellington's support without legally binding yourself to the man."

"I know." Which was why Dexter had asked her to marry him now. It would show they were choosing this instead of being forced into it. "I want to marry him. He treats me as an equal." And he was passionate about his people. He embodied everything she found important.

"I need to get back to work," Gordon said. "I'll see you later today."

She exited the tent, making her way over to the sparring area. When she reached it, Dexter and Ackley weren't sparring as Gordon had suspected. Instead, Ackley was working with Idina on some basic self-defense moves. A few soldiers watched, encouraging her. Reid hadn't been sure how Ellington men would feel about women being in the army. Maybe, just maybe, they saw the value of women knowing how to fight.

Standing next to Dexter, she watched Idina throw a punch. "Does she know it would be easier in pants?"

"I told her that," he responded. "She said she intends to wear dresses, so she needs to know how to move and fight in one." He shrugged.

"We're getting married." Hopefully, nothing would interrupt the ceremony this time.

"We are."

"There's still so much I don't know about you."

"What would you like to know?" he asked.

"Well, for starters, I want to know what it's like to spar with you."

"You would?" He chuckled, the sound deep and throaty. "Let's rectify that right now. Come on."

"I don't have my swords." She'd left them inside her bedchamber.

"If you're disarmed, you need to be able to defend yourself."

"True."

"I've been training for years. I think it's safe to say I could easily overpower you."

Where was he going with this?

"I'd like to work with you."

"Okay."

They stood opposite one another. "I'm concerned about someone sneaking up on you," he said. "If someone comes up behind you, what do you do?"

Easy. "Flip them over my shoulder."

"What if you don't know they intend to harm you?"

Whenever she'd fought, it had always been with the assumption the person meant her harm. "I'm not sure."

Placing his large hands on her shoulders, he turned her until she faced away from him. "Let's say I come up behind you. I hit your head, knocking you to the ground. What do you do?"

She'd never practiced a situation like this one before. "I'd roll over to face my attacker."

"Then he knows you're still conscious."

"So I should pretend I'm knocked out?"

"Yes. And hope he moves on." He instructed her to stretch out on the ground as if she'd just been hit. "Your attacker will probably kneel to check to see if you're conscious." He knelt next to her, feeling her neck. "When he does this, you make your move."

She twisted, grabbed his wrist, and pulled, applying pressure as if attempting to break his arm.

"Excellent." He helped her to her feet. "Another concern is someone snatching you to use against me or someone else who cares for you." He turned her so her back was to his front, then he wrapped his arm around her body, pinning her arms down. "Pretend I have a knife pointed at your throat. What do you do?"

A good question. It was hard to think logically so close to Dexter. With his arm around her body, her back pressed against him, all she could see and smell was him. Closing her eyes, she chided herself. She needed to focus. Opening her eyes, she attempted to think rationally. "If you were shorter, I'd throw my head back and hit your head." The top of her head didn't even come up to Dexter's chin. What else could she do that would be effective? Well, he was a man. Reaching back, she patted his groin. "I could squeeze until you let me go." She heard him suck in a quick breath.

He released her, quickly retreating. "Yes, that will work." He rubbed a hand over his face. "When your attacker lets go, you run like hell."

CHAPTER EIGHT

For the second time in Reid's life, she stood before a mirror, readying herself for her wedding. Hopefully, they'd get through the entire ceremony this time. If they did, she'd be married in a couple of hours.

Ironically, the last dress she'd worn had also been a wedding dress. The one she wore now, Idina had confiscated from Kamden's bedchamber. Even though it wasn't made for this occasion, it suited Reid just fine. The light blue fabric covered her shoulders and arms, fitting snugly against her chest and hanging straight to the floor. It was simple, yet elegant, and it made her feel pretty.

"I hope you don't mind," Idina said as she came into Reid's room, "but I went into the field and picked some flowers." She set a bundle of wildflowers, lavender, and ferns on the desk. "I can braid a couple into your hair, and you can carry the rest during the ceremony."

Reid smiled. This was starting to feel like a good-old country wedding.

"It's nice to see you happy," Idina commented.

"Having the ceremony with only a couple of people makes it feel more like a wedding and less like a merging of counties or a business deal." It also made it more intimate, more personable, and more real.

"Regardless, that element is there. Never forget that no matter what you feel for Dexter, you are a representative of Ellington, and you will be the queen of Marsden. That comes with a lot of responsibility."

Even though Reid knew she could handle the position, it was the social interactions she would have to get used to. Especially since Axian and northern Marsden were vastly different. She would need to find a way to merge the two, forging a new future for all involved. She just had to survive the next couple of weeks.

Eldon had put out a kill order on all the Knights. If the king managed to capture Reid, he'd order someone to eliminate her. She rubbed her temples, thinking about the Knights. Hopefully, Ackley would be able to control the small contingent of Knights in northern Marsden. If Anna maintained control over the organization, who knew what havoc they'd cause. There were so many unknowns.

Idina tied several of the flowers together, making a crown for Reid. She set it atop Reid's head. Placing her hands on Reid's shoulders, she looked into her eyes and said, "Tonight is about you and Dexter. But come tomorrow, you two need to focus on what's ahead of us. Understand?"

"Yes." And since it was just them, she decided to ask, "Did you tell your mother we plan to assassinate Eldon?"

"I did."

"How did she take it?"

"After he attempted to strangle her, she realized her son had changed and is a danger to the entire kingdom. My mother supports us, and she will do what needs to be done to secure peace in Marsden. Dexter is part of our family—and, very shortly, you will be, too."

Someone knocked on Reid's door. Idina answered it, talking to whoever was on the other side. When she shut it, she smiled. "It's time."

Reid took one last look in the mirror. The flower crown added a nice touch. She picked up the remaining flowers, tying a ribbon around the stems to hold them together.

As they exited Reid's room, Idina said, "I hope you don't mind, but we rearranged the great hall for tonight."

Reid wasn't sure what they could move other than the table. "I'm sure whatever you did is fine."

Idina glanced over her shoulder, smiling at Reid. "Don't look over the mezzanine and ruin it."

Keeping her focus on Idina, Reid descended the stone stairs to the first floor, wondering what they could have done.

Idina stopped. "Wait here until the music starts."

"Music?" Where'd they get music?

A sly smirk spread across Idina's face before she turned the corner and disappeared from sight.

Rolling her shoulders back, Reid tried to calm her excitement as she waited for her wedding ceremony to start. She was moments away from marrying Dexter in an intimate setting in her own home. The only thing that could make this more perfect would be if her family were there. She banished that thought since they'd be in attendance for her formal wedding in Axian.

A lute started playing a melodic tune. Reid assumed that was her cue, so she rounded the corner. Her father stood in the hallway dressed in his formal tunic with the Ellington family crest on the front.

"What are you doing here?" she asked, shocked.

"When I heard my baby was getting married, I rushed home." He took hold of her upper arms, giving her a squeeze before kissing her forehead. "You look beautiful." Tears filled his eyes.

"You rushed back just for me?"

"Of course." He released her, then held out his arm. "Are you ready?"

"Yes." Although, if he'd asked that question a few weeks ago, she would have given a vastly different answer.

"I think Dexter is a good man, and you two are well suited for each other."

She took her father's arm, and they continued to the entrance of the great hall.

The table had been moved off to the side. Candles lined a path from where Reid stood to the other side of the room where the marriage binder waited, Dexter on his left. Leigh, Idina, Ackley, Gordon, and Harlan were all there, smiling encouragingly at Reid. One of her father's soldiers stood in a corner, playing the lute.

Duke Ellington patted his daughter's hand, and they walked down the candlelit aisle. Growing up, Reid had never envisioned how her wedding day would be—she'd never even given it a thought. In Axian, the almost-wedding ceremony had been more of a show for the people. However, as she moved toward Dexter, all she could think about was how perfect the candles, music, and having her friends there was. And Dexter —his eyes were alight with excitement as he waited for her, dressed in solid black. This ceremony was for them alone, which made it even more special. When she reached the marriage binder, Duke Ellington handed Reid over to Dexter.

His large hand took hers. "You look beautiful," he whispered before they faced the binder.

The musician stopped playing, and the binder thanked everyone for coming. With a warm smile, he started talking about the importance of marriage and joining two families together to make a new one. "And, of course, part of creating that new family is procreation."

Dexter had the nerve to squeeze Reid's hand. She tried not to elbow him. After all, her father was only a few feet away from them.

"And now, we will begin the vows. Please face one another."

Reid handed Idina her bouquet, then turned to Dexter, their hands joined. While she hadn't known him that long, she couldn't believe how much had changed between them. Reid recalled the first time they'd encountered one another in his parents' bedchamber in Axian. She'd broken into the palace in an attempt to steal the box Eldon needed. Dexter had caught her, and they'd briefly fought before she'd been apprehended. Dexter had intimidated and scared her during that encounter. Then, at the beginning of their engagement, he'd wanted nothing to do with her. Now, everything was different. Everything had changed.

Once Reid got around Dexter's rough exterior and saw the man underneath, her heart had started to fall for him. She admired the man he was, understanding his loyalty to his family, his people, and his kingdom. Marriage to him would be a true partnership. They would work side by side to not only make Marsden a better place, but to support one another as well.

"Prince Dexter Winston, do you take Lady Reid Ellington to be your wife?"

"I do." His deep voice echoed in the room, confident and loud.

A surge of happiness swept through Reid at hearing Dexter say those words.

"Do you promise to be true to her, to love and respect her?"

"I do," Dexter answered, his eyes focused on Reid, as if trying to convey the enormity of what he promised.

"And do you, Lady Reid Ellington, take Prince Dexter Winston to be your husband?"

"I do." As the reality of what was happening hit her, she smiled. She was actually marrying the man before her.

"Do you promise to be true to him, to love and respect him?"

"I do." While the uncertain road ahead would be difficult at times, she would honor her marriage vows every day of her life.

The binder pulled out two silver rings. Reid took the larger one, sliding it onto Dexter's finger. He, in turn, took the other and slid it onto her finger.

"I now pronounce you husband and wife."

Dexter leaned down, pressing his lips to hers in what was supposed to be a chaste kiss. However, a surge of desire swelled inside her. She wanted to show him how much she cared for and loved him. Deepening the kiss, she slid her hands around his neck, pulling him toward her.

He chuckled, the sound deep and throaty. "There'll be plenty of time for that later," he murmured in her ear.

Dexter laced his hand with Reid's, and they turned to face their family. And just like that, Reid was a married woman.

"I officially present Prince Dexter Winston and his wife, Lady Reid Winston." When they held the ceremony in Axian for all to see, she would be crowned at that time.

Everyone applauded. Duke Ellington hurried forward. He shook Dexter's hand, then hugged Reid.

Two Ellington soldiers entered, and Idina directed them to move the table back to the center of the room. Harlan ran around placing candles along the perimeter. Once the room was back in order, the soldiers returned with several plates of food. They set the plates on the table before congratulating the happy couple.

"If everyone will please take a seat," Leigh said. "We have a special meal prepared to celebrate."

As everyone sat, Reid scanned the faces of those present. She wanted to remember this moment for the rest of her life. Duke Ellington sat tall and straight, his chest puffed out a little more than she'd seen as of late, pride radiating from him. Gordon, on the other hand, sat slightly slouched, his face blank with indifference. Leigh had never been particularly warm toward Reid, and now was no exception. Her being involved and helping had to do with the fact Dexter was her nephew and Henrick's son. Idina kept glancing at Reid with smug satisfaction, as if she knew a secret. Reid sincerely hoped it didn't have to do with what came after dinner. However, knowing Idina, she'd probably done something in regard to a marital suite for the night. Reid shoved all thoughts about that aside. For now, she wanted to enjoy the moment. Harlan smiled warmly from where he sat beside her, seeming genuinely happy for his friend. When she looked at Ackley, his brows drew together and his forehead wrinkled in confusion. His attention remained on his spoon as he tapped it against the table, lost in thought.

Dexter rubbed her back. "Are you okay?" he mumbled so only she would hear.

"Perfect." When she turned toward him, her breath caught.

This man was her husband. And he was watching her as if she were the most important thing to him. Leaning in, she placed a soft kiss on his cheek.

His lips curved into a smile. "I don't think I'll ever get used to that."

Duke Ellington stood, capturing everyone's attention. "Thank you all for being here tonight to celebrate my daughter's marriage to Dexter. I'm honored to gain such a worthy son-in-law. When I look at my youngest daughter and see how her face lights up when Dexter walks in the room…well, I can tell you that, as a father, I can't ask for anything more than my daughter's happiness." He raised his cup. "Dexter, thank you for being Reid's partner in life."

"Here, here," Gordon said, raising his cup.

Everyone took a drink, then started eating. Her father reminisced about his wedding day. Leigh shared a story about the day she married Hudson. Harlan even joined in to offer a few things about the day he married Sophie

"It is getting late," Gordon said, "and I am departing before the sun rises. Mother, Idina, I assume you are packed and ready to go with me?"

"We are." Idina sighed. "I suppose I should retire for the night." She stood, then exited the room.

"Come, Harlan," Reid said. "I'll walk you out."

He thanked everyone for including him, then followed Reid to the front door. "I'm glad you're happy," he said. "I was afraid Dexter would have stifled you. Or resented you. Clearly, I was wrong. If anything, he's helped bring you out of your shell."

Reid hugged her dear friend. "I'm glad you'll be coming with us. I've missed you." She wanted to hear more about his life with his new bride, how things were going at the apothecary's, and what else he'd been up to since Reid had been in Axian. The journey to the City of Buckley would afford them plenty of time to catch up.

"Me too." He released her before trying the door. Only, it wouldn't budge.

"That's strange. Is it locked?"

"It doesn't appear to be."

Maybe it was just stuck. "Let's try another door."

They headed past the great hall toward the servants' quarters where the back door was located.

"Do you smell that?" Harlan asked, pulling Reid to a halt. "It smells like damp dirt or the ground after a heavy rain."

She took a deep breath. "I smell smoke."

"It's valerian root. I'm certain of it." He ran his hands through his red hair while pacing back and forth. Stopping, he sniffed. "Is someone burning it? It only works as a sedative if it's ingested, not burned."

"Sedative?"

Harlan headed toward the kitchen, sniffing as he went.

"What are you doing?"

"Trying to find the source of the smell."

"The smoke is probably from all the candles being blown out. I'm sure everything is fine."

"Even so, what about the valerian?" As he pushed the kitchen door open, they were greeted by flames—the entire kitchen engulfed.

The sheer heat pushed Reid back. "Idina!" she screamed. Idina's bedchamber was located right above the kitchen. Turning, Reid took off running up the stairs to warn her friend. She found Idina coming out of her room.

"What's going on?"

"There's a fire in the kitchen." Reid grabbed Idina's arm,

dragging her downstairs. Thick black smoke poured out from under the kitchen door, filling the hallway.

Dexter stood at the bottom of the stairs, waving them on. "Everyone's in the great hall."

"All the doors are jammed," Gordon said as Dexter, Reid, and Idina entered the room.

Ackley cursed. "Let's bust a window. We can get out that way." Picking up a chair, he banged it against one of the windows, shattering it. After setting the chair down, he broke a leg off and used it to clear the shards away. "Gordon, go first. Organize the soldiers. We need buckets of water. Get lines going."

Gordon rushed over to the opening as smoke started filling the room. The fire was quickly spreading to other parts of the castle.

"Wait," Harlan said. "I still smell valerian. Something is wrong."

"I smell it, too," Ackley said, leaning against the wall next to the window.

"We need to get out of here before the fire reaches this room," Gordon said. "The smoke is getting bad." He moved to put his leg through the opening to climb out.

An arrow shot into his calf. He crumbled backward, falling to the floor. "Everyone down," he ordered.

Reid slid to the floor. Were they under attack? How could that be when there were hundreds of soldiers outside? Who would be attacking them and why?

Gordon slid across the room, propping against the wall near Reid.

"How bad is it?" she asked.

He made two fists, took a deep breath, and then reached

down, pulling the arrow free. Blood gushed from the wound. "I'll be fine."

Harlan squatted next to Gordon, ripping one of the curtains down. He tore a strip of fabric off, using it to tie a tourniquet around Gordon's leg. "This will help stop the bleeding."

"I don't see anyone out there," Ackley announced as he peeked out the broken window.

"Wait here," Dexter commanded. "I'm going to the second floor to take a look." He ran from the room.

Leigh put out the last of the candles, sending the room into darkness.

Duke Ellington sat next to Reid. The smoke intensified as the flames moved to the sitting room next to the kitchen. "I need to get a few personal items from my office. Do you have the duke's ring on?"

"No." She'd left it in her room for the wedding ceremony.

"Go upstairs and get it. Then come right back here. Don't worry about anything else. Understand?"

"Yes." Reid rose, hurrying from the room. Thick smoke filled the hallway, making it hard to breathe. She sprinted up the steps, holding her breath. In her bedchamber, she could feel the heat from below through her shoes. Going straight to her dresser, she plucked the ring from her drawer and slid it on her finger. Since her pants were right there, she pulled them on, ripping the dress off and replacing it with a tunic. Her swords were lying on her desk, so she grabbed them, strapping them to her waist.

Someone went running past her room. "Dexter?" she called.

"What are you doing up here?" he asked, coming into her room.

"Getting the duke's ring. What did you see outside?"

"The soldiers appear to be asleep."

"Can you tell who shot the arrow?"

"No." He took her hand, pulling her from the bedchamber and down the stairs. "Whoever shot Gordon must be watching us from the tree line. We need to get out of here without them seeing us."

She realized if it were simply one person out there, they could create a distraction at one window while everyone snuck out another. However, that couldn't be the case since hundreds of soldiers were passed out, most likely from the valerian Harlan had smelled earlier. How could it have been distributed to so many?

Reid and Dexter rejoined everyone in the great hall. Dexter quickly told them what he'd seen. "We need to get out of here without anyone seeing us. I don't suppose you have any secret tunnels?"

The duke shook his head. "The only thing we have is a root cellar. And that's in the kitchen."

"We don't have much time," Dexter said. "We'll have to fight our way out. Do you have shields and weapons?"

Duke Ellington nodded. "They're old, but I have a couple of shields in my office."

Dexter rose, pulling the duke with him. They left the room, quickly returning with three shields.

"Harlan and Idina, you two will use this one." Dexter thrust one of the shields at Harlan. "Tatum will use one. And the last will go to Reid and Leigh."

"What about the rest of you?" Reid demanded, panic starting to set in at the prospect they might not all make it out of this alive.

"We'll use chairs." Dexter pointed at the heavy chairs around the table. "When you exit with the shields, squat and keep it raised above your head. Move fast. Go straight to the stables. Whatever you do, don't stop. It's harder to hit a moving target. Understand?"

Reid nodded, taking a shield from Dexter.

"Since the doors are stuck, each pair will use a different window to exit the castle. You have five minutes to get out of here. While you're doing that, the three of us," Dexter pointed at Ackley, Gordon, and himself, "will cause a distraction at this window. Hopefully, we'll keep the archer focused on us while the rest of you escape."

"Leigh and I will exit the front office," Reid said. "Harlan and Idina, use the window in the sitting room. Father, use the window in the receiving area."

"Go!" Dexter shouted.

Hefting the shield up, Reid held onto it as she and Leigh sprinted to the front of the castle where the office was located. Thick smoke filled the space. Thankfully, it was free from flames. Not having much time, Reid set the shield down.

"These windows open," she explained. Twisting the levers, she popped the windows outward. She feared breaking the glass would be too loud and attract attention.

Leigh moved toward the open window.

"Wait," Reid said, ducking below the opening. "I want to make sure this window isn't being watched."

When a slew of arrows didn't rain down on them, Reid peeked outside. The soldiers were to the east of the castle, so she couldn't see them. The stables were diagonal from here. "I'll climb out first to hold the shield for you. Once it's up, climb out."

Leigh nodded.

"You might want to pull your dress up and tie it, so you don't trip." Reid was glad she'd put pants on. Without waiting for Leigh's response, Reid lifted the shield, sliding it out of the window. Since she wasn't strong enough to climb out with it, she dropped it on the ground, then quickly crawled out the opening. Grabbing the shield, she covered her body. Her heart beat frantically as she waited for an arrow to strike. Nothing happened. With shaking hands, she held the shield up and moved forward, giving Leigh enough room to climb out. A moment later, Leigh fell beside her.

"Stay right next to me," Reid whispered.

Leigh nodded and grabbed one of the handles on the shield, helping hold it upright. The two women squatted and moved forward, keeping the shield angled above them as they went. Reid mentally pictured the path they took, trying to keep them on course. No screams or grunting noises sounded in the night. Hopefully, everyone else had made it out safely.

Breaking glass sounded somewhere behind her. She wanted to look to see what was going on, but she couldn't. Her arms shook from the weight of the shield, her thighs burning from squatting.

When they neared the stables, Royce urged them on. He stood at the entrance with the door open a couple of inches. Reid and Leigh turned so their backs were to the door, then Leigh slid inside first. Royce reached down, helping Reid into the stables.

"Is anyone else here?" she asked, dropping the shield. Her throat stung from all the smoke she'd inhaled.

"Duke Ellington is here," Royce replied as he kept watch at the door.

"Harlan and Idina?"

"Not yet."

If anything happened to her friends, Reid would be devastated. What could she do to help?

Leigh's shoulders started shaking, and Reid realized the woman was crying. She wrapped her arms around Leigh, despite not being close to her. "I'm sure Idina will be fine."

She wiped her eyes. "I don't understand how Eldon can do this. How can he be so cruel?"

Even though Eldon seemed the likely culprit, they didn't have proof he was involved in tonight's events.

"They're coming," Royce announced.

A minute later, Idina and Harlan stumbled inside. "Sorry," Harlan said. "We ended up on the wrong side, and we had to sneak around the corner to get to the door."

Reid released Leigh, waving Idina over. Idina hugged her mother while assuring her everything would be okay.

Peering outside, Reid scanned the area for Dexter, Ackley, and Gordon. A chair protruded from a window as someone started to climb out.

Duke Ellington rubbed his face. "There should be some bows and arrows in the back room."

"I'll fetch them," Royce said. He returned with two bows and a couple dozen arrows.

Reid took one of the bows, then nocked an arrow. She didn't know what she was aiming at. A person? Movement?

An arrow sailed through the air, landing on the underside of the chair just as Ackley jumped to the ground, causing him to stumble. He held the chair in front of his body as he regained his footing. Once steadied, he moved toward the stables. Another arrow shot through the air, this one landing toward the top of the chair's seat, much too close to Ackley's head for Reid's liking. Based upon the way the arrow stuck out of the chair, Reid determined the general direction it had been shot from.

Holding the bow like Markis had shown her, she aimed for

where she thought the archer was. She had to either draw the person out or distract him enough so Ackley and the others could get safely to the stables.

"Idina," Reid said as she prepared to shoot. "Come up with a plan. We don't want someone setting the stables on fire."

Reid released the arrow. It sailed toward the trees. She hoped she didn't accidentally strike one of her father's soldiers.

"There's a ladder in the back," the duke said. "It'll take you to the loft where there's a small lookout. You'll be able to see if anyone is approaching."

"Mother," Idina said, "I need you to go up there and keep watch. If anyone besides Ackley, Gordon, or Dexter approaches, holler. Can you do that?"

"Yes." The tears were gone, and Leigh's voice sounded stronger.

Reid nocked another arrow and shot again, unable to see where it landed. Her fingers stung from pulling the heavy string back. Loading arrow after arrow, she shot again and again until Ackley reached the stables.

"Where's Dexter and Gordon?" she demanded, scanning the area surrounding the castle.

"We made a slight change to the plan," Ackley said after he dropped the chair, breathing heavily. "When'd you learn to shoot?"

"I've always known how to shoot, but in Axian, I learned how to hit."

He laughed. "Well, that is a handy skill to have."

Reid remained perched in the doorway, which was only cracked a couple of inches, the loaded bow at the ready. "What's the new plan?" She continued to scan the area.

"I was the bait."

"Explain." She lowered the bow, not sure she wanted to know what her husband and Gordon were up to.

"I came out the window with the chair, keeping the archer's focus on me so the other two could escape out a back window. They are going north about a mile and then looping around, hoping to come up behind the archer and take him by surprise."

"Whose idiotic idea was that?"

He smiled sheepishly.

She whacked his shoulder. "Why?"

"We need to discover who wants us dead."

Reid shook her head, focusing again on the land surrounding her home. She couldn't actually look at the castle, which now had flames licking out of the windows. Everything she owned was burning—her father's books, her treasured weapons, her sister's dresses. It would be ashes by morning. A deep pain stabbed at her chest. She shoved it away—now was not the time to feel. It was the time to act.

"What are you thinking?" Idina asked.

"Anna loves her poisons," Ackley murmured. "And all those soldiers were given a sleeping tonic. I don't know how she managed to give it to so many."

"It could be Eldon," Duke Ellington pointed out.

"I agree," Idina said. "We plan to assassinate him and take control of the kingdom. It seems only logical he'd try to prevent us from doing so."

"I suppose you're right," Ackley said. He came up behind Reid. "Give me the bow. I'll take a turn keeping watch."

After handing the weapon over, she leaned against the wall. Her head throbbed, her eyes stung, and it hurt to breathe.

"I'm sorry," Idina said. "I'm sure this isn't how you imagined your wedding night."

Reid snorted. Her wedding night wasn't on her mind right now. All she could think about was her home burning. And Dexter, who was out there somewhere, in danger. She couldn't sit in the stables while he was trying to flush the archer out. She had to help.

Pushing off the wall, she went to the door.

"Where are you going?" Ackley demanded.

"To save my husband."

CHAPTER NINE

"Then I'm going with you," Ackley said, swinging the bow over his shoulder. After stocking up on arrows and finding a suitable sword, he picked up one of the shields.

Reid withdrew her twin swords. "Hurry up." A sense of panic started to take root.

"When people hurry, mistakes are made. We need to be smart. I will lead the way, and you will follow behind me." He pointed at the shield, making his point.

"Fine."

"Reid," Duke Ellington said. "I think you should remain here. Let Ackley handle it."

Ten nasty retorts came to mind. As if she shouldn't go out there simply because she was a woman? That she needed to let a man handle it? However, now was not the time to argue. Her father was simply worried about her well-being. She could understand that.

Instead of replying, she ignored him and opened the door. Ackley slid through it, lifting the shield. He clicked his tongue twice, and Reid assumed that was her cue to move. With her swords in hand, she exited the stables, keeping her body right behind Ackley's. He headed south, remaining against the stables for cover.

The archer was somewhere to the east near the tree line.

When they reached the end of the building, Ackley whispered, "Ready?"

"Yes."

He squatted, covering most of his body with the shield. Then he steadily moved south. Out in the open, Reid felt exposed. The shield suddenly felt too small for them both. She kept expecting an arrow to come their way. When Ackley moved, she moved. When he paused, so did she. It seemed like it was taking them forever to reach the tree line.

A loud moan cut through the night, followed by a rumbling crash. Reid jumped.

"Go." Ackley jumped up, then took off running.

Reid scrambled to keep up with him. They made it to the first set of trees. With the trunks providing cover, they slowed.

"What was that?" she demanded, glancing over her shoulder. The sky above the castle glowed bright orange from the fire.

"I think part of the roof collapsed." Tossing the shield on the ground, he headed deeper into the forest.

Trying not to think about the destruction of her home, Reid scrambled to keep up. "Why'd you run?"

"The castle served as a distraction. I used it to our advantage."

Adjusting her hands on the hilts of her swords, she realized she was shaking. If she wanted to be of any use out here, she needed to calm her nerves so she'd be ready to fight. "Thanks for coming with me."

Ackley shook his head. "I didn't do it just to save your arse," he said. "Gordon is out there, too."

Helping Dexter had consumed her so much she'd forgotten about Gordon. "What's the plan?"

"Either they push the archer forward, toward the castle, where my mother will spot him from her elevated position. Or they push the archer east and we lose him."

"What about the soldiers?" How would they rouse them? Or did they simply have to wait for the draught to wear off?

"I'm counting on Harlan to deal with that." He froze, head snapping up as he scanned the treetops above.

What had Ackley heard? Afraid to move, Reid examined the area, not seeing anything. She took a step back, bumping into someone. Before a yelp could escape her lips, a hand slid over her mouth, the tip of a knife pressing into her side.

She didn't want to be taken hostage and used against her family, so she had to get out of this situation. Plus, Dexter would be furious if her trying to help him turned into him needing to save her. Letting go of the sword in her right hand, she reached back, grabbing the man's groin. The second the man jerked, withdrawing the knife from her side, she dropped to the ground, intending to kick his legs out from under him. Only, he collapsed next to her, a dagger protruding from his chest.

Scrambling away, Reid was about to question how Ackley had moved that fast when a twig snapped in the tree above her.

Ackley swung the bow over his shoulder while nocking an arrow. He shot. Someone fell from the tree, crashing on the ground next to Reid, an arrow sticking out of his stomach.

Reid sprang to her feet, moving away from the two dead bodies. How many men were out there?

Ackley scanned the area. His head cocked to the side as he

listened to something Reid couldn't hear. Then he took off running through the forest, dodging between the trees. She sprinted after him, only one sword in hand. She cursed herself for not picking up the one she'd dropped.

Grunts came from up ahead. Nearing the commotion, Reid saw Gordon fighting with two men. While still running, Ackley nocked an arrow and shot, striking one. Gordon swung, punching the second attacker. Ackley nocked another arrow, killing the second man as well.

"Where's Dexter?" Ackley demanded.

"North. There are two more." Gordon pointed to his left while bending over, trying to catch his breath.

"Keep Reid with you." Deftly jumping over the bodies, Ackley took off running.

While Reid wanted to go, she stayed in place, knowing she couldn't fight the caliber of men they were up against.

Gordon dropped to his knees, examining one of the bodies.

"What are you doing?" Reid asked while trying not to look at the blood oozing from the puncture wound. The metallic smell made her nauseous.

"Searching for anything that might tell me who he is or who sent him."

Knowing it could either be the king or Anna, Reid went over to the other body. Setting her sword aside, she knelt next to the man and pulled his sleeve up. No tattoo. Relief filled her. She checked the man's pockets, not finding anything. "Now what?"

Gordon rose, wiping his face. "We need to wake the soldiers, regroup, and prepare for the journey to the City of Buckley."

"What about..." She pointed at the bodies.

He closed his eyes. "I'm trying not to think about the fact

my brother—my own flesh and blood—just sent assassins to kill us." He looked at Reid. "How you feel about your mother is how I feel about my brother. It's like I don't even know him. Yet, somehow, it doesn't surprise me that he did this." He kicked a nearby tree. "Let's go."

"What about Dexter?"

"My guess is Ackley went to keep one of Dexter's attackers alive so he could question him. That's not something you want to witness."

She followed Gordon to the edge of the forest. The castle still stood, flames licking out of the windows. In one section, the wooden roof had collapsed. Tears filled her eyes as a deep pain pierced her heart.

"I'm sorry," Gordon said. "But at least we're all safe."

He'd never been well spoken.

Not wanting to talk about her destroyed home, she asked, "Do you think the assassins are the king's Shields?"

"No. I didn't recognize them." He started walking toward the sleeping soldiers.

"How do we know it's safe?" There could be more assassins lurking nearby.

"We don't. But we need to rouse these men and get the fire out."

Reid had no idea how they would do either of those things.

"Are you coming?"

She nodded. "I'll be right there."

Wiping the tears from her eyes, she attempted to rally her strength and courage. Right now, her energy had to be on rousing the soldiers and providing help where needed.

A distinct, pungent smell permeated the air, reminding Reid of the smell Harlan had noticed earlier in the castle. A twig snapped behind her just as an arm snaked around her body. A cloth was shoved over her mouth and nose.

Before she could protest or fight back, everything went black.

The first thing Reid became aware of was the bouncing. Her arms hung above her head, her stomach pressing against something bony as someone gripped her legs. That was when she realized a man carried her over his shoulder as he ran.

Reid's head throbbed—whether from the valerian or the bouncing, she couldn't be sure. Her stomach rumbled with nausea as it pressed against the bony shoulder of the man carrying her. She couldn't even think straight in this position. A light mist covered the ground. The sky—at least what Reid could see of it upside down—was a dull gray, the crisp air cold. How long had it been since she'd been abducted?

Even though her wrists were bound together, she pressed her hands against the man's back, trying to steady herself so she wouldn't be jostled so much. After what felt like several hours, the sun started to set, the sky darkening.

The man carrying her finally stopped. "We can't follow standard protocol," he said. "Let's set up a perimeter fifty feet out."

Reid peered around him, trying to see who he was talking too. She counted eleven men, plus the one holding her, so twelve in total. They broke into three groups, each heading in a different direction.

When the man finally set Reid on her feet, she swayed and collapsed on the ground, her head pounding, her throat raw. One of the men handed her a piece of bread. She grabbed it, devouring the food. When she finished, he handed her a sack of water, which she drained dry.

Once her stomach had sustenance, she was able to start thinking clearly. Why couldn't these men use standard protocol? Who were they? And what did they want with her? Reid observed the four men, immediately recognizing them as belonging to the unit of Knights in Gordon's army—the men Ackley was in charge of.

Reid wanted to pull her sleeve up to reveal her tattoo, proving she was a Knight. However, her wrists were bound together, preventing her from doing so. Instead, she said, "Why did the Knights kidnap me?"

The four men stilled. Then one jumped to his feet, withdrew a strip of fabric, and tied it around Reid's head, fully covering her mouth. She rolled her eyes.

He squatted in front of her, then reached out, gently pushing a strand of hair away from her face. "You're safe. That's all you need to know. Nobody here is going to hurt you." He stood, then walked away.

A cold chill slid over Reid's body. The way the man had touched her felt intimate. She wasn't used to feeling vulnerable. Instead of arguing and making a scene, she remained quiet, choosing to listen instead of fight—at least for now. Once she knew why the Knights had taken her, she would decide how to proceed.

After the men ate, three went to sleep while one remained on watch, a sword in hand. Not having many options, Reid laid down, trying to get comfortable. It was impossible to with a gag around her mouth and her hands and feet bound.

In the darkness, she tried to think rationally. Why would the Knights abduct her? Ackley was in charge of these men. However, he hadn't given the order to kidnap her. Which meant these men were following someone else's orders. Anna, perhaps? To complicate matters, the men who'd drugged the Ellington soldiers and set fire to Reid's castle hadn't had the mark of a Knight. So who were those men and why had they destroyed her home? Why had they been trying to kill Reid and her friends? Were those men working with the Knights or independently? Maybe that was the reason the Knights had intervened—they were trying to keep Reid safe? If that were the case, why the bindings and the gag?

Well, one thing was for certain, ever since she married Dexter, nothing had gone the way Reid thought it would.

She must have dozed off, because she startled awake, the sky still dark. Remaining still, she tried to figure out what had awoken her.

"Any concerns?" a man whispered.

"No, nothing. It's been quiet during my watch."

"Good. I'll be glad when we reach the stables tomorrow where the horses are stashed. Then we can travel faster."

"It's been a long time since I've been to our headquarters."

"Don't you think it's strange she tasked twelve Knights with this assignment?"

It was quiet for several minutes.

"Maybe she just wants her daughter protected."

Reid realized Anna had tasked these men with bringing her to the Knights' headquarters. But why?

"What I don't understand is why we took her from Ackley. Why not work with him?"

There was a shuffling noise as the man who'd been on watch laid down. "I heard she said she needs Prince Dexter controlled. Something about him being a liability and the way to keep him in line is through her."

A few minutes later, the man's breathing evened out as he

fell asleep. Unable to sleep herself, Reid decided to get to work. Since there was one man on watch, she had to be as quiet as possible. Moving slowly, she used her shoulders to shove the gag away from her mouth. After ripping off a piece of fabric from her tunic, she raised it, using her teeth to tear it into smaller pieces. Tomorrow, she'd leave a trail.

The next morning, the group rejoined the others shortly before sunrise. Once again, a soldier threw Reid over his shoulders like a sack of flour. Only today, she didn't mind. It afforded her the opportunity to drop pieces of fabric, hoping Dexter would be able to track her. The task seemed futile—the Knights probably had too far of a head start. Nevertheless, doing so gave Reid hope.

Just before sunset, they reached a small town, the group stopping on the outskirts. Two of the twelve men went into the town to inquire after the horses. Reid sat, leaning against a tree. Her stomach growled, her head throbbing from being upside down for so long.

"I feel bad we're doing this behind Ackley's back," one man mumbled. "It doesn't seem right. He's always been our leader."

"I agree," another replied. "And you know Ackley—when he gets mad, he turns into a beast."

Reid recalled the couple of times she'd seen Ackley kill. He fought like a panther and killed without remorse. When the mercenaries attacked them in the middle of the night, he'd slaughtered them all without hesitation. He was so different from Dexter, who let the Melenians get away when Colbert had been struck by the knife. Of course, Ackley had been trained by the Knights to be an assassin.

Reid's skin prickled. Something was wrong. Sitting up, she scanned the area, trying to figure out the cause for her unease.

"It's taking too long," one of the Knights said.

"We'll give them five more minutes. If they're not back by then, you two will go check on them."

Reid's wrists were tied together, her hair knotted from traveling upside down for two days and sleeping on the ground, and she had a gag around her mouth. Dread filled her. If Ackley saw her like this, he would strike down every single one of these Knights.

The pieces of the puzzle started to fall into place as Harlow's words came back to haunt Reid. What was Anna's end goal? Anna wanted to destroy the Winston family and control Marsden through Reid. The Knights were a stumbling block because they took an oath to protect the kingdom—not support Anna's warped agenda. Which meant Anna didn't want the Knights to take Reid to their headquarters so she could control Dexter. No, she wanted Ackley to think Reid was in danger, so he'd kill the Knights for her.

Reid tried warning the men, but the gag made her words unintelligible.

"I think she's trying to tell us something," one of the Knights said.

One of the men squatted before her, looking into her panic-stricken eyes. He reached forward, gently pushing the gag down so she could speak clearly.

"This is a set up," she said, tears filling her eyes.

The man remained in front of Reid. "Why do you say that?"

What if she were wrong? When she opened her mouth to speak, the man in front of her collapsed.

CHAPTER TEN

eid jumped, fearing a dagger struck him. She didn't see anything protruding from his body. One by one, the men around her fell to the ground.

Ackley stepped around a tree trunk, examining the scene. "Are you okay?"

"Did you kill them?" she demanded.

"Why do you ask?"

"They're your Knights."

"Yes, I know." His face remained unreadable.

"There are two more. They went into town."

He nodded. "Dexter is dealing with them."

Dexter was there?

Ackley knelt before her. "Because these men are Knights, I'm assuming they did not harm you?"

"I'm fine."

He cut her bindings. "Don't want Dexter to see this. He might change his mind."

"What are you talking about?"

"He insisted we not kill them." He stood, pulling Reid up along with him.

"So these men aren't dead?" Relief filled her.

"No." Ackley rubbed his forehead. "I wanted to kill them, but Dexter convinced me otherwise."

A hundred different questions came to mind. Before Reid could voice any, Ackley must have sensed her confusion because he chuckled. "As we tracked you, Dexter thought this may be a setup. I wasn't so sure. However, I had two days with Dexter where I had no choice but to hear him out. We argued. A lot. In the end, we compromised."

"I didn't think you capable of compromise."

He smiled ruefully. "Not normally. And if we'd found you that first night, I would have killed every single one of these men for taking you."

"Why?" They were his Knights. His friends. He'd known them far longer than her.

Instead of answering, he said, "I agreed to shoot the men with some of the sleeping tonic we found near the drugged soldiers at your castle."

"These men are asleep?"

"For now." He rubbed his forehead, examining them. "What do they want with you?"

"They said Anna instructed them to take me to the Knights' headquarters so she could maintain control over Dexter. However, that doesn't make any sense." She chewed on her bottom lip, working it out in her head.

"What are you thinking?" Ackley asked.

"That Anna wanted you to assassinate them. I think she's trying to kill all the Knights. In order for her plan to work, she has to eliminate the organization."

"Then we need to proceed as if that's what happened." Ackley nodded at the three men heading their way.

As they got closer, Reid noticed Dexter's focus was pinned solely on her.

Ackley chuckled, the sound anything but funny. "I'm pretty sure if he came here alone to deal with these men, he would have killed them all when he saw the state you're in."

"That's because you don't know him," Reid insisted.

He didn't reply.

When Dexter was close enough to hear her, she said, "I'm fine." He scanned her body, obviously searching for injuries.

The two Knights with Dexter knelt to examine their comrades.

"As promised," Dexter said, "they're asleep, not dead."

Ackley tilted his head. "How'd he get you to come willingly?"

"He's our prince," one answered. "He ordered us to stand down. Said Anna had sent an assassin after our unit. He said if we came willingly, he would ensure none of my fellow Knights were harmed."

"And you believed him?" Ackley asked.

"I wasn't sure. I figured I'd come and if I didn't like what I saw, I'd kill him."

Reid didn't think the Knight would have been able to kill Dexter so easily. However, she kept that opinion to herself. "Now what?" she asked.

"We proceed as if the assassinations took place," Ackley replied. "Anna can't know Dexter thwarted her plan."

"Did you figure out who set my castle on fire?" Reid asked. "And is everyone still okay?" They had been the last time she saw them.

"Everyone is fine," Dexter assured her. "As for who burned

your home, after questioning one of the men we found in the forest, it appears the king gave the order."

"Then what were the Knights doing there?" Reid asked.

"Anna heard the king sent soldiers north to assassinate Duke Ellington and whomever was with him," Dexter explained. "So she must have used them as a cover for the Knights to sneak in and kidnap you. Ackley wasn't supposed to know the Knights took you. He was supposed to think they were the king's men. Anna must have hoped he'd kill them before realizing who they were."

Reid rubbed her temple, trying to think it through. In order to stay one step in front of Anna, Reid had to figure out what her mother intended to do next. "We proceed as if everything went according to Anna's plan. Ackley saved me, these Knights were eliminated, and now we're traveling to the City of Buckley to gather what's left of the Marsden army."

"Correct." Dexter turned to Ackley. "How long until they wake up?"

"I gave them a low dose, so ten, fifteen minutes."

"We need to get moving," Dexter said. "Anna could have someone in town who reports to her."

"Assuming Ackley just slaughtered a dozen men, what would he do next?" she asked.

"I'd burn the bodies."

"Then we need to make it look like that's what you're doing."

Ackley nodded. "I'll go shoot some deer. We can use the blood and bones at the scene of the massacre. Then we'll set the area on fire."

Once he left, Dexter turned to the two Knights. "I'm going to take Reid and get her cleaned up. You stay here with your men. When they wake, let them know the plan."

"Yes, Your Highness," they replied.

"What are your names?"

"He's two, I'm one."

"Very well." Dexter took hold of Reid's hand, gripping it. "I'll be back with my wife in twenty minutes. When Ackley returns, help him prepare the area."

When Dexter called Reid his *wife,* both men's eyes widened. They'd probably only thought of her as Anna's daughter.

Dexter pulled Reid up the hill and out of sight from the Knights. He walked so quickly Reid almost tripped over a tree root. However, his grip on her remained firm, keeping her upright. They wound their way between the trees until they reached a narrow river.

Dexter's shoulders heaved up and down. "Are you okay?"

"Yes." She squeezed his hand before letting it go. Kneeling on the bank, she splashed refreshing frigid water on her face.

"I assume no one...*touched* you?" While he asked it as a question, his tone held a menacing threat.

She could feel him watching her, so she glanced over her shoulder, meeting his eyes. "No. I was not harmed in any way. I'm fine."

Closing his eyes, he gave a brief nod, his shoulders finally relaxing. "The water looks deep enough for you to bathe in if you want. I can keep watch."

"Thank you. I'd like that."

When he turned his back to her, she peeled off her clothes, tossing them on the ground. Stepping into the water, she tried not to slip on the slick rocks. She went deeper, gradually adjusting to the chilly water. Once it reached her waist, she went under, washing off the accumulated dirt and grime.

Resurfacing, she peered over at Dexter. He now faced her

direction, scanning the surrounding area, looking everywhere but at Reid.

"I'm coming out now," she announced, curious to see what he'd do. Would he watch her?

He turned around, his back to her once again.

"You know you can look." As she said the words, she felt her face flush. Normally, she wasn't so bold.

He stilled.

Afraid she'd been too forward and had somehow offended him, she said, "You know, because we're married. It's okay for you to keep watch while I exit the river." Now she sounded like a bumbling idiot.

He shook his head. "Oh, Reid." The way her name rolled off his tongue sent a shiver through her. "The first time I see you —*my wife*—naked, will be when we have all night to spend together."

She slipped on a rock, stumbling under the water. Scrambling to her feet, she tried not to focus on images of being in Dexter's arms all night. What would it feel like to be with him?

"It doesn't sound like you're out yet."

"I'm not." Shaking her head, she climbed out of the river and put her clothes back on. A large boulder stood a few feet away, so she climbed on top of it and sat. Pulling her boots on, she tied them, hoping she'd warm up now.

Dexter flicked a gaze over her. "All dressed?"

"Yes." She patted the spot next to her on the boulder. "Sit with me."

"We should get back to the others."

Instead of responding, she patted the spot again. He came over, collapsing on the boulder next to her. "I want to thank you."

"For what?" he asked.

"Coming after me."

He rubbed his face.

"What's the matter?" she asked.

"Do you remember the conversation we had the night of our engagement party?"

"Yes." He'd said he didn't want to love someone because he feared it would make him a slave to that person. She wrapped her arm around his large shoulders, resting her head against him, not knowing what to think. Was he upset he had feelings for her?

"Reid." He sighed. "When I realized you'd been kidnapped, I've never felt terror like that before."

"I'm sorry."

"It's not your fault." He twisted toward her, taking her hands in his. "I hate feeling helpless. I thought you'd been taken to get to me. That someone knew my weakness. And when I found your abductors, I planned to kill them. Then I realized that's what Anna, or whoever is behind this, wants. I had to force myself to calm down. To think rationally."

She didn't want to be his weakness—she wanted to be his strength.

"When I saw Ackley, he transformed into someone I didn't recognize. I realized, he, too, was falling into the trap that was set for us. It took every ounce of strength I had to think logically instead of with my emotions."

"I'm glad you didn't fall for it." Reid's voice sounded small. Where was he going with this? What was he trying to say?

"I'd been so afraid of something like this happening."

"Are you trying to say you don't want to be with me anymore?" Tears threatened.

He focused on her as he reached up, gently cupping her

cheeks. "I've been so afraid of loving another person. I want you to understand—I watched my parents. I saw how much my mother loved my father. And I saw my father pining over another woman. While he came to care for my mother, it wasn't the same intense love she had for him. I've been afraid of that. I didn't want to love someone who didn't love me back. I couldn't handle that feeling of rejection."

"What are you saying?"

"That I *want* to be with you, to love you. I want kids with you. A future with you. Because the thought of losing you, of not having you in my life, is unbearable. What I'm trying to say is—despite my fears of you not loving me or me losing you—it's worth it. Being with you is worth it." His eyes shone with intense sincerity.

Movement off to the side caught Reid's attention as one of the Knights approached. "Sorry to interrupt," he said, "but Ackley's back. It's time to set the fire and get moving."

"We'll be right there," Reid replied.

Dexter's brows drew together. He still hadn't released her face.

She knew she needed to express her feelings. However, articulating such things was difficult for her. All her life, she'd been so careful to keep others at a distance that it was hard to let him in. And right now, the nearness of him overwhelmed her. "I have a lot I'd like to say, and I don't want to be rushed. Can we finish this conversation later?"

His hands slowly slid from her face to her shoulders. "Of course."

When they neared the other Knights, one who appeared to be about Reid's age twisted to face them, sweat trickling down his forehead.

"Are you okay?" Reid asked.

"I think I'm going to be sick."

Dexter maneuvered his body, blocking Reid's view of the other Knights. "I want you to take this Knight to the river. Wait there for me."

Some of the men were directing where to put more blood. Reid looked at Dexter in question.

"Trust me."

She nodded. Taking the Knight's arm, she pulled him away from the others. "You're not bothered by the blood, are you?" Given the fact he was not only a Knight, but also a soldier in the army, she couldn't imagine he'd be ill over something like that.

He pulled the collar of his tunic away from his neck. "I can handle a lot of things. However, animal mutilation is not one of them."

Wanting to change the subject, she asked about how he became a Knight, what he liked most about being a member of Ackley's unit, and if he preferred the long or short sword. Sitting on the boulder, the Knight—who said he was identified as number twelve—dutifully answered Reid's questions. While he chattered away, she thought about what Dexter had revealed and how she would respond. She grappled with how to put her feelings for him into words.

The Knights wordlessly joined them a few minutes later, just after sunset. The group headed east. Once they'd gone about two miles, Reid asked if they'd be stopping soon since it was becoming difficult to see.

"We're too close to the town," Ackley said. "We can't stop until we're farther away."

They exited the forest. Reid didn't like the idea of traveling out in the open without trees to provide cover. However, Ackley insisted they traverse this route because it would take them directly to the City of Buckley. According to him, no one would expect them to travel this way.

After a couple of hours, Ackley finally halted everyone. He ordered three men to stay on watch while everyone else got a few hours of sleep.

Reid was just about to lie down when Ackley approached.

"Can I please speak with you privately?" he asked.

She felt Dexter tense next to her, but he didn't say anything.

"Of course." She followed Ackley about a hundred feet away from their campsite. "What is it?"

"Are you okay?" he asked, his back to her.

"Yes." He'd already questioned his Knights. They'd given him a full report of what had happened from the moment they took Reid until Ackley recovered her.

He shook his head. "You got married, watched your home burn, and then were kidnapped." He finally turned to face her. "I want to know how you're holding up." There was a gentleness to his voice she rarely heard.

"I haven't allowed myself to think about it." Which was the truth. If she did, she'd be overwhelmed. There was too much to do right now to allow that.

"Reid." He reached out, taking her hand. "You know you're like a...sister...to me."

"I know." She considered him the brother she'd never had.

"If you need anything at all, even if you just want to talk, I'm here for you."

"Thank you." She squeezed his hand, then let it go. It dawned on her that something was bothering him. "What's on your mind?"

He rocked back on his heels. "I'm afraid of Anna. I've been

so focused on Eldon and what he intends to do that I never saw her attack coming. I fear I'll miss something else."

"It's not your fault." Anna was responsible for burning Reid's home and kidnapping her—not Ackley. "If it makes you feel any better, she scares me, too." Anna had years to plan this. "But if there's anyone who can outsmart her, it's you."

"I'm glad you have so much confidence in me."

While he probably meant the comment as a joke, his voice held a hint of sadness, making Reid pause. "Is something else bothering you?"

"No, it's nothing."

"Ackley…"

"Fine." He ran his hands through his hair. "Your kidnapping really threw me off."

"You found me. Everything is fine." She kicked at the ground with the tip of her boot. "And it's not like you can plan for every possible scenario. I know you pride yourself on having a plan and several backups, but sometimes things just don't go the way you think they will."

"You're right. But that wasn't what I was referring to. When I realized you were gone, something in me snapped."

She couldn't imagine if the roles had been reversed. If she'd discovered her father, Dexter, or Idina were missing, what would she have done to save them? How would she have felt?

"I realized I've been lying to myself about something. Your kidnapping forced me to face it. And now I don't know what to do." He looked everywhere but at Reid.

She had no idea what her kidnapping had forced him to face. Instead of inquiring about it, she said, "You're a good man, Ackley. I think you expect too much of yourself. No one is perfect." She smiled, trying to reassure him.

"Let's get back," he whispered. "We have a long day ahead of us tomorrow."

When they returned to the others, Ackley walked Reid over to where Dexter waited for her. Ackley then left, saying he had the first watch.

"Since we're short on bedrolls," Dexter said, "I told them we'd share one."

Reid simply climbed under the blanket. Dexter stretched out next to her, wrapping his arm around her waist. Nestling against her husband, she fell into a blissful sleep.

The following days fell into a routine. The group rose early and traveled until it was too dark to walk any farther. Then they would set up camp only to do it all over again the next day. After a week, Ackley finally declared they would arrive at the City of Buckley tomorrow.

Unease filled Reid. Anna knew they were headed to the castle. Not only that, but it also felt wrong to be going to Eldon's home while he remained in the City of Radella—Dexter's home. However, there weren't any other options since they needed to organize the army, and this was where a majority of the army was located.

After stretching out her bedroll, Reid plopped on top of it, exhausted.

Ackley laid out his bedroll next to hers. "Tomorrow, the Knights will break into smaller groups before heading into the city. I have a few safe houses Anna knows nothing about."

"Do you think she has other men in the city?" Reid was afraid her mother would somehow be watching them.

"No. We'll still need to be vigilant, but she only has the Knights at her disposal."

Reid untied her boots, then removed them. "When will Gordon and the others reach the castle?"

"Even though they had a head start, since they're traveling with Ellington's soldiers, it'll take them another four to five days before they arrive." Ackley stretched out on his bedroll. "Did Dexter tell you that your father decided to remain behind?"

She nodded. The castle burning had caused quite a lot of concern in the City of Dorsot, so Duke Ellington thought it best to stay there with his people. Since he'd given his ring to Reid, she was able to make decisions on Ellington's behalf. And now that she was married, the duke no longer felt like it was his place to take care of Reid.

"When we reach the City of Buckley, what's the plan?" she asked. Even though Dexter had been the commander of the Axian army, since he was going to be the king, he was relinquishing control of his soldiers to Gordon, who was the commander of the Marsden army.

"I want to go through Eldon's possessions to make sure there's nothing we're missing. Then Dexter can start organizing the soldiers. That way, when Ellington's soldiers arrive, we'll be ready for them."

She absently nodded, pulling at a piece of grass.

"What's the matter?" he asked. "There's nothing to be worried about."

At that, she raised her eyebrows.

"I'm serious. We've got this under control."

That was precisely why she was nervous. If there was one thing she'd learned, nothing ever went according to plan.

Ackley reached out, taking Reid's hand. "Stop worrying."

Dexter approached them. "Perimeter check is done. Four men are on watch." He sat next to Reid, rubbing his face. He opened his mouth to say something, but stopped. Instead, his focus zeroed in on where Ackley held Reid's hand.

Ackley immediately let go. "I better go to sleep—I have the next watch." He rolled over, his back to them.

Reid wondered if there was something else bothering Ackley that he wasn't telling her. Not wanting to push the matter, she laid down. Dexter stretched out next to her. She wondered what tomorrow night would bring once they were in the castle. Would she and Dexter share a bed as husband and wife? She still hadn't told him how she felt. Somehow, the words eluded her. But maybe there was another way. She closed her eyes, imagining how she could express her love to him.

Reid opened her eyes. The sky was only just starting to lighten, a thick fog coating the ground. What had woken her? Usually, she was one of the last to rise in the morning. Rolling onto her side, she noticed Ackley lying there. He stared blankly into space. She mouthed, "Everything okay?" Hopefully, no one was planning to attack them. Reid didn't think she had enough energy to fight someone right now.

Ackley nodded before rolling over, facing away from her.

Unable to fall back asleep, Reid snuggled closer to Dexter, the morning air cold and crisp. Once the sky lightened some more, the Knights started to wake up.

After eating a quick breakfast, Ackley put the men into groups of three, giving each a different route to take to the City of Buckley along with a different safe house to stay at. Once the Knights left, Dexter, Ackley, and Reid set out.

"Why are you fidgeting?" Ackley asked.

She hadn't even realized she'd been playing with the edge of her tunic. "What if the king told the soldiers manning the gate to be on the lookout for us? What if he told them we're enemies of the crown?"

Ackley shook his head. "I'm a prince. So is Dexter. They have no choice but to listen to us. And the king isn't here to give them any orders."

Eldon had stripped Ackley's title. "Technically, you're not a prince any longer," Reid pointed out.

"We'll be fine. Eldon's plan only works if he maintains peace here in the city. If people catch word he intends to overthrow the dukes, chaos will ensue. He can't manage the army on his own. My father saw to that."

"How so?" Dexter inquired.

"Given what my father had been through," Ackley said, "he believed each of his sons should control a different element of the kingdom. Eldon was tasked with politics, and Gordon was put in charge of the army."

Reid knew there was no way Gordon was capable of stepping into the role of king. Not only did he not know how to handle the dukes, but his public-speaking skills were also severely lacking, and he didn't have the political savviness Eldon did. She just didn't realize he was that way because of a lack of education and training manufactured by his father.

"And you?" Dexter said. "What did your father expect from you?"

"Originally, he intended for me to handle the kingdom's finances. However, I pretended to be abysmal with numbers so I wouldn't be stuck at a desk all day. When he taught me sword work, I excelled. He told me I could help Gordon with the army." He shrugged. "I honestly don't think he knew what to do with Idina."

As they exited the forest, Reid became anxious at seeing the city again. She tried to remain calm, knowing the king wasn't there.

"I'm surprised there aren't agricultural fields near the city," Dexter commented.

"Not much grows right around here," Ackley replied.

"Where does your food come from?"

"This city is only a fifth the size of the City of Radella. A lot of it is brought in."

Reid didn't want to point out the rampant poverty. Dexter would see that for himself.

"My father wanted to make sure the army was well funded, the castle cared for, and there was plenty of food on his plate. I hate to say it, but taxes are high. People don't have a lot here. Northern Marsden is vastly different from Axian."

Reid hoped to change that. She wanted to take Axian's prosperity and bring that way of life into Marsden. People here didn't understand how much it hurt them by not allowing women to work or own a business.

They ascended the hill overlooking the castle. When Reid reached the top, she came to an abrupt halt, the color draining from her face.

Ackley cursed.

Hundreds and hundreds of soldiers surrounded the city.

CHAPTER ELEVEN

"Those aren't Marsden soldiers," Ackley stated. "Nor are they from Melenia."

"Who are they?" Reid didn't see a universal uniform among them.

"Based upon what I'm seeing, I think they're from Cartr, Alder, and Bridger. I'll know for certain once I get closer."

"Do you think they're here to support us?" Dexter asked.

"I sure hope so." Ackley headed down the hill, toward the city, Reid and Dexter following suit. "Because if they're not, we're in a heap of trouble."

"With this many soldiers amassing, word is going to reach the king," Reid mumbled.

"Probably," Ackley replied. "But then Eldon will realize he has nowhere to retreat to since Dexter has his men in the south, and we are here in the north."

"I think we need a plan in case those soldiers aren't here to support us," Dexter said. He stopped, crossing his arms and observing the scene before him.

"Get moving," Ackley commanded. "I'm sure someone is

watching us. If you stand there, you'll attract attention. Pretend like you know where you're going and what you're doing."

Dexter started hiking down the hill again. "What's our plan?" His voice held a hint of worry, so used to being the one in control that it had to be hard for him to trust Ackley.

"Our first order of business will be to announce ourselves at the castle," Ackley stated. "Then, we'll get to work."

Reid wondered who Eldon put in charge in his absence.

When they reached the bottom of the hill, Ackley led them slightly north, toward the main entrance. Reid tucked her hair under her tunic, wishing she had a hat to hide it with.

"Stop fidgeting," Ackley hissed.

Rolling her eyes, Reid put her hands at her sides, not knowing how Ackley had managed to see her playing with her hair since she was behind him.

"The gates are open," Ackley mumbled. "That's a good sign."

Dexter pursed his lips. Reid knew he had questions, but now was not the time to ask them. During her stay in Axian, she hadn't seen a single city surrounded by a wall. Rumor had it Hudson built it to protect himself from his own brother.

They reached the main entrance. Most of the people meandering about were merchants, probably because of all the soldiers nearby. Hardly any citizens were coming and going. Four Marsden soldiers manned the gate. As Ackley, Dexter, and Reid entered the city, the soldiers barely even glanced their way.

Ackley took the main road cutting directly through the city. Malnourished children ran about, people slept in alleys, and others begged for food. Since the road was dirt, dust kicked into the air, making Reid sneeze. When they reached the portion of the city where the wealthier shops were located, the scenery changed. People here wore heavier clothes without holes, all had shoes on, and, instead of rotting trash, the smell improved to baking bread and roasting meat. Every single woman they passed wore a dress and was escorted by a man. Reid kept her head down, hoping no one noticed she was a woman wearing pants.

They finally reached the interior wall separating the castle from the city. Ackley rolled his shoulders back, stepping in front of Reid and Dexter to address the soldiers manning the gate. "Everything secure?" he asked, his voice deep and commanding.

The one soldier's eyes widened, clearly surprised to find Prince Ackley in front of him.

"Yes, Your Highness," he answered.

"Excellent. My mother and sister will be arriving in the next couple of days. Please be on the lookout for them."

The soldier nodded, then granted them entrance.

They headed straight for the castle.

"The bells didn't ring to announce you," Reid commented. The soldiers manning the main gate for the city were usually the ones to ring the bells, announcing when a member of the royal family had arrived. However, Ackley hadn't revealed himself to them.

"No, they did not," he replied. "I didn't want whoever is in charge to know I'm coming. Catching them by surprise will be so much more fun."

"This is Eldon's home?" Dexter asked, eyeing the castle.

Ackley shrugged. "Idina, my mother, Gordon, that miserable wife of his, and I all live here."

His brows drew together. "It's...not what I expected."

"Rarely is anything what we expect it to be." Ackley threw

open the front door. "I'm home," he announced. No one responded. The castle smelled musty, and there were no candles lit. Not a single servant was in sight. "Let's see if anyone is in the great hall." Ackley strolled down the hallway, whistling as he went.

"Hudson grew up in the palace at the City of Radella," Dexter mumbled as he followed Ackley.

Reid nodded.

"I thought he would have built something far grander here. No wonder Eldon wants the palace for himself."

This castle was more in line with Reid's grandparents' manor. "Now you can understand some of my astonishment at seeing the palace for the first time."

Entering the great hall, they found it unoccupied. The curtains were drawn shut, the room was dark, and the fireplace empty.

"Is no one here?" Reid asked. The place felt abandoned.

Ackley tilted his head to the side, cracking his neck. "Let's go to the barracks."

They exited the castle, heading to the adjacent building that housed the army. Several soldiers stood outside, talking to one another.

"You there," Ackley barked, addressing the closest man. "What's going on?"

The man snapped to attention. "What do you mean, Your Highness?"

"Who is in charge and who are the soldiers outside the city wall?"

The man's eyes widened, then he swallowed. "Shortly after you departed, the king left with the rest of the royal family, accompanied by half our soldiers. The castle was closed down since he didn't know when he'd be returning. We were told to maintain our position here." He pointed at the barracks. "We are to keep a secure perimeter of the castle and city. There are three armies outside the wall. Soldiers from Cartr, Alder, and Bridger."

Ackley folded his arms. "Why are there soldiers here from the neighboring counties?"

The man glanced between Ackley and Dexter. "To face the invading army from Axian?" He said it as if asking a question instead of giving an answer.

Ackley tapped his chin with his pointer finger. "I want you to announce there will be a meeting tomorrow morning in the courtyard of the barracks. Dismissed."

The man agreed and left.

"I need a drink," Ackley muttered before heading back toward the castle. "What are you thinking?" he asked Dexter.

"That these three counties are heeding the king's letter. The duchesses are here with the soldiers he requested. They're probably waiting for the remaining counties to join them. Once they do, they will march together into Axian, joining with the Marsden and Melenia soldiers already there. With those numbers, Eldon will be able to easily gain control of Axian, thus taking over the entire kingdom."

"I agree."

"Hopefully, the duchesses in the north received Reid's letter asking for help. I'm optimistic Reid convinced them to join us instead of following Eldon's orders."

"What's the purpose of the meeting tomorrow?" Reid chimed in.

"I want to introduce the men to Dexter. Then we'll start getting them organized so we can plan our own assault."

Inside, Ackley went straight to the staircase.

"I thought you needed a drink?" Reid said, wondering why he wasn't going to the sitting room or the great hall.

"I just said that in case anyone overheard me."

Now that she was thinking on the matter, she rarely saw Ackley drink. "Then what are we doing?" Because he was clearly walking with purpose.

He glanced over his shoulder. "We're going to my mother's room."

Instead of questioning him as to why they were headed there, Reid and Dexter quietly followed him. When they arrived, the door hung open on one hinge. Inside, clothes were strewn everywhere, the curtains shredded, and the bed flipped upside down.

"What happened?" Dexter asked.

"After Eldon tried strangling my mother, I snuck her out of the castle and hid her at Reid's home. Once Eldon realized she was gone, he probably had her room searched for the letters." Ackley went farther into the room, stepping over a drawer.

"I still can't believe Eldon tried killing Leigh." Reid moved around a ripped dress, peering into the bathing chamber. It, too, was a mess with wooden buckets smashed into pieces and towels strewn about.

"I'd never seen him so angry before." Ackley rubbed his tired face.

"Do you think Eldon found the letters?" Dexter asked.

Ackley picked up a chair knocked on its side, setting it upright. "No. They're hidden." He knelt on the hearth.

"How did you manage to steal the letters from me?" Reid asked. "They were in a locked box."

The corners of his lips rose in a half smile. "Mother gave me the key. When I was at your castle, I saw the box sitting on your bookshelf. I used the key, stole the letters, and put that chess piece in there."

"Why?" By then, she'd been a Knight. He could have been honest with her and told her the truth. She may have even given them to him.

He shrugged. "I was being selfish and doing what I wanted —not what the Knights dictated. And I didn't want Eldon to have the letters. I also wanted to see his reaction when he found the chess piece, and he realized he was going to be challenged for the throne. You have to understand, at the time, I suspected he'd killed Father, but didn't have any proof." He yanked out one of the stones near the bottom of the fireplace. Reaching his hand in, he pulled out a handful of papers. "Here they are."

"Those letters prove Eldon is not the rightful king?" Dexter asked.

"They prove Eldon is the son of Leigh and Henrick."

Which meant Eldon wasn't Hudson's legal heir. Which, in turn, meant he had no right to be sitting on the throne. Either Gordon—Hudson's first-born son—or Henrick had the right to be king. However, since Henrick was considered dead, and Dexter had legally been declared his heir, then Dexter could inherit the throne.

"What's our next move?" Reid asked, biting her thumbnail.

Ackley stood. "Dexter is going to officially announce his bid for the throne."

***

They spent the next several hours holed up in the sitting room, trying to decide how best to word the letters to the dukes and duchesses. When they finished, Reid was impressed at the eloquent way Dexter presented the issue of Eldon not being the rightful ruler and declaring himself the true king. He also stated he wouldn't move forward without the complete support of the dukes and duchesses. He welcomed everyone to the castle where they could discuss the matter in greater detail. Once those letters were complete, Dexter wrote one to Eldon as well, stating his case.

"I don't know about you two," Ackley said around a yawn, "but I'm exhausted. I'm going to bed." He headed toward the door.

"Do you care where we sleep?" Reid asked.

Without turning to face them, Ackley answered, "You know where the guest wing is." He left without giving Reid a chance to say anything else.

Silence filled the room, making her suddenly nervous to be alone with Dexter.

He leaned back against the sofa, resting his feet on the low table.

"So," she said, contemplating the sleeping arrangements. Their marriage hadn't been consummated yet. Would Dexter want to do that tonight?

He tilted his head as she sat on the chair across from him, unsure what to say or do. Apparently, he wasn't going to offer his opinion on the matter. Of course, he'd bared his soul, telling her exactly how he felt about her. She had yet to do the same. Not because she didn't want to, but also because she was embarrassed and unsure how to do so.

Fidgeting with her wedding ring, she tried to decide how to proceed. Should she lead him to a bedchamber, then ask him if he wanted to consummate their marriage? Or would it be better to try to seduce him? Maybe she should just remove her clothes, making her intentions clear.

Dexter let out a long sigh. "Reid, don't look so panicked. If you're not ready, you're not ready. We can wait."

But that was the problem—she didn't like the idea of waiting any longer. She wanted him to know how she felt. "I don't want to be alone tonight."

"I'll stay in the same room with you," he assured her. "You can take the bed, and I'll take the floor." He stood and stretched.

Reid rose, then led the way to the guest wing of the castle where she chose a bedchamber at random. Inside, she lit a few candles before going over to the armoire, hoping to find something suitable to sleep in. After finding a large undershirt, she headed to the bathing chamber. It was small and nowhere near as luxurious as the one in Axian. However, it had water and soap, which was all Reid needed right now. She scrubbed away the dirt and grime that had accumulated on her body over the past week from traveling. When finished, she pulled on the undershirt.

Her legs were exposed. Chewing on her bottom lip, she tried to summon the courage necessary to go out there with bare legs. She could do this. They were married—there was nothing improper going on. Besides, showing Dexter how much she loved him was easier than telling him.

Taking a deep breath, Reid entered the bedchamber. Dexter knelt in front of the low-burning fire, stoking the flames to life. His hair was wet, and he had on a clean shirt and pants. He must have bathed in one of the adjacent rooms.

Going over to the bed, Reid pulled back the blankets. Since Dexter hadn't looked her way, her anxiety eased. "Can I ask you something?"

"Anything."

"Do you want to be king?" She sat on the bed, crossing her legs.

He stood, shoving his hands in his pockets as he turned to face her. "That's a good question, and one I can't answer." His eyes darkened as he took her in where she sat on the bed in a thin undershirt.

Her wet hair clung to her back. "You did just announce to the ruling families your intention to take the throne." If he didn't want to be king, why go through all this trouble?

"Yes, I did. But that wasn't your question." He sat on the edge of the bed, two feet away from her. "All my life, I've been groomed to lead. Whether that's as a commander for the army or as a ruler of the Axian people, I have had it drilled into me that I am a servant to my people."

"So you're willing to lead, whether you want to or not?"

He leaned back on his elbows, dangerously close to her legs. "Let me ask you something. Do you want to be queen?" His deep voice rumbled in the quiet room.

"No." She hated being the center of attention.

"But you married me knowing the outcome?"

"Yes."

"Why?"

Well, that was two-fold. "It's the best thing for the kingdom."

He nodded, as if expecting that answer.

"And I wanted to," she revealed.

Dexter went very still, almost as if holding his breath, waiting for her explanation.

"We need to join Axian and Ellington together in order to save Marsden. I understand that. But somewhere along the way, it went from me *needing* to marry you to me *wanting* to. Marrying you opens so many opportunities for me. I can change Marsden into the kingdom I want it to be—a place where everyone is equal, women can work and own land, where businesses can thrive, and people don't go hungry." She played with the edge of the blanket as she spoke. "And the thought of living my life with you at my side is very appealing. You make me feel things I've never felt before. You accept me for who I am, you challenge me, and you treat me as an equal. I want to be your partner in life. And...I want you." She couldn't believe she'd just said all that. Biting her lower lip, she waited for his reaction.

"I really want to kiss you right now."

A jolt of pleasure surged through her at hearing him say that. "The feeling is mutual."

He crawled on the bed until he was in front of her. She brought her hands up, sliding them around his neck and into his hair. When she tilted her head, his lips brushed hers. Dexter gently pushed her back onto the bed as he kissed her, carefully lowering his body over hers.

Reid didn't know what he intended to do. However, instead of worrying about what was coming next, she decided to just relax and trust him. What he was doing felt good, so she let him kiss her, his large hands roaming up and down the sides of her body.

And she kissed him back, savoring the taste and smell of Dexter.

They kissed for hours.

Reid woke up in Dexter's arms, well rested and content. Not wanting to wake him, she remained there, watching him. He seemed so peaceful while sleeping. Last night, all he did was kiss her—her lips, neck, ears. Not once did he push her to go further.

"Why are you staring at me?" he mumbled.

"I thought you were sleeping."

"I was until I felt you watching me." He opened his eyes, the corners of his lips rising. "Morning, beautiful."

She laughed. She'd always been so concerned with looking like a man and not attracting attention that she'd never allowed herself to feel beautiful before. For her husband to see her that way made her heart swell with joy.

"We need to get up," he said, rolling onto his back. "We have that meeting this morning with Ackley and the soldiers."

Reid pushed back the covers, sliding out of bed. The fire had died, making the room chilly. Grabbing a blanket off the bed, she wrapped it around her body. "I'll be back." Needing something to wear, she went to Idina's room. On her way to the princess's dressing closet, something caught her attention. She froze.

"Didn't mean to scare you," Ackley said, his voice groggy. He sat in a chair facing the window, his gaze meeting hers in the reflection.

"What are you doing in your sister's room?" She pulled the blanket tightly around her body, trying to ward off the cold.

"I've been in here waiting for you."

"Why?" She meandered over to the window, gazing outside. A thin fog covered the hills in the distance.

"I figured you'd come here looking for something to wear."

"That's not what I asked." She leaned against the windowsill, facing him. A bottle sat on the floor, and Ackley smelled of mead. "What's going on?"

He hadn't shaved, his hair stuck up in all directions, and

dark circles shone under his eyes. "You know Anna plans on killing Dexter, don't you?"

"I do."

"I won't let that happen," he promised. "I see how much you care for him."

"Once the Melenia army is dealt with, we'll worry about Anna." She waited for Ackley to say what was bothering him. When he didn't, she prodded, "Please talk to me."

"You know, the one good thing to come out of this is I don't have to marry Duke Lyndr's evil spawn."

Reid laughed. "Yes, being stripped of your title so you don't have to marry is definitely a good thing for you."

"I never wanted to marry."

"I know."

"You used to not want to marry either. But look at you. A married woman." Something dark flitted across his eyes.

"Yes." Where was he going with this?

"Dexter's a good man." He stood and stretched. "Which room did you take—so I can make sure to avoid the honeymoon suite?"

"Dexter and I...we haven't...I think we're going to wait..." Her face flushed. Why was she telling any of this to Ackley? Pushing off the windowsill, she went over to the closet, trying to find a simple dress to wear.

Most of Idina's outfits were rather ostentatious. Reid combed through them until she found one that was solid green without any frills. The neckline was high, the sleeves long. It would do nicely. Taking the dress, she exited the closet.

Ackley hadn't moved. He sat there, blank faced.

"What is it?" she asked.

He shook his head. "Nothing."

"I'll see you at breakfast." She exited the room, heading

back to the bedchamber she was staying in. When she arrived, Dexter had already changed.

She tossed the blanket on a chair. Stepping into the dress, she pulled it up to her waist. Now for the tricky part. Peering over at Dexter, she saw him studiously fixing the blankets and fluffing the pillows in an obvious effort not to watch her while she changed. She quickly pulled off her undershirt before sliding her arms into the sleeves of the dress, shimmying it onto her shoulders. "Um, can you help me?"

He wiped his hands on his pants. "What do you need?"

"Can you please tie the back for me?"

Dexter's hands went to her shoulders, twisting her so her back faced him. Heat radiated from his body. Licking her lips, she wondered why she was more nervous now than when lying in bed kissing him last night. He gently gathered her hair, setting it over her right shoulder. He trailed his hand up her bare back before pressing his lips against her lower neck. Heat seared down her spine.

"I just pull the strings and knot them?" he asked, his voice husky, his breath tickling her.

"Yes." Oh, holy hell, her voice sounded all breathy. She was fully clothed, and all he'd done was kiss her. How could he have such an effect on her?

He tugged the strings, cinching the back before tying it. "Finished."

"Now what?"

"Now it's time for us to save the kingdom."

Reid took Dexter's hand, and they exited the room.

CHAPTER TWELVE

While waiting for Gordon and the others to arrive with Ellington's soldiers, Ackley, Dexter, and Reid spent the days strategizing. They came up with several plans on how to move forward, each one dependent on what Eldon may or may not do. The days passed quickly. At night, Reid and Dexter continued to sleep in the same bed, though all they did was kiss before falling asleep in each other's arms.

On the day word came Gordon had been spotted a few miles out, a letter arrived from the king.

"What does it say?" Reid asked, biting the tip of her thumb.

Ackley handed it to Dexter so he could read it for himself. "It basically says Dexter is in no position to make demands since Eldon is in possession of all the dukes."

Reid started pacing. They'd planned for this scenario. They knew several of the dukes had previously sided with Eldon. Was Eldon holding those dukes hostage as well? Or did they still side with him? That was what they needed to discover. "Have we heard anything from your men?" she asked Dexter.

"No, not yet."

"Most of the counties supporting the king have soldiers stationed outside the city wall," she mused.

"Once we hear from the duchesses," Ackley said, "we'll know how to proceed. For now, I'm going to prepare for my brother and the Ellington soldiers." He exited the sitting room.

That was the question. Would the duchesses send troops to Eldon as he'd demanded? Or would they stand with Reid and fight? If the women did what their husbands told them, then those in favor of the king would send their soldiers. Not knowing where each county stood was the hardest part. Reid hoped the women would read her letter and decide on their own. She hoped they were strong and would stand with her.

Dexter took a deep breath. "I'm glad I'm not here by myself." He pushed off the edge of the table, standing before her. "Thank you for supporting me."

"We're doing this for the people of this kingdom. They deserve better."

"I had no idea how northern Marsden was."

"No one here realizes how good things can be. I plan to change all that."

He kissed her forehead. "We will. I promise."

A red-faced Gordon entered the castle, Idina, Leigh, and Harlan behind him.

"Welcome home," Reid said, hugging Idina in the entryway.

"It's good to be home," the princess said. "I never realized traveling with so many men would be so…tedious. I'm going to bathe." With a flourish, Idina swept up the staircase.

"Now that the three of you are safely deposited," Gordon

said, "I need to go finish up with Ackley over in the barracks." He exited the castle.

"Is he all right?" Dexter asked.

"He's never been one for words," Leigh explained. "And he's upset there are soldiers camped outside the city walls. He'll calm down. Eventually." Leigh smiled. "I'm going to bathe as well."

"You might need to use a guest room," Reid said.

Closing her eyes, Leigh took a deep breath. When she looked at Reid, there was a sadness there she couldn't begin to comprehend. "Of course." She hurried up the stairs.

"I never thought I'd be back here," Harlan mumbled, clutching his hat.

Reid hugged him. "It's good to see you."

"I'm sorry about your home."

She waved her hand, not wanting to talk about it. The pain was still too fresh in her mind. "I'm just glad the soldiers are okay." And that no one had needlessly died because of the attack.

"Come," Dexter said. "I'll show you to your room."

With his bag in hand, Harlan followed Dexter to the guest wing. Reid meandered into the sitting room, taking a seat on the sofa.

A few minutes later, Ackley and Gordon entered.

"Everything okay?" Reid asked.

Gordon plopped on the sofa, his boots covered with dried mud. He rubbed his tired face. "I'm just going to rest for five minutes, then I will oversee the Ellington soldiers."

"I told you it's taken care of," Ackley said, sitting next to his brother. "I put men in charge of setting up the tents."

"But there are men from Cartr, Alder, and Bridger here."

"It'll be fine," Ackley insisted.

Dexter and Harlan entered.

Ackley crossed his legs. "We're going to have to order all the servants back to work."

"Why is that?" Reid rather enjoyed having the castle empty.

"Word just came—the duchesses from Cartr, Alder, and Bridger will be here tomorrow. Apparently, they received both Dexter and Reid's letters."

Reid sat up straighter. Those were the three duchesses most likely to side with Eldon since their husbands supported the king. What was their purpose for coming to speak to Reid? Would they give her a chance to explain her position? Or would they automatically side with Eldon?

"Any word from the other duchesses?" Dexter asked.

"Not yet."

"Make sure some sort of watch is set up," Dexter commanded. "I don't want anyone giving the soldiers any sleep tonics again."

"Will do." Gordon stood. "Now, if you'll excuse me, I am going to pay Sir Gilbert, Lord Fesher, and Lord Drider a visit."

"The men from the party?" Reid asked, recalling the people she'd met when she went undercover with Gordon.

"Yes. And, Ackley, I need your Knights. I want to know what's being said at the local taverns and what the general feel for the soldiers stationed outside the city is."

"That may be problematic since my Knights are supposed to be dead," Ackley drawled. He quickly explained how Anna had sent them in to kidnap Reid, hoping he'd mistakenly assume the king's men had taken her so he'd assassinate them.

"That sounds like something you'd do." Gordon rubbed a hand over his face. "Did you?"

"Anna's plan would have worked if she'd known Dexter any better. He stopped me."

Gordon eyed Dexter. "I don't understand Anna's motives."

Idina and Leigh came into the room, both clean and smelling like flowers.

Gordon leaned against the doorframe. "I understand Anna hates our family for taking her parents' land, but her actions seem a bit extreme. She's the leader of the Knights. Why try to eliminate them?"

Leigh perched on the sofa, her back straight. "Anna has more than just her land to be upset about." She laced her fingers together.

"You know my mother?" Reid asked. She hated referring to Anna as *her mother*. It felt wrong.

"Yes."

"Can you tell us about her?" Dexter asked. "It may help us understand her better."

"And then we'll know how to stop her." A wicked smile spread across Ackley's face.

Leigh pushed her hair behind her ears, then clasped her hands in her lap. "I only know bits and pieces," she said. "But I do know she was madly in love with Hudson."

Reid raised her eyebrows, surprised by the admission.

"Hudson told me he met Anna at a royal function where he'd been impressed by her beauty." She peered over at Reid. "After a brief correspondence, he went to visit her under the guise of a hunting trip. Duke Axian took Hudson hunting, and that's when the tragic accident happened." Leigh focused on her hands, shaking her head. "Hudson liked doing a lot of things, so he never perfected any one thing. Hunting was no exception. According to him, he'd been too busy talking and thinking about Anna. When he went to shoot the deer, he accidentally shot Duke Axian instead. It was at close range, and the arrow shattered the duke's knee."

Reid had often wondered why her grandfather wasn't able to walk.

"Hudson helped the duke home, then fetched a healer. While the duke was being tended to, Hudson and Anna snuck out of the manor." Leigh twisted her hands. "Hudson told me they were intimate."

"I'm assuming this is before Anna married my father?" Reid asked.

"Yes. This took place a couple of months before they married."

"What happened next?" Idina asked, enraptured by the story.

"Anna wanted to marry him. However, he revealed his father had entered into marriage negotiations on his behalf."

"With whom?" Reid asked.

Leigh took a deep breath before revealing, "A princess from Melenia."

Reid's stomach twisted, and she felt like she was going to be ill. Since Hudson was originally supposed to marry someone from Melenia, it couldn't be a mere coincidence Melenia was in Marsden now.

"Hudson said his father wanted to unite the two kingdoms. After he left Anna and returned home, I believe Anna followed him. She dressed as a man in order to spy on him. This is how she discovered he wasn't as attached to her as she thought." Leigh shook her head. "I was so wrapped up in my relationship with Henrick that I never knew. Not until it was too late."

"Never knew what?" Ackley asked.

"That Hudson wanted me. Probably because I was the one woman he couldn't have since I was in love with his twin brother."

No one spoke for a moment as they all processed what Leigh had revealed.

Gordon cleared his throat. "Wasn't Henrick the king's heir?"

Leigh nodded.

"So why did Grandfather want Hudson to marry a Melenia princess instead of Henrick?" he asked.

"Broc always had a soft spot for romance. He knew Henrick and I were in love, so he gave us his blessing to marry. When Melenia's king wrote seeking an alliance, Broc agreed and offered Hudson."

"How did Father feel about the union?" Idina asked.

"Hudson was upset. He didn't understand why Henrick was allowed to choose who he married when he couldn't. Shortly thereafter, the king met with an untimely death. Hudson was declared the heir. Henrick believed Hudson forced those two men to change Broc's successor on his deathbed." Her eyes filled with tears as she told her children a story they'd never heard before. "Hudson confided in me years later. He said Anna came to him declaring her undying love. She said she'd killed Broc for him—so he could be king, and he wouldn't have to marry someone he didn't love. She claimed they could be together. What she didn't foresee was Hudson's vicious side. He told her she was crazy, and he'd never marry her. Then she threatened him. She said she would never leave him alone, that she would always be nearby watching. She claimed to know all about the hidden passageways throughout the palace. She could come and go, and he would never know."

A chill slid over Reid's skin. "Then what happened?"

"Hudson took control of the army to try to stop her. However, she disappeared. Hudson declared I was to marry him. He produced a signed contract. His behavior became erratic. I sent Henrick into hiding, fearing for his life. I didn't know if Hudson would do something to harm him. Everything fell apart."

"At what point did Anna marry my father?" Reid asked.

"Not long after that. When she returned home, she discovered her father had signed her marriage contract without her input. I know Duke Axian was concerned since he had no heir and his land had reverted to the king. He wanted Anna cared for. Marrying her off was his way of making sure she was provided for."

"At what point did Henrick gain control over Axian?" Idina asked.

"Hudson couldn't stand to be in the palace any longer. He believed Anna was always watching him. It was driving him mad. He had to leave, but he didn't want to abandon the county. I think he pretended Broc deeded Axian to Henrick, knowing Henrick would come out of hiding and govern Axian."

Reid rubbed her temples. So many lies and misconceptions. When would it end?

"Did my uncle truly hate my father?" Dexter asked.

Leigh stood then, then went over to the window, gazing outside. "The brothers had their moments. They were so vastly different but both highly competitive. I'd like to think if they were alive today, they'd be friends if I hadn't come between them. And that is something I'll never be able to forgive myself for."

"I appreciate you sharing what you know," Dexter said, his voice gentle.

Leigh glanced over her shoulder. "You look so much like your father. I see him in the way you carry yourself. But you have your mother's genuine smile."

Dexter slid his hand over Reid's, squeezing it.

"Let's focus on Anna," Ackley said as he stood and started pacing. "What can we glean from this?"

"She loves to use poisons," Leigh said, coming to stand behind the sofa, resting her hands on the back. "And she can hold a grudge. I'm sure she has something special planned for me since I married Hudson."

Ackley went over to his mother, sliding his arm around her shoulders. "We won't let anything happen to you. I promise."

"Eldon—*my own son*—tried to kill me. Then, at Duke Ellington's, we almost died. I'm not sure you can make that promise."

Ackley pulled his mother into a hug. "I can make that promise."

Reid wondered if Ackley had told Leigh about him being a Knight and his association with Anna over the years.

A thought suddenly occurred to her. If Anna held grudges, were her grandparents in danger? After all, her grandfather had been the one to sign Anna's marriage contract with Duke Ellington. And what about her father? He'd let Anna go, so that had to count for something. However, he'd also fathered five daughters with her. And, Reid suspected, that was five daughters too many.

Rubbing her temples, she ignored her headache, wanting a few minutes alone to sort through this. Reid abruptly rose, exiting the room. As she went along the hallway, images of her life while growing up swirled in her mind. Reid always assumed she was at a disadvantage for not having a mother. She felt as if her life were missing something. Now, she realized how wrong she'd been. If Anna had remained at home to raise her, Reid's life would be vastly different. For the first time, she was glad her mother had abandoned them. They were better off without her.

"Reid," Harlan said, gaining her attention.

She stopped, waiting for her friend to catch up.

"Are you okay?" he asked.

She rolled her eyes.

"Never mind—that was a stupid question." He folded his arms, observing her. "I keep trying to imagine how I'd feel if my parents came back from the dead. You know, figuratively speaking."

"How can I be related to someone like her?" Reid asked. And just like that, she understood what bothered her the most. Was Reid inherently evil like her mother? Would she become bitter like her one day?

"You're your own person. You choose how you behave." He glanced up and down the hallway. "You don't suppose we could get out of here? Maybe we can go to a tavern for a bit?"

While that sounded like just what she needed, she didn't think it wise to leave the safety of the castle with all the turmoil going on. "Actually, I have an idea. Follow me."

Reid led Harlan up the stairs to the royal family's wing.

"What are we doing?" he asked, trying to keep up with her.

Glancing over her shoulder to be sure no one followed them, she whispered, "Investigating."

Harlan groaned. "Reid." He pulled her to a stop. "Tell me what's going on. Who don't you trust? We can leave the castle if you want."

"That's not it." She trusted everyone who was currently in the castle.

"Then what is it?"

Not wanting to say it out in the open, she nodded down the hallway. "Come with me."

He pinched the bridge of his nose. "Fine."

She reached the door to the king's private chambers,

assuming Harlow's room was attached to it. The locked door wouldn't budge. Unfortunately, picking a lock was not one of her skills.

"Do I even want to know what you two are up to?" Leigh asked as she glided down the hallway.

"No, you don't," Harlan responded. "Come on Reid, let's go."

"I want to investigate. Do you have the key?" Whenever Reid was around Leigh, she got the feeling the woman didn't much care for her. However, given the vast changes over the past couple of weeks, she hoped Leigh had warmed up to her enough to give her the key to Eldon's rooms.

"Harlow keeps a key sitting on top of the doorframe," Leigh said. "Ackley told me he already combed through Eldon's room." She lifted her hands, palm up, in a silent question.

"We're going to look through Harlow's," Reid answered.

Leigh nodded. "Let me know if you need anything else." She continued down the hall, stopping outside her own bedchamber a moment later. Maybe she intended to start cleaning the mess in there.

Reaching up, Harlan felt along the doorframe until he found the key. After unlocking the door, he put it back.

Reid stepped inside the king's private sitting room. This was where Eldon had first asked her to go to Axian to retrieve the letters for him. Shivering from the memory, she moved farther into the room. Off to the side were two doors leading to the king and queen's bedchambers.

Harlan whistled. "This is fancy."

The sitting room reminded Reid of a room from the palace in Axian. She went over to the first bedchamber, peering inside. The large four-poster bed had a light green bedspread and a handful of pillows situated at the head, perfectly aligned according to size. At the foot of the bed was a chaise lounge. Reid entered, afraid to touch anything. Two armoires, one chest of drawers, and two chairs were also placed in the room. A soft area rug woven from light blues and greens adorned the floor.

Reid stood there for several minutes, observing her surroundings. Everything looked perfect. Too perfect. Which meant she was missing something. Whatever she was searching for wouldn't be in plain sight. Unsure of where to start, she scanned the room again, trying to see it from Harlow's point of view. If Reid were the queen, where would she put her personal items she didn't want anyone else to see?

"What do you want me to do?" Harlan asked from the threshold of the room, not stepping a single foot inside.

"I'd like for you to search the king's room."

"Didn't Ackley already do that?"

"Yes. But Ackley knows Eldon. I'd like you to take a look, too."

His shoulders rose and fell. "What am I looking for?"

"Correspondence, maps, anything you feel might be useful."

He nodded, then left, mumbling something.

Seeing no other way, Reid started searching under the mattress, in drawers, through the closet, behind the curtains, and in the hearth. She didn't find a single personal item. This room could easily belong to a guest instead of the queen. When she had first met Harlow, Reid had considered her a mindless young woman who didn't know anything. How wrong she'd been. Otherwise, the queen wouldn't have warned Reid, nor would Harlow have known her way around the palace. Harlow's appearance and personality were a façade— just like this room.

A chill slid over Reid.

"Find anything?" Harlan asked from the doorway.

"No." She stood with her hands on her hips, scanning the room again.

"What are you thinking?"

"That we must be missing something. And that is a scary thought." What had Harlow said? Sometimes, the quietest one in the room was the most dangerous?

"Maybe she just doesn't have anything," he suggested. "If she were forced to marry the king, she could have chosen to leave her belongings behind. It could be her own way of protesting the marriage?"

Possibly. But Reid didn't think so. "Do you know why Eldon chose to marry Harlow?"

He shrugged. "You'd have to ask Ackley, Idina, or Gordon."

While Reid wasn't certain, she had an inkling Harlow had managed to fool all three siblings into believing she was a mindless twit.

"Why do you look like you've seen a ghost?" Harlan asked.

"Because we're missing something. I'm sure of it." They had enough to deal with without adding Harlow to the list. However, Reid knew she couldn't ignore the queen. Harlow could very well be working against Eldon, but to what end? Was she a friend or a foe?

***

"There you are," Idina said as she swept into the great hall. "I've been looking all over the castle for you."

Reid had snuck in here to be alone for a few minutes before supper. She wanted time to sort through everything Leigh had revealed about Anna.

"I've been dying to talk to you about Dexter." Idina plopped on the sofa. "Tell me everything."

Knowing Idina would push until she got what she wanted, Reid decided it was easier to comply than argue. "What do you want to know?" She twisted on the sofa to face the princess.

"How is it?" she asked with a devilish smile.

"How is what?"

Idina raised her left eyebrow, looking at Reid as if she were daft. "You can't be that dense, Reid. How was your first time with Dexter?"

"Oh." Why would Idina want to know something so personal?

"We're practically sisters." She nudged Reid with her elbow. "You can tell me anything."

Would Reid normally share something so intimate with her sisters? Probably Kamden, but that was it. "There's nothing to tell."

"I imagine he's quite good."

Reid's face flamed red—whether from the subject matter or the fact Idina was fantasizing about Dexter, she couldn't be sure. "I'm going to pretend you didn't just say that."

"Oh, please," Idina chided her. "If you won't tell me what sort of a lover he is, at least tell me how he kisses."

Mortified, Reid covered her face with her hands. "We haven't been intimate yet."

"Why the hell not? You're married."

"There hasn't been any time." She removed her hands, unable to look Idina in the eyes.

Idina burst out laughing. "No time? What have you been doing at night?"

"We're exhausted at the end of the day." A partial truth.

Idina shook her head, not buying it.

"Fine. I'm not ready."

"But you wanted to marry him." Her brows scrunched in confusion.

"Yes. And we've kissed and spent the past few nights in each other's arms. The next step will come after we're a little more comfortable with one another that way."

Ackley and Gordon entered, talking in hushed whispers.

"Do the man a favor, Reid," Idina whispered. "Don't make him wait too long."

"I think he feels the same as me. He isn't ready." He hadn't once pushed her to do more than kiss.

Idina rose, patting Reid on the shoulder. "You can think that all you want. But the man wants you."

CHAPTER THIRTEEN

"I feel awkward being in the throne room," Reid mumbled to Dexter. The last time she'd been in here, Eldon had revealed she'd be marrying Dexter and he was sending her to Axian as a spy.

"It's strange for me to be in this castle." Dexter turned in a slow circle, taking in the room. It was a fourth the size of the one in Axian and not nearly as grand. "Everything is so...stark."

Reid chuckled. "Compared to your grand palace in Axian, yes, this is rather bland. But compared to most castles in Marsden, it is fancy."

"Our."

"What?"

"You said *your palace*. It's not mine, it's *ours*."

She hadn't thought of that before.

"Try not to look so overwhelmed." He took her hands in his. "Ackley is leading the three duchesses here as we speak. When they see you, you can't let them think they outrank you.

Stand tall and don't let them intimidate you." He squeezed her hands in reassurance.

Reid rolled her eyes. That was easier said than done. She still felt uneasy in high society. While she was becoming more comfortable being a woman in public, she still preferred pants and spending time with men to putting on a dress and socializing with women. "Wouldn't it be better to meet them in the sitting room?"

Shaking his head in exasperation, Dexter pulled her toward the dais. "We've been over this. In order for me to assert I'm the rightful king, I need to conduct formal business here in the throne room."

She sighed. "Fine." Reid had already agreed to this. She just hadn't realized being in the throne room would make her nervous. After running her hands down the front of her dress, she rolled her shoulders back and faced the doors.

"Don't forget to smile, Reid Winston."

Unused to hearing that name, she smiled.

"That's better. Now you don't look like you want to murder someone."

She punched his arm, making him chuckle.

The side door opened, and Idina and Leigh entered the throne room.

"We thought we should be here to show our support for you two," the princess said. Her red hair was unbound, set off by the pale yellow dress she wore. Idina positioned herself on one of the lower steps to Reid's right.

Donning a navy dress, Leigh stood on Dexter's left, also on a lower step. "Gordon and Ackley are escorting the three duchesses here."

A moment later, the doors flew open, revealing Ackley, a sly smirk on his face. "Your Highnesses." He bowed.

"Enter," Dexter replied. Since he'd been raised as royalty, he knew the proper protocols and procedures for this sort of thing.

Reid pasted on a pleasant smile, trying not to laugh at Ackley for addressing her as *Your Highness*. She hadn't been crowned yet. That wouldn't happen until she returned to Axian with Dexter.

Sauntering forward, Ackley led three women, Gordon right behind them. Reid didn't know what she imagined the duchesses would look like, but this wasn't it.

"May I present Duchess Amille Cartr," Ackley said, indicating the woman to his left. Amille was short—shorter than Reid—with her hair slicked back into a severe bun. Her slightly weathered skin indicated her age to be closer to fifty. She wore a simple brown dress with no jewelry.

"Duchess Jane Alder," Ackley said, indicating the woman in the middle. Jane was a plump woman of no more than thirty. Her blue eyes scanned both Dexter and Reid, her face giving nothing away. She wore a simple dark green dress which complemented her black hair.

"And last, but not least, Duchess Camille Bridger." Ackley indicated the woman on his right. Without being told, Reid knew this was Harlow's mother. Like her daughter, Camille had pale blonde hair, blue eyes, and pasty white skin. Her short-sleeved gray dress revealed thin, bony arms.

Reid wondered if these women normally dressed so demurely, or if they'd donned the simple attire for traveling purposes.

"Duchess Cartr, Duchess Alder, and Duchess Bridger, may I present His Highness Prince Dexter Winston and his lovely wife Lady Reid Winston."

All three duchesses curtseyed.

"And Queen Mother Leigh Winston and her daughter, Princess Idina Winston." Ackley moved out of the way, taking his place at Idina's side.

After closing the doors, Gordon positioned himself next to Leigh. Not a single sentry stood guard in the throne room, per Dexter's instructions. He wanted the duchesses to be able to speak freely without worrying about spies.

"Thank you for coming," Dexter said.

"Shall we cut out the pleasantries and get to business?" Amille asked.

"Please." Dexter lifted his hands palm up, indicating for her to continue.

"Before my husband left, he gave me his ring. He said if Duke Ellington could do it, he could, too." Amille held her head high as she spoke, jutting out her proud chin. "The king sent me a letter demanding I send my soldiers to Axian. That's where my husband went in order to attend your wedding. The problem is, I haven't heard from him. I know something is wrong."

"I concur," Jane said. "My husband also gave me his ring before he left."

Shocked, Reid couldn't believe the dukes had done such a thing. She'd mistakenly assumed they were as backward as the king and wanted to suppress women.

Jane continued, "Eldon is a young and inexperienced king. His father died under mysterious circumstances. The king is now in the south while you are here. I haven't heard from my husband either. Therefore, I am withholding my decision until I know more." Jane looked at Camille.

"I don't even know where to begin," Camille stated, her voice soft like honey. "My interests are torn. On one hand, my daughter is married to the king. I won't pretend it to be a love match. But I do have a vested interest seeing my daughter remain on the throne."

"I understand," Dexter said.

"However, the king is raping my county. He told the Melenians they could come to Bridger and mine our precious stones. They trample our farms, take our natural resources, and leave us with nothing for compensation. My husband has done everything the king has asked. Unfortunately, the mining has only increased. Our livelihood is being ruined." She turned her hand, revealing she wore Duke Bridger's ring.

"We're willing to hear you out," Amille said. "Then we will decide how to proceed."

Joy surged through Reid. These women were taking charge and not letting the men control everything. Which meant it was time for her to step forward and speak. Pushing her nerves aside, she spoke with all the authority and conviction she could muster. "By now, you have received two letters. One from my husband, and one from me. We believe the king is trying to lure you to Axian to murder you. He intends to do away with all dukes, duchesses, and counties. He wants total and complete control. The purpose of the Melenia army is to help him achieve this goal."

"I've heard my son discussing his plans," Leigh said. "After he kills you and your husbands, he will use your soldiers against your own people to suppress any uprisings."

"Why?" Jane asked.

Camille stepped forward. "My Harlow has confided in me. She discovered Eldon is not the true heir. When she confronted him, he revealed he intends to kill all the dukes before they can strip him of the crown. He knows they will side with the law, and the law is not with him."

"We have been functioning as independent counties under

one king for over a century," Amille said. "We have a duty to preserve our way of life."

"And we have a duty to protect our people," Reid pointed out. She wanted it clear they were not doing this for power, but for the citizens of Marsden.

"You must understand the precarious position this puts me in," Camille said. "Save my husband but doom my daughter? How can I choose?"

"Why does supporting me doom your daughter?" Dexter asked.

"Eldon won't step down," Camille pointed out.

"No, he will not," Dexter agreed.

"The only choice you have is to either arrest or assassinate him. Since my daughter is married to him, I assume you will do to her what you do to him." Her eyes became glassy.

"There are no plans, nor will there ever be, to harm your daughter in any way," Dexter replied with conviction. "You have my word."

"What will happen to her? She becomes a widow? No one will want anything to do with her."

"I understand your concerns," Reid said. "However, I believe Harlow can choose how she lives her life. She is a strong, capable woman."

Camille nodded, seemingly satisfied with that response. "What about the Bridger mines?"

"The mines will be restored to your control," Dexter answered. "Will you help us remove the imposter king, get rid of the Melenia soldiers, and restore peace to the kingdom?"

"Yes," Camille replied. "Bridger will stand with you."

"As will Cartr."

"Alder will stand with you."

"Thank you for upholding the laws of Marsden," Dexter

said. "Please prepare your soldiers for war. Our commander, Prince Gordon, will be leading the soldiers south when the time comes."

The three women took their leave, Ackley and Gordon escorting them from the throne room.

Once they were gone, Idina snorted. "Who knew the women of Marsden would be the ones calling the shots to save the kingdom."

"We still have a long way to go until the kingdom is saved," Reid pointed out. However, the fact the women were stepping up and taking charge made her proud and reinforced her belief that women were just as capable as men.

"You know, this is only possible because of you." Idina patted Reid's shoulder as they exited the throne room.

She wasn't so sure about that. "We only have three counties siding with us. There are several more to speak with."

The group made their way along the corridor.

"Ryder and Lyndr are the only two who might pose an objection," Leigh said. "I am confident the rest will stand with you. Especially when they see the Winston royal family is united in their agreement on who should be and is legally the king."

When Reid had spoken with Dukes Willer, Tucker, and Slader, they'd all voiced their support for righting the royal line. "I just don't want to be overconfident," Reid said. "We still have my mother and the Knights to contend with."

A loud bang resounded from up ahead. "What was that?" Idina asked.

"It sounded like the front door was kicked in." Dexter led them down the corridor.

A raucous sound came from the entryway. When they got

closer to the commotion, Reid recognized one of the voices. She started running, Dexter right behind her.

"I will not yield," Gytha hollered.

When Reid reached the front door, Gytha had one of the sentries wrapped in a headlock.

"Gytha!" Reid wanted to hug the warrior woman. "You're here!" And she looked well—no obvious injuries from her scuffle in the underground passageways.

Gytha tilted her head toward Reid. "Obviously, I am here."

"Gytha," Nara said, stepping inside the castle. "Let him go. He's only doing his job."

"Mother." Dexter wrapped Nara in a hug. "I'm so glad you're safe."

Gordon and Ackley joined them.

"Looks like you broke the door," Ackley said, pointing to the busted handle.

Gytha released the red-faced sentry.

"Is Dana with you?" Gordon asked, his voice tight.

"No, she's not with us. I'm sorry," Nara answered. "Princess Dana is still at the palace with the king."

"Is she okay?" Gordon ran his hands through his hair.

"She's fine," she assured him.

Gytha pointed at the sentry. "Someone, tell him to go."

Gordon ordered the sentry back to his post.

"I'm glad the both of you are here," Dexter said. "Any word on Colbert?"

"No," Nara said. "But we have much to tell you."

"How did you two get here?" Reid asked.

"We rode horses until we reached the mountain pass," Gytha answered. "Then we walked the rest of the way."

"No one else is with you?" Ackley asked.

Gytha shook her head.

"Nara?" Leigh said, her eyes wide as she and Idina reached the front door.

"It has been a long time," Nara replied.

Reid wondered if the two women had seen one another since Leigh ordered Nara to hide Henrick—the man they both loved.

"I'm sorry to hear about Henrick passing," Leigh said, her voice soft.

Nara pursed her lips, but nodded. "Captain Gytha and I have been traveling for days. We need to freshen up."

"I'll show you to the guest wing," Reid offered. "Then we can all speak over supper." She hooked her arm with Nara's, leading the woman up the stairs, Gytha following.

"No one knows?" Nara whispered.

"No. That's the only way for it to work, right?" If people found out Henrick was alive, then he would have to be the king. Honestly, Reid would prefer it if that were the case. Then she would be a princess instead of the queen. However, Henrick didn't want the responsibility and would do whatever he could to avoid it—even going so far as to fake his own death.

Reid opened a door. "You can stay in here."

Nara smiled before going inside.

"Gytha, you can stay next door." Reid opened that door.

"I am glad you are still alive," Gytha said. "I didn't know if you would make it."

"Likewise. I was afraid you'd be stuck in the passageways with no way out."

"It took some time, but I was able to make my way back into the palace. That's when I found Nara. We waited a couple of days before leaving." Gytha went into the bedchamber, examining the room. "Shouldn't I stay in the barracks with the army?"

"We need you here." Reid leaned against the doorframe, relief filling her. Her friend was just as she remembered.

"Ackley looks like he lost some weight."

Reid hadn't noticed.

"Is he okay?"

"Why do you ask?"

"No reason." The warrior woman went over to the window, peering outside. "This does not seem like a prosperous city."

"It's vastly different from the City of Radella."

"Do you think Ackley can give me a tour? I've never been out of Axian before."

Reid chuckled. "I'm sure that can be arranged." She closed the door, leaving Gytha alone to bathe before supper.

Heading down the hallway, she was just about to pass Nara's room when a bang resounded from inside it. Pausing, she listened, hearing mumbling coming from the other side. She knocked, wanting to make sure everything was okay.

Nara didn't answer. Reid hesitated before pushing the door open. "Nara?" The princess was sitting on the floor, her back resting against the foot of the bed. "Is everything all right?" Reid sat next to her.

Nara wiped the tears from her eyes. "This is the first time I've been alone in weeks. And seeing Leigh is a lot to take in right now."

Reid wrapped her arm around the woman. "I'm sorry." The words didn't seem adequate, but she didn't know what else to say.

"I thought I was strong enough to do this," Nara whispered. "But now, I'm not so sure."

"To do what?"

"Live without him. Not that he gave me a choice."

She was talking about Henrick then. "What does he plan to do?" Where would he go? Where would he live? How could he just abandon his family like that?

"I have no idea. Seeing Leigh brought up all sorts of feelings I'm not prepared to deal with right now. I mean, he always loved her. Probably more than me."

"But he loved you, too." Reid was certain of it. Nara had given him two children. Had stood by his side through all those years.

She wiped her eyes again. "He always respected me. We were dear friends. But he never genuinely loved me like he did her."

Reid's heart broke for Nara. "That's his loss." Nara was a wonderful woman who deserved so much more.

"I have to put on a brave face for my children. For my county. I just didn't think it would be this hard."

Reid realized it was like Henrick had truly died for Nara. She didn't have the heart to tell the woman they'd seen Henrick at Reid's grandparents' manor. If Dexter wanted to reveal that information to his mother, he could. It wasn't Reid's place to do so.

"Enough about me," Nara said, patting Reid's hand. "How are you doing?" Surprise coloring her features, she blinked and lifted Reid's hand, examining the wedding ring.

"Dexter and I got married."

Nara grinned. "I'm glad."

"We still plan to have another wedding—an elaborate one—in Axian." She didn't want Nara to feel like they'd gone behind her back.

"I think that's wise."

"We had a small ceremony at my home." Reid's voice broke

on the word *home*. Not wanting to go into details, she left it at that.

"I hope you and Dexter have a long and happy marriage. Welcome to the family, Reid."

Over supper, Gytha explained the king was livid when he discovered the city was void of people. He flew into a fit of rage, screaming at the remaining people in the palace. Furious, he moved as much of the Melenia army as possible to the palace lawn, forcing them to camp alongside the Marsden soldiers who'd accompanied Gordon to the palace. When he questioned the palace servants—undercover Axian soldiers—where the Axian army was, they said it was small, unorganized, and spread throughout the county.

"Do you know if they've rendezvoused at Camp Lival?" Dexter asked.

"No," Gytha replied. "I didn't receive word from Colbert."

"What about the dukes?"

"They are being held in the dungeon."

"The palace has a dungeon?" Reid asked. She hadn't seen it while there.

"Yes," Nara replied. "It's quite small and rarely used. There is a bigger one at the barracks."

"Thank you for the report," Dexter said. "When you're done eating, please let Duchesses Cartr, Alder, and Bridger know the state of their husbands."

"I'll show you where they're staying," Ackley said.

"Then I need to spar," Gytha replied. "Ackley, you will be my sparring partner. You look like you need to liven up a bit." She shoved a spoonful of mashed potatoes in her mouth.

"What's that supposed to mean?" Ackley took a sip of his wine, eyeing Gytha.

"I think you know." She resumed eating, not bothering to explain any further.

A soldier entered, carrying a piece of paper. "A message for the commander."

Both Dexter and Gordon held out a hand. The soldier hesitated.

"Sorry," Dexter mumbled. "Habit. Prince Gordon is the commander."

Reid knew it was hard for Dexter to relinquish control of the army. However, with him declaring his right to be king, someone else had to be in charge of the soldiers. Since Gordon was the commander for the Marsden army, it only made sense for him to continue in that position.

Gordon reached for the paper, quickly reading it. "Duchesses Ryder and Lyndr will arrive tomorrow." He rubbed his forehead. "They will require some coaxing to get them to join us."

"When will the duchesses from the north be here?" Dexter asked.

"Our reports indicate they'll arrive by the end of the week."

"Then let next week be the agreed-upon time. We will take our kingdom back and dethrone the king."

That night, lying in bed alongside Dexter, Reid was restless. She rolled over, fluffing her pillow. Again.

"What's wrong?" he mumbled.

"I can't sleep."

"Obviously."

Sighing, she rolled onto her back. "Something about Leigh is bothering me." She couldn't work through it in her mind, so she didn't know how to explain it.

"She's a fairly reserved person," Dexter admitted. "It's hard to figure her out."

"I know she loves her children." Reid was about to say *what mother wouldn't* until she remembered her own mother.

"She also doesn't talk much," he said. "She rarely gives her opinion."

"That's a Marsden thing." Most women didn't give their opinion.

"Then how do you explain Idina? She learned to be strong from someone."

"True." But that wasn't what was bothering Reid. "How can Leigh not protest our plan to kill Eldon?" Even knowing her son was evil, how could she stand by while those around her plotted his demise? "And Eldon is your half-brother."

"Are you advocating we not assassinate him?"

"No. But…Leigh only had one child with the man she loved. And that's Eldon."

"Huh. I never thought about it that way before. Are you afraid she'll try to stop us?"

"She hasn't protested. Not once. She hasn't even asked if we can put him in the dungeon instead. Don't you think that's odd?"

"It's not odd if she's planning something."

And *that* was what Reid was afraid of. Only, she had no idea what Leigh could be planning. In order to figure it out, she had to discover Leigh's end goal. What did Leigh want to accomplish?

"And now that my father's dead, it makes me wonder."

"You think he might seek Leigh out?"

"I don't know. I've been so focused on organizing soldiers and preparing for an invasion with minimal loss of life and property, that my father and Leigh haven't been on my mind."

Reid slid her arm around Dexter's torso. "Maybe I'm overthinking it." But seeing Nara crying on the floor had stirred something inside of Reid.

"I don't think we should ever doubt or question our intuition." He ran his hand through her hair. "For example, my intuition is telling me I should kiss you right now."

"Then I suggest you take your own advice."

"Gladly." His lips devoured hers.

Sleep was a long time coming that night.

CHAPTER FOURTEEN

From where she stood on the roof of the castle's northeast tower, Reid couldn't believe how many soldiers camped outside the city wall. If they joined forces to march under Marsden's banner, they would defeat Eldon. She was sure of it.

"What are you doing up here?" Nara asked as she joined Reid.

"Just looking."

"Dexter wants to see you. I offered to find you. He's at the barracks."

"I'll head over there." She pushed off the low wall.

"Before you go," Nara said, "I'd like to apologize for my behavior the other day. I didn't mean to cry like that. It had been a long journey, a trying day, and I was hungry."

"You don't need to explain yourself to me."

"I know, but I'd like to. I want you to understand that even the strongest have times of weakness. These moments don't make us less. We can become more when we acknowledge all parts within us." She wrapped her arm around Reid's shoulders, hugging her.

Now it was Reid's turn to tear up.

"What's the matter?" Nara asked.

This woman—this warrior princess—was more of a mother to Reid than her own mother had ever been. Reid shook her head, not wanting to talk about it.

Nara rubbed Reid's back. "Let's discuss something else then."

Reid didn't have anything to say.

"I don't want to sound too presumptuous," Nara said, "but I'm guessing with your upbringing, you don't have a lot of *experience* with men."

Oh, good gracious, was this woman turning the conversation to a more intimate topic?

"Now that you and Dexter are married, do you have any questions about anything that occurs in the bedroom?"

Reid covered her face with her hands. They were not going to talk about this.

"I know you don't have a mother to ask any questions you may have." She wrung her hands together. "If you'd like, I can fill that role. Remember, I don't have a daughter of my own."

Reid sucked in a large breath of air, a funny little cry-snort escaping. Had no one told Nara that Reid's mother was alive? "Brianna now goes by the name Anna. And she is running the Knights of the Realm."

"Come again?" Nara blinked.

"My mother is alive."

"Oh."

Reid had forgotten to fill Nara and Gytha in on that vital detail.

Nara opened her mouth several times to speak, but nothing

came out. Finally, she rubbed her forehead. "I have no idea what to say to that."

"Which is fine because I don't want to talk about her right now. I'm not ready."

Nara nodded. "Back to what I was trying to say then. Since you grew up without a mother and were raised as a man, do you want to discuss bedroom matters?" Her voice lacked emotion. It sounded very matter of fact. Almost as if she were just as uncomfortable as Reid.

"No, I do not."

Leaning on the low wall, Nara gazed out at the city and soldiers beyond it. "During my first month of marriage, I remember not having anyone to discuss such things with. I had questions..."

"Dexter and I haven't done *that* yet."

"Haven't done what?" Nara asked, tilting her head toward Reid.

Was Nara going to make Reid say it? "Dexter and I haven't been intimate."

"Why not? You're married. You should enjoy one another."

Reid wanted to crawl into a hole.

"What are you afraid of?"

"I'm not afraid." She just wasn't sure what to do.

Nara took Reid's hand. "One thing I can assure you of is when you love someone, it comes naturally. You don't have to think about what to do."

"Did you love Henrick?"

"Very much so." She squeezed Reid's hand, then released it. "I didn't plan on marrying or even loving him. But when he came to my estate to hide from his brother, we became fast friends. I found his intelligence appealing. He wasn't interested in me that way—he only had eyes for Leigh. However, when

Leigh married Hudson, he was devastated. When he learned she was with child, and the child was born six months after the wedding, he knew it was his and it nearly killed him. I was there for him through it all." Nara pulled her single braid over her shoulder, running her hands along it. "He had to take control of Axian, but he was still dealing with the death of his father and his brother's betrayal. He needed a partner, so he asked me to marry him out of necessity, not want. I agreed, even knowing how he felt. I thought, with time, he'd learn to love me. And he did. It was different from how he loved Leigh. I gave myself to him in hopes of expressing that love."

"You two seemed to have a good marriage." From what Reid saw, they respected one another, had raised two wonderful boys, and appeared to genuinely enjoy each other's company.

"We did. Children helped form our family. Henrick was an excellent father. We were happy. And like I said, he did love me. We had many good years together."

"Dexter and I have so much going on that I'm in no way ready for children." Which was one of the reasons she didn't want to be intimate with him.

"I understand. Have you spoken to your friend Harlan?"

Why would Reid discuss something so personal with one of her friends?

Nara chuckled. "Oh, Reid, with four sisters, I thought one would have told you there are herbs you can take to prevent a pregnancy."

"No, I did not know that." After all, her father had raised the four girls—not their mother. She doubted he would have spoken about such matters.

"Ask Harlan. He'll supply you with what you need."

While Reid knew she should request the herbs—and doing

so from Harlan would be the easiest way—she still wasn't sure. Once she had them in her possession, there would be nothing stopping her from being intimate with her husband.

"What is it?" Nara asked.

"I've just never been good getting close to other people. Especially physically."

"I can understand why. But don't you think it's time to change that?"

"Possibly." And if being with Dexter were anything like kissing him, Reid was sure she'd enjoy it.

Reid arrived at the training yard in the barracks. In one corner, Gordon was busy teaching Idina more self-defense moves. Despite the dress she wore, her movements were fluid, her strikes fierce.

In another corner, several soldiers ringed the perimeter, watching Ackley spar with Gytha. Reid had always thought Ackley cat-like when he fought, and now was no exception. He moved so fast Gytha barely had time to block his strikes. She always managed to counter with one of her own, but he'd dart away before she'd get a hit in.

"I wish I could say I taught Gytha everything she knows," Dexter said wryly from behind Reid. "But she knew how to fight long before I met her."

Reid twisted to him, scanning his leather vest and pants, his well-defined shoulders and muscled arms nicely on display. She cleared her throat, forcing herself to meet his eyes. "Who taught her to fight?"

"Her two older brothers." He nodded at one of the corners. "Want to go a round with me?"

Reid was about to tell him that she needed to prepare for their meeting with the duchesses when he grabbed her around the waist, effortlessly tossing her over his shoulder. She was too shocked to protest.

Setting her on her feet in one of the empty sparring areas, he said, "Your swords are over there." He pointed to the corner.

Furious he'd thrown her over his shoulder like a sack of flour, she stomped over and grabbed her weapons, withdrawing them from their sheaths. When she faced him, he stood with his legs shoulder-width apart, his hands at his sides.

"No weapon?" she asked.

"I don't need one." His fingers twitched as he prepared to spar.

She couldn't best him physically—which meant she had to outsmart him. An idea formed. Lifting her sword, she pretended as if she were going to strike his side. When he went to block with his arm, she twisted her hand awkwardly. Crying out, she dropped her sword, then grabbed her wrist, cradling it.

"Are you okay?" Dexter took her hand, examining it. "Does this hurt?"

While his attention was on her hand, she withdrew her dagger, placing the tip at his neck. "I win."

He chuckled. "You didn't hurt yourself, did you?"

"Nope." She grinned.

"Then, yes, I concede this round." His foot shot out, hooking around Reid's ankle and flipping her to the ground.

Lying flat on her back, she blinked at the bright sky. "That was a bit excessive."

He straddled her. "Was it?" His dark eyes danced with mischief.

"Your Highness," a soldier shouted as he ran into the

training area. "There's someone here to see you. He says it's urgent."

With his eyes still trained on Reid, Dexter asked, "Did he give his name?"

"Yes, Your Highness. He said his name is Seb."

Dexter went unnaturally still, a dozen emotions flitting across his face. Finally, he jumped to his feet. Reaching a hand down, he pulled Reid up.

"Is he an older gentleman?" Dexter asked the soldier.

"He is."

"Is he alone?"

"No, Your Highness, he is not."

Everyone had stopped sparring to watch the exchange between Dexter and the soldier.

"Then I guess we better go see what Seb wants."

Entering the great hall, Reid and Dexter approached their guest. Seb sat on the sofa, a man kneeling on the floor beside him. Ackley, Gordon, Idina, and Gytha fanned out in the room.

"Seb," Dexter said. "I didn't expect to see you here."

"Some matters cannot be entrusted to another person," Seb replied, standing to shake Dexter's proffered hand.

"Who's this?" Dexter asked, pointing at the kneeling man.

"This is Prince Owen of Melenia."

Shock rolled through Reid. One of the Melenia princes was here? Why hadn't she heard about him before now? Like the other Melenians she'd encountered, he had short blond hair, blue eyes, and pale skin. However, he wasn't wide shouldered or muscled. She put his age to be closer to her own—eighteen or nineteen.

"Are you certain?" Dexter asked.

"I can verify Prince Owen's identity," Gordon said. "I met him when I spoke with the Melenia officers stationed outside the palace. He is the fourth-born child of the king and queen of Melenia. He was sent here to assist Commander Beck with the soldiers."

Dexter observed the young man. "Captain Gytha, wait here with the prince. Everyone else, come with me."

"I'm going to stay with Gytha in case she needs backup," Reid said. If the prince were here learning military strategy and how to invade another kingdom, he had to be intelligent and skilled with the sword.

Dexter lifted a single eyebrow, but he didn't question her. "That is an excellent idea," he replied. With a flourish, he handed her a dagger before exiting the room with the others.

Reid slid the dagger into the back of her pants in case she needed it. This man obviously didn't have any weapons on him. Seb would have made sure to remove them before traveling with him. However, something told her not to underestimate him—that he was far more lethal than he seemed.

Prince Owen's wrists and ankles were tied together. Did Seb bring him here on his own? Or had he traveled with additional soldiers? Perhaps the prince was utterly useless, and he didn't have any sword skills. Maybe his father had sent him to get him out of the way or to instill some sort of work ethic in him.

She watched the prince where he knelt on the floor, trying to get a read on him. His eyes were trained on her, making her feel oddly exposed.

Gytha placed a hand on Reid's arm, pulling her away from the prince.

A slow smile spread across his face. "I was trying to determine who you are," he said. "Now I know." His voice had a thick accent.

"You could have asked. I would have told you." Reid saw no harm in him knowing her identity. She sat on one of the chairs across from the prince. Gytha insisted on standing next to her, hovering like a protective mother.

Prince Owen's intelligent eyes narrowed, taking Reid in again, assessing.

Wanting to gain the upper hand, Reid crossed her legs, trying to pretend he didn't rattle her. "Tell me, Prince Owen, you seem like a spry young gentleman. How did you manage to be captured by an old man?"

He sprang to his feet, ankles and wrists still tied together.

Gytha was already there, a knife at his throat. "Don't move, prince."

Reid chuckled. "So temperamental. Often a trait in the youngest sibling."

"You would know, Lord Reid."

Drumming her fingers on the arm of the chair, she said, "You didn't let Seb capture you, did you?"

Instead of replying, he sat on the sofa.

"Do you think he wanted to come north?" Gytha asked, her knife still pointed at Owen.

"I do. The question is why."

Gytha shook her head. "I told you, I don't like these Melenians. There aren't any women in their army."

Owen chuckled. "We're not any different from Marsden."

"In Axian, we let women fight."

"Too bad your king has gained control of Axian. Last I saw, he was rounding up women wearing pants and tossing them in prison."

Reid bristled. The only people left at the palace were soldiers. And the women had all worn dresses so as not to upset the king. If what the prince said were true, that meant the king had sent soldiers to the nearby cities. Panic began to grow for the Axian people. They needed to overthrow Eldon as soon as possible.

Standing, she started pacing behind the chair, trying to figure out why Prince Owen would have wanted to leave the Melenia army and come north. What was here that he'd be interested in? "Your king and queen want control of Marsden," she said, thinking aloud. "I've heard they are enamored with our mines." Ships had been transporting jewelry to Melenia for quite some time.

His face remained impassive, indicating there was some truth to what she said.

"Did you come north to check on the mines?" She gripped the back of the chair, closely watching his reaction.

The corners of his lips rose, whether it was from her guessing the truth, she couldn't be sure. Maybe she should ask Ackley for lessons on interrogation.

The only other reason she could think of for him being here was to check on the Melenia ships off the northern coast of Marsden.

Dexter, Gordon, Ackley, and Seb returned to the great hall. Reid wondered where Idina had run off to.

"Gytha, you and Ackley will escort Prince Owen to the barracks," Dexter ordered. "He will remain there for now."

"I assume in a locked facility?" Gytha asked.

"Ackley will show you."

Reid wasn't sure what that meant. Was there a dungeon or some sort of holding cell in the barracks?

Ackley chuckled, the sound cold, dark, and humorless.

"This should be fun. Come, Prince Owen, it seems we get to play."

Once Gytha and Ackley left with the prince, Reid turned to Dexter. "You're having him interrogated?" The thought of Ackley torturing another person made her sick.

"There's no need," Seb said. "I already know everything of importance."

"Then why did Ackley imply he'd be interrogating the prince?"

"I'll find Duchess Bridger," Gordon said.

"And I will accompany you," Seb said. They exited the room, leaving Reid and Dexter alone.

"What am I missing?" Reid asked.

"Word came from Melenia," Dexter explained. "Duchess Bridger has the letter." He went over to the fireplace, putting one hand on the mantle while hunching forward. With his back to her, he said, "Russek slaughtered the entire Melenia royal family, and he gained control of the kingdom. Most of the Melenia army has been killed as well. He ordered heads placed on spikes along the entire border. It was brutal."

Reid collapsed on the sofa, dumbfounded. "Does Idina know?"

"She does. She's in her room, crying."

The princess had to feel awful since she'd written to Russek letting them know a substantial portion of the Melenia army was in Marsden.

"If this forces the Melenia army to return home, then Princess Idina will have managed to accomplish something with minimal loss of life to the Marsden people," Dexter said as if reading from a book.

"I agree, she very well may have saved our civilians' lives, but at the cost of Melenians?" How many people had been ruthlessly slaughtered? Reid's stomach twisted at the mere thought.

"War is never pretty," Dexter said as he took a seat beside her. "It brings out the worst in people." He took hold of her hands. "And when we march south into Axian, we will be at war. People will die."

She didn't want to think about people she knew and loved dying. "Who is going to tell Prince Owen?" He was the only surviving monarch. "I mean, King Owen?"

"Gordon went to ask the duchess to give the letter to Owen. Then we will release him so he can gather his soldiers and return home."

"Do you think he'll retaliate against us?"

"He can never know of our involvement in the matter. I've already told Idina she isn't to say a word to anyone about what she did."

Reid agreed. However, an ominous feeling took root. Secrets rarely stayed hidden.

Since Duchess Willer, Duchess Tucker, and Duchess Slader had each sent a messenger with word they would stand with Reid, only Duchess Ryder and Duchess Lyndr remained undecided. And both duchesses had arrived with their soldiers outside the city wall only an hour or so ago. Reid stood in Eldon's office, staring out the window, wondering if Duchess Ryder and Duchess Lyndr would stand with Reid or side with Eldon. If they stood with Reid, then Dexter could proceed with removing the king. Dexter had yet to release Owen—she didn't know what he was waiting for. However, she hoped once he was allowed to go, he'd pack up his soldiers and sail back home. If he didn't, then Dexter would have to fight the Melenia soldiers as well. She chewed on her thumbnail, hoping it didn't come to that.

Ackley poked his head in the room. "What are you doing in here?"

"Thinking."

"Want to snoop with me?"

"What about the duchesses?"

He rolled his eyes, then stepped into the room. "Duchess Lyndr is refusing to meet with you. She said she supports the true king. I informed her the *true king* stripped me of my title so I wouldn't be marrying her daughter. Once the shock wore off, she said she was taking her soldiers south as her husband and the king requested. Good riddance is what I say."

Reid leaned against the window ledge. "I suppose it would have been too much to ask that all the counties support us."

"You invoked the ring," he reminded her. "That means if we win, her land and title will be stripped."

Reid pinched the bridge of her nose. "What about Duchess Ryder?"

"She will only speak with Gordon, her son-in-law." Ackley folded his arms. "She's here with her two sons. Idina asked to accompany Gordon to speak to her."

"I'm not needed?"

He smirked. "Thus, the snooping."

She smiled. "Okay." More than anything, she was curious what he was searching for.

"Go change out of that dress. I'll meet you at the barracks."

"Who do you need me to be?" A man, woman, merchant, servant?

"I need you to be yourself."

Walking along the street in the City of Buckley, Reid adjusted her hat, making sure she hid her hair beneath it.

"Will you focus?" Ackley mumbled.

"Sorry." They were nearing the gate in the wall, and they needed to make it past the soldiers without anyone recognizing them.

Since it was afternoon, there were still a lot of people coming and going, allowing the two to easily blend in with the crowd, no one stopping or questioning them as they left the city.

"Care to tell me where we're going?" she whispered. When he'd said they were snooping, she thought he meant in the castle, not out here. As far as she could see, soldiers were camped in tents.

"To the mines."

"In Bridger?" she squealed. They were leaving the area completely? Bridger was almost a day's walk from there.

"We're going to *borrow* some horses."

"Even on horseback, it'll take us a couple of hours. Each way." People would question where they'd disappeared to.

"I told Dexter I was taking you to do some reconnaissance."

"We won't be back until after dark."

"Exactly. It'll be easier to sneak inside the castle under the cover of night."

Not having the energy to argue, Reid followed him toward the forest. Just before they reached the cover of the trees, they came to a large fenced-in area where the horses for the Slader officers were kept.

Acting as if he belonged there, Ackley opened the gate, then began saddling one of the horses. Not wanting it to take any longer than necessary, Reid joined him. Picking up a smaller saddle, she put it on one of the horses. Once they finished, they led the animals out of the pen, heading toward the trees. Reid kept waiting for someone to scream or stop them; however, no one did. When they were far enough away for anyone to see them, they mounted.

"We'll need to travel fast," Ackley said. "Ready?"

Instead of answering, she leaned forward, squeezing her legs into the horse's flanks as she commanded it to run. The animal took off. Reid smiled as the wind whipped through her hair, the land rushing below the horse's hooves.

CHAPTER FIFTEEN

After securing the horses to trees, Ackley and Reid crept toward the mines, trying to get a better look. When they neared the large hole in the ground, they got on their hands and knees, crawling to the edge.

"It's still light out," Reid mumbled, silently cursing Ackley for bringing her along. "Someone is going to see us."

"No one is expecting us to be here."

At the edge, they stretched out on their stomachs, observing the hundred-foot-wide circular hole before them. Like the last time Reid was there, over a hundred miners were excavating precious stones along the sides. Also like before, the men had short hair and wide shoulders, indicating they were from Melenia.

"If Duchess Bridger is so upset over Melenia taking her resources, why isn't she trying to stop them?" Ackley mused.

"Since her daughter is married to Eldon, she probably doesn't want to cause any problems." Besides, most of Bridger's soldiers were currently at the City of Buckley with the duchess.

"Where do you think they take the stones?" he mused.

That was a good question. Once a miner dislodged a stone with his hammer or spike, he put it in a basket around his waist. The men stood on ledges built into the sides of the hole. At the end of the day, they probably came out of the hole and emptied their baskets somewhere. Reid scanned the area, not seeing any place where they'd do so. "Where do the men go at night?" she asked, not spotting any tents or homes nearby. The men had to sleep somewhere. And they needed food. "Why is any of this important?"

"I'm curious. I think there is more to it than we know." He started scooting backward, away from the hole.

Reid did the same.

When they were safely back under the cover of the forest, Ackley started pacing. "I want to find out where they're keeping the stones until they ship them to Melenia."

"Why?" Reid asked, leaning against a tree.

"Once Owen learns of his kingdom's fate, what do you think he's going to do?"

"Rush home." Hopefully with his soldiers in tow.

"And what of the stones?"

"He'll leave them?" Reid suggested.

"Most likely. The problem with that is he could come back for them. Especially if he's financially strapped for cash." Ackley stopped pacing. "We need to find the stones and gain control of them. They are too valuable to leave in Bridger. If the duke gets his hands on them, it'll throw off the balance of power."

Who was Ackley more concerned about? King Owen or Duke Bridger? "Doesn't the duke own the mines?" Which would make the stones his in the first place? And hadn't

Dexter promised the duchess full control of the mines would return to Bridger?

"Part of Eldon's marriage negotiations to Harlow included these stones. I know for a fact he hasn't received full payment yet."

Reid rubbed her temple. "Ackley, why are we really here?" She had a feeling she wasn't going to like his answer.

He gestured over her shoulder. "Perfect timing."

Reid glanced back, seeing Ackley's Knights approaching. "What are they doing here?"

The Knights moved like shadows cast by the setting sun.

"They're here to help us."

The group formed a loose circle around Reid and Ackley.

"Our mission is two-fold," Ackley said, wasting no time. "Half will stay here to find out what the Melenian miners do at the end of the day. Where do they take the stones? Are they stored somewhere? If so, where? My guess is they're somehow using the Modig Mountains."

"Once we have the information, what do you want us to do?" one of the Knights asked.

"Two will report back to me while four stay to monitor the situation."

"We'll take that task," the Knight said, pointing at half the circle.

"The second group will be with Reid and me," Ackley said.

Reid didn't want to know what he had planned—she was certain she wouldn't like it.

"Let's get the horses. We don't have a lot of time."

The group headed twenty or so feet away, deeper into the cover of the trees, where the horses were. Reid untied hers and mounted, the six Knights accompanying them doing the same. Once everyone was ready, Ackley led them east.

"Where are we going?" Reid asked, steering her horse alongside Ackley's.

"To the duke and duchess's manor."

Why did Ackley want to go to Harlow's house? What did he hope to discover? "Is this regarding the stones or something else?"

He looked sidelong at her. "What do you think?"

"That it's about Harlow."

"Why do you say that?"

He didn't seem shocked or surprised by her answer. "I don't know. But something isn't right with her."

"How so?"

"Harlow knows secret passageways in the palace not even Nara knows about. One night, she spoke to me about people's motives...it was some kind of warning." They exited the forest, then headed up a small hill. "What about you? What do you think is going on with her?"

"I have no idea—which is the problem. She never speaks, never shows emotion, and doesn't seem to care about anyone or anything. The only thing I can deduce is she's hiding something."

"And you hope that by going to her house, we're going to discover what it is?"

"We probably won't learn anything." He adjusted the horse's reins. "Since I've combed through her bedchamber in the castle and found nothing personal to indicate she's living in the room, I'd like to see where she grew up. Is her childhood bedchamber just as impersonal? If so, that will tell me something about her. If not, it will indicate she's hiding something."

At the top of the hill, Reid observed the valley before them.

A well-kept manor was situated between towering pine trees. "Is anyone home?" she asked.

"There are probably some servants around."

"Why are the Knights with us?"

"To distract the servants so we can get in and snoop." He winked.

"The place looks pretty quiet." No one was out and about, the stables were still, no smoke rose from the chimneys, nor did any lights shine from within.

Ackley ordered two of his men to investigate. Reid watched them ride down the hill, approaching the square manor. The building was three stories tall, with a turret at each corner and two more at the front entry. Green grass and thick pine trees surrounded the home.

The Knights went around back, out of sight. Ackley handed Reid a chunk of bread. She ate it, waiting for the Knights to return. About twenty minutes later, the two men rode up the hill.

"The place is closed up," the Knight on the right said. "All the servants are gone."

"That makes sense," Reid said. "The duke is south with a contingent of his men, and the duchess is at the City of Buckley with the rest of Bridger's soldiers."

"I suppose." Ackley nudged his horse, then began to descend the hill.

Reid followed.

At the front of the manor, they tied their horses to the trees. Ackley broke them into groups of two, putting Reid with him. So they could finish quickly, each group was assigned to investigate a different section of the manor. The sun was about to set, and it would be dark soon.

As Reid and Ackley headed to the front door, she worried

about being gone for so long. She hoped Dexter didn't think something bad had happened to her—like being kidnapped again.

"Focus on what you're doing," Ackley snapped. "I'd prefer you not to get anyone killed because you're busy daydreaming."

She froze three feet from the front doors. "What am I missing?" Nothing appeared dangerous.

"I don't know. But they could have the place filled with traps." He withdrew something from his pocket, then reached forward, picking the lock. The front door squeaked open. Ackley peered inside. "Let's go," he whispered, stepping into the manor.

Reid followed, being careful not to make a sound. The large entryway revealed a grand staircase and a sitting room. Two Knights entered behind Reid. Ackley pointed up before signaling with two fingers. They nodded, heading to the second floor to investigate. The other Knights were entering from the back, and they would cover the entire first floor.

Ackley waved Reid forward. After carefully closing the front door, she followed him up the staircase to the third floor. She was about to head to the left when Ackley grabbed her arm, pulling her to the right. Even though they could cover more ground if they separated, she understood the reasoning for staying together.

They peered in bedchamber after bedchamber. Most were simple, containing only a bed and dresser. Reid assumed they were guest rooms. The duke and duchess had adjoining rooms. Both were elaborate with thick, heavy drapery on the beds, curtains on the windows, perfumes and smelling salts on the vanities, and closets bursting with clothes. In the duke's room, Ackley went through his desk, complaining there weren't any worthwhile letters or ledgers. Exiting the room, they went into the last bedchamber down this wing. This one boasted hunting knives and skins from various animals. Reid assumed it belonged to one of the lords. Moving to the other wing, they checked bedchamber after bedchamber. They encountered another young man's room, but none of the bedchambers felt like they belonged to Harlow.

"Do you think they got rid of her room once she married?" Reid whispered.

Ackley shook his head.

It didn't make any sense for them to do away with Harlow's room since, clearly, they weren't lacking in space.

They reached the last room in this wing. The bed had a knitted blanket folded neatly on it, dresses packed the dresser, and the hearth had some black markings on it, which indicated use over the years. Could this be Harlow's bedchamber? There weren't any books, letters, or drawings. Was Harlow truly that bland and lacking in personality? No, she couldn't be. The last time Reid thought so, she'd been mistaken. Appearances could be deceiving.

If Harlow could look like a docile woman when she was actually something else inside, maybe her room could be a cover, too. Reid examined the space with renewed interest. There was nothing under the bed or between the mattresses. Opening every single drawer, she checked under the clothes. She moved curtains, lifted rugs, and peeked behind the armoire. Nothing.

The entire time, Ackley stood in one spot, examining the room with only his eyes. "Move next to the window," he whispered. "Do you feel any air coming from outside?"

Reid did as he asked. When she didn't feel anything, she shook her head.

"Move to the empty wall next to the dresser. Do you feel any air coming from there?"

Instead of questioning him, Reid stood where he indicated. A slight brushing of air flitted a strand of her hair. She turned to examine the plain wall. None of the stones looked different or out of place.

Ackley came over, then started pushing on the stones. Nothing happened. Then he stood and closed his eyes. After a minute, he stuck his hand out, moving it toward the wall. Reid assumed he was trying to feel where the air was coming from. When his hand hit the wall, he opened his eyes, examining the joint where the two stones met. He knelt, feeling the edge of the wall.

Reid tried to remember how Harlow had opened the door in Reid's room back in the palace. Harlow had pushed on it. "Watch out."

After Ackley moved, Reid stood in front of the wall and pushed. Nothing happened. If it were a door, maybe it swung the other way. Feeling to the left, she tried to see if there was another hint of wind. Not finding any, she went the other direction until she came across a trickle of air. She pushed. The stone door sprung open.

"I'm impressed," Ackley mumbled as he poked his head inside. "Not a passageway, just a closet." Reaching down, he pulled out a trunk. "Look through that. I'll investigate the rest."

Kneeling, Reid opened the lid and found a treasure trove of personal belongings. There were a few dolls, a couple of scarves, a handful of books, some drawings. Nothing out of the ordinary. Reid was glad to have finally found something that revealed Harlow was a normal person. After she closed the lid, she stood.

Ackley exited the closet with his hands on his hips. "Nothing." He sounded disappointed.

"Same here."

He shoved the trunk back inside while Reid held the door open for him.

"The inside of the door is covered with wood paneling," Reid mumbled, more to herself than Ackley.

"Maybe it has something to do with how the door is made? Or it helps conceal the draft?"

"Where's the draft coming from if this is just a closet?"

"Good question." Ackley stood back, observing the door.

"There are knife marks on the wood," Reid pointed out. Almost as if someone had thrown knives at it. A chill spread over her skin.

Ackley moved closer to inspect it. "The wood isn't thick enough for a knife to lodge into it."

"You're right." Reid wasn't thinking clearly. She was so determined to find something nefarious about Harlow that she was letting her imagination get the better of her.

"Let's go see what the others have to say."

They exited the manor, heading back to where they'd left the horses. The six Knights were already waiting for them.

"Report," Ackley said.

"I found a letter from the duke to the king offering his support. He agreed to send another shipment of the blue stones. The king said not to bother since there was no one to sell them to."

"Interesting," Ackley mumbled.

Reid recalled the sailor Dexter had questioned. He'd been in Melenia selling jewelry. "Do you think the king knows Bridger is selling the stones in Melenia? Maybe Eldon is taking a cut of the profit for allowing it?"

"Could be." Ackley's head suddenly whipped to the side as he withdrew a dagger.

"Put your weapon away," Gytha said as she stepped out from behind a tree. The sun had set and the sky was almost dark, making it hard to see the warrior woman's face.

"What are you doing here?" Ackley demanded.

"I followed Lady Reid."

"Why?" He sheathed his dagger.

"To make sure she is okay. She will be crowned as our queen. As such, she should have a guard."

Ackley huffed. "What do you think I am?"

"A hot-headed man who is only thinking about what he hopes to accomplish and not what is best for Lady Reid."

"You don't know that."

They both glared at Reid. "I'm not getting in the middle of this," she said as she untied her horse. "It has been a long day, and I am tired."

The other Knights wordlessly mounted their horses. Having no other option, Gytha and Ackley followed suit.

As they rode, Ackley and Gytha continued to argue.

"I would never let anything happen to her," he said.

"I know. But you have to consider what it looks like to other people. You two should not be alone."

"We weren't. My Knights have been with us."

"I know that. You know that. But no one else does. Prince Dexter wants a strong, unified kingdom. He needs people to believe in the monarch. You will do nothing to jeopardize that."

"I don't plan on it."

"The next time you think about using Lady Reid for an assignment, a mission, or whatever it is you're doing, take me instead."

There was a long pause. "Thank you for the offer," Ackley replied. "I will take you up on it."

One of the Knights said, "I think it's too dark to travel any farther."

"I concur," another said.

Reid didn't want to stop. Stopping meant sleeping alone out here instead of at the castle with her husband. He would be worried when she didn't return. "Does Dexter know you are with me?" she asked Gytha.

"I asked his permission to be your personal guard. He knows I went after you."

Gytha had asked to protect Reid?

"Don't look at me like that," the warrior woman said. "I just don't have anything else to do in this county. Once I get back to my army in Axian, you won't be seeing much of me."

"I hope that's not true. I'd like for you to work alongside me in some capacity."

Gytha eyed Reid. "We shall see."

Reid laughed. That was all she could ask for.

The group found a spot to sleep for the night. The situation wasn't ideal since they didn't have any supplies for bedding. However, Reid didn't care. As soon as it was light out, she could resume her trek to the castle where her husband was waiting for her.

"Reid, wake up." Gytha shook Reid's shoulder.

Reid groaned. The sun hadn't fully risen yet. It was too early. Reid rolled over, her face hitting a rock. She was up. Rubbing her eyes, she stood.

The Knights were gone.

"Let's go," Ackley said. "If we ride fast, we can reach the castle in a couple of hours."

Eager to see Dexter, eat some food, and bathe, Reid mounted and followed Ackley and Gytha without complaint.

When they reached the outskirts of the City of Buckley, they returned the horses to the pen they'd taken them from. Since they were delivering horses, no one questioned them.

"Let's enter through the side," Ackley suggested. He led them around the wall surrounding the city. When they reached the door, they found it closed and locked. No one was manning it. "That's strange," Ackley mumbled as he withdrew his lock picks, then popped the door open. He quickly ushered them inside before locking the door. They were on the grounds surrounding the castle, having bypassed the city entirely.

"Do you think there's a problem?" Gytha asked, reaching for her sword.

"I don't know."

When they neared the barracks, a flurry of activity was going on. Soldiers ran about, some saddling horses. Gordon was off to the side, his face red as he barked out orders to a group of men. Ackley jogged over to him, Reid and Gytha right on his heels.

When Gordon saw them, he bent over, his hands on his knees.

"What's going on?" Ackley demanded.

"There was an attack on the castle." Gordon straightened, then cleared his throat. "Idina has been kidnapped."

Reid's heartbeat sped up. "What?" Maybe she'd heard him wrong.

"Two men took Idina. She put up quite a fight, but she wasn't strong enough. Then, we couldn't find you." Gordon waved his hand in Reid's direction.

"Where's Dexter?" she demanded.

"In the castle speaking with the duchesses."

Reid took off running. Inside, she headed straight for the great hall where she found the duchesses sitting on the sofas alongside Dexter. When he saw her, he jumped to his feet.

She ran straight to him, throwing her arms around his neck and holding him close. "I'm here. I'm okay."

His large hands slid around her back, clutching her tightly against his body.

"She was with me the entire time," Ackley said as he came into the room. "We were riding horses, and we couldn't make it back once the sun set. I apologize for the delay."

Dexter released Reid before whirling on Ackley. His eyes darkened as he fought to control his emotions in front of the duchesses.

"Captain Gytha was also with me," Reid said. "At first light, she woke us, and we returned as soon as possible. Now tell me what happened and what I can do to help."

Dexter took a deep breath, focusing on Reid. "A group of men infiltrated the palace a few hours ago. They kidnapped Idina."

"Any idea who took her or why?" she asked.

He shook his head. "I'm asking the duchesses if they heard or saw anything suspicious. Perhaps a group of men from one of the armies outside the city wall who is unhappy with the duchesses uniting?"

"But why Idina?" Ackley asked, folding his arms. "If Reid had been kidnapped, that would make sense. But not my sister."

"Maybe they took her because they couldn't find Reid?" Dexter suggested.

Ackley flinched. He sat on one of the chairs, not looking at anyone. "What is being done to retrieve her?" He rubbed his face.

"Prince Gordon is putting together search parties. He intends to comb through the camps. First, I want to make sure the duchesses are okay with this."

"Do we have a choice?" Duchess Cartr asked, her eyes trained on Dexter, watching him carefully.

"Yes. They are your soldiers. I will not have my soldiers search yours without your permission."

Duchess Tucker stood. "Give us until sunset to question our soldiers. Let us see what we can glean from the situation before Prince Gordon intervenes."

"Very well," Dexter said. "If you discover anything, please let us know at once."

After the duchesses left, Ackley started pacing. "I'm going to kill whoever took Idina."

Reid sat on the sofa the duchesses had just vacated. "Gordon and Ackley should not be in charge of searching for their sister."

A string of curse words flew out of Ackley's mouth.

"You are too emotional," she said, cutting him off. "You're not thinking clearly. We can't have that right now."

"My sister is in danger," he snarled. "Who knows what they're doing to her right now."

"If they wanted her dead, they would have killed her. But they didn't—they took her. Whoever did this knows how you'd react." She stood, pointing at his chest. "You need to calm down—don't play into their hands."

"She has a point," Gytha said, coming into the room.

"I can't sit around and do nothing." Ackley threw his arms in the air.

"I understand," Dexter said, his tone placating. "And no one is asking you to. However, we can't have you out there tearing through the city."

"While a search is being organized," Gytha said, "we can investigate here. Come with me. We can find out where the men entered, and if they left any traces of who they are behind."

"I think I'm going to be sick," Ackley mumbled, following Gytha.

As he exited, Reid said, "We'll find her. I promise we won't rest until we do."

CHAPTER SIXTEEN

Once Reid and Dexter were alone, he wrapped her in a hug. "I feel awful I'm secretly glad it's Idina and not you," he murmured in her ear. "If they'd taken you...I don't know what I would do."

"Then I guess it's a good thing I left with Ackley." And they'd searched the duchess's manor, which delayed them from returning home last night. She released Dexter and sat on the sofa, thinking over everything that had happened in the last twenty-four hours. It wasn't like Ackley knew someone was going to sneak into the castle. He never would have left if Idina were being threatened. But if he knew Reid were in danger... she shook her head, banishing those thoughts. Again, she was trying to find something where there wasn't anything to be found.

Dexter plopped on the sofa next to her. "I miss having my father and brother nearby to bounce ideas off."

"I understand. But you have me. So let's figure this out together."

"The main contenders are Anna and Eldon." He sighed.

Reid wondered if he'd slept at all last night. Focusing on the task at hand, she said, "Whoever took her did so for a reason." She just needed to figure out why so they could bargain to get her back. "What about Prince Owen?"

"He's in a holding cell." Dexter rubbed his face.

"Have you considered the Melenia soldiers might want him back?"

"I hadn't thought of the possibility, but it makes perfect sense. If they're the ones who took Idina, do you think they'll demand an exchange? We give them Owen in return for her?"

"It's a possibility."

He placed his hand at the nape of her neck, gently massaging it. "I guess we should discuss it with Owen. See if he has any insight."

"How is the new king?" Reid had only spent a few minutes with the man, so she wasn't sure how he'd react to the murder of his entire family. Would he be like Ackley and fly into a fit of rage? Or would he be so devastated he couldn't rally his men to fight back?

"He hasn't spoken since reading the letter."

"Let's see if he'll talk to us. Then we can determine if the Melenians are suspects or not." She stood, reaching her hand out for Dexter. He grabbed it, and she pulled him to his feet.

Instead of letting go, he yanked her toward him. She squealed since she hadn't expected it. When their eyes met, he slowly lowered his head, placing a soft kiss on her lips.

"I have a confession to make," he whispered, leaning his forehead against hers. "I'm jealous you spent last night with Ackley."

"You know nothing happened. He's like a brother to me. And Gytha was there."

"I know. It still doesn't change the way I feel."

"I'm sorry."

"You have nothing to be sorry for. I'm just trying to be honest with you."

Taking a deep breath, she said, "We'll talk more about this later." She wanted to try to be as honest with him as he was being with her. Since she had difficulty putting her feelings into words, she hoped to express herself by other means.

"I'll hold you to that." They exited the great hall. "Given what happened here, I think you need a bodyguard at all times. Gytha asked for the position, and I am going to give it to her."

While Reid didn't want someone following her around all day, she understood the necessity for it. Plus, Gytha had become a friend to Reid, so she didn't mind the warrior woman. "What about you?"

He smiled wryly. "You sound like my mother. She always said the very same thing to my father and me when we tried to assign a guard to her."

"I want you protected as well. What if you're ambushed?"

"I've decided if you have a guard, then I should as well."

"Who are you going to choose?" There weren't many men who were more proficient at fighting than Dexter.

"If Markis were here, I'd pick him. However, since he's with my brother, I'll have to ask Ackley if there's someone here he trusts."

"What about Ackley?"

Instead of responding, Dexter pushed open the door. They exited the castle. When they entered the barracks, Reid heard two people arguing from down the hall. She headed that way, realizing it was Ackley and Gytha.

Entering Ackley's office, she found him bent over an open chest filled with weapons. "What's going on?" Reid demanded.

Gytha's shoulders heaved up and down. "He thinks he is going to search for his sister alone."

Reid understood why he wanted to look for her. She knew there would be no changing his mind. Coming farther into the office, she leaned against the wall, watching Ackley. "Do you know something we don't?" she asked, voicing one of her concerns.

Not looking at her, he withdrew several vials, placing them in his vest. Then he picked up a handful of daggers, sliding them in pockets sewn in his pants and shirt.

"Will you at least let me talk to Owen before you leave? He may know who has her."

Ackley went still. "Owen?"

"We captured him. Maybe the Melenians want an exchange?"

He tilted his head, eyeing her. "You're not going to try to stop me from leaving?"

There was no stopping him. "No, I'm not. I just want to see if Owen knows anything. Will you give me thirty minutes?"

Gytha glared at Reid.

Ackley nodded. "Thirty minutes. No more."

Reid exited the room, finding Dexter waiting for her in the hallway. "Where's Owen?" she asked.

"Holding cell below the barracks."

Reid had never been to the subterranean level.

Gytha stomped out of the office. "Ackley is going to get himself killed."

"I have an idea," Reid said. "Stay here and watch Ackley. Don't let him leave until we return."

"You have my word." The warrior woman took up watch in the doorway, effectively blocking Ackley from exiting.

Dexter and Reid went to the end of the hall where a lone

soldier guarded a narrow door. The man unlocked it, ushering Reid and Dexter down the steep, narrow staircase to the subterranean level. A long corridor extended before them with a dozen doors on either side, torches hanging on the walls at even intervals.

The soldier led them to the third door on the right. After unlocking it, he opened the door and examined the room. "You can go in."

Reid stepped inside.

A single candle on a small desk lit the room, revealing Owen lying on a cot, facing the wall.

"This isn't as dreary as I thought it would be," Reid said by way of greeting.

Owen didn't acknowledge her.

"Dexter told me what happened to your kingdom. I'm sorry."

He still didn't respond.

"You do see the irony of the situation, don't you?"

He rolled onto his back, peering over.

"You came here under the guise of helping the king. Only, you planned to turn around and overthrow him once the dukes were removed from power."

"It's not the same thing," he replied, his voice gruff.

"It's not?"

He sat up, twisting to face her. "I didn't plan to slaughter the royal family."

"What did you intend to do with them?" She folded her hands, patiently waiting for him to explain.

His eyes finally met hers. "Melenia's purpose for being here is to secure access to the mines. Since Commander Beck can be a little…intense sometimes, I'm here to make sure things don't get out of hand. If Melenia happened to gain control of the kingdom, I'd be here to oversee everything."

"I'm failing to see how what you're doing is any better than what Russek did. You both seek to take what's not yours."

He chuckled, the sound humorless. "And what about you? Dexter wants an occupied throne."

Now they were getting somewhere. "He is the rightful heir."

"According to you."

"According to our laws."

"Why are you here?" He tilted his head, observing her.

"Men snuck into the castle and kidnapped Princess Idina."

"The redhead?"

Reid smiled. "Yes, but don't let her hear you calling her that."

"Her hair color is unique." His eyes remained focused on Reid. "You didn't answer my question. Why are you here?"

"I need to find Idina." She glanced back at Dexter hovering in the doorway, appreciating he was letting her handle this on her own. Taking a steadying breath, she asked Owen, "Do you know who took her?"

"I've been down here in this holding cell," he pointed out.

"I'm wondering if it's some sort of standard protocol. If you're captured, your men are to kidnap one of the reigning monarch's family members in order to do an exchange."

"Has anyone asked for me?"

"No." She supposed if it were his men, they would have left a ransom note.

He reached forward, picking up the cup on the desk and drinking a sip of water. "That would have been a smart move." He set the cup back down. "I doubt any of my men would have thought of it. And I'm certain Commander Beck is not eager for my return."

Reid was sure there was a story there. However, now was not the time to inquire about it. "May I ask you a question?"

"Only if I can ask one in return."

The last time she'd made a deal like this it had been with Ackley at the lake. She briefly hesitated before replying, "Okay."

"I'll go first." He stood, then took a step closer to her. "Why are *you* the one questioning me?"

That was easy to answer. "Because Ackley and Gordon are not fit to speak to you or anyone else at the moment. They are both too worried about their sister."

"Why not Dexter?"

Glancing back, she shrugged. "I had questions for you so I'm asking them. If he wants to say something, I'm sure he will."

Owen shook his head. "I didn't ask that right. Why is a man allowing a woman to be in charge?"

She pursed her lips. "Why not?"

"Because you're a woman." He scanned her from head to toe. "In pants. You're very strange."

Dexter chuckled but made no move to enter the room.

"Now what is your question for me?"

Reid wasn't sure how to say what she wanted without sounding too eager. As calmly as possible, without trying to appear invested, she said, "It seems you are now the king of Melenia. I'd say congratulations, but I know that's not what you want to hear at the moment. As king, you have the authority to withdraw your troops from Marsden and return home to retake your kingdom from Russek."

"I've been considering that." Moving over to the desk, he

sat on the edge. "I don't think I have enough men to retake my kingdom. It's bigger than yours."

And now for her actual question. "What if we work together?"

"Together how?" Dexter asked, coming into the room.

"I have an idea." Which she probably should have ran by him first, but she'd been too afraid he would say no.

"I'd like to hear it," Dexter said, standing alongside her.

"So would I," Owen stated.

She chose her words carefully. "If you help us, we'll help you."

"How so?" Owen asked.

"I want you to accompany Ackley to find Idina."

"Why me?"

"Several reasons. I need someone who isn't connected so intimately with the situation, someone who can be objective and see things clearly, to go with Ackley."

"I'm sure you have plenty of people who fit that bill."

"I do." But she didn't have any men who were stealthy, intelligent, and skilled with the sword whom Anna didn't know about.

"Reid, don't you think we should discuss this first?" Dexter asked.

"Now that Owen is Melenia's king, we have an opportunity to work with him."

"His army is in our kingdom," Dexter pointed out.

"I know. But consider this: Owen could have gotten away from Seb at any time. Yet, he came with the man. In addition, Owen just lost his entire family, his kingdom, and his friends. If you were in his position, you'd want someone to help you."

Dexter pursed his lips, his indecision clear.

"I want to be sure I'm understanding you correctly," Owen

said. "If I help you retrieve Idina, you'll support me in my bid to reclaim my kingdom?"

"Yes. We'll send soldiers to Melenia with you to ensure you retake your kingdom."

He held out his hand. "Deal."

She shook it, hoping she hadn't just made a huge mistake.

After drawing up a wordy treaty and signing it, Dexter led Owen and Reid to Ackley's office where Gordon and Gytha waited with Ackley.

"The duchesses are saying their soldiers had nothing to do with it," Gordon said as he paced in the small office. "Where do you plan to start looking?" He warily eyed Owen.

"I agreed to help because I have an idea of who took her," Owen said. He went over to Ackley's chest and rummaged around, picking out weapons to use for the journey. After sheathing a longsword, he faced Gordon.

"You agreed to help so you'd have access to our soldiers." Gordon clenched his hands into fists, glaring at Reid.

"Enough," Reid chided. "There are too many people in here. Gordon, return to your soldiers. I'm sure you have things to do to prepare for our march south into Axian."

After Gordon stormed out of the office, Owen chuckled. "That would never fly in my kingdom."

"Focus," Reid snapped. "You said you had an idea of who took the princess?"

Dexter went around the desk and sat on the chair, watching their exchange.

"I know something you don't." Owen peered into the

hallway, then closed the door. Lowering his voice, he whispered, "Why do you think Melenia is here?"

Dexter narrowed his eyes. "You're here because Eldon requested aid in exchange for access to the mines."

Reid leaned on the window ledge, folding her arms. Ackley closed and locked the weapons chest, then sat on top of it.

"That is what everyone is supposed to believe. However, there is more to it than that. My mother received a letter from a woman in Marsden seeking our help. She said King Eldon was evil and murdering his own people. She offered an enormous sum of money if we'd send soldiers to help overthrow the king."

A sick foreboding overcame Reid. She rubbed her forehead, fearing she knew who sent the letter. But why? Thinking back over everything she'd learned these last few weeks, she recalled Leigh telling her that Anna had been in love with Hudson. However, Hudson was supposed to marry a princess from Melenia. Knowing what she did about her mother, Anna probably still held a grudge against Melenia and wanted them destroyed as well. Reid abruptly stood, another horrible thought coming to mind. What if Idina had written the letter to Russek encouraging them to take over Melenia because Anna had put the clues in front of her?

"What is it?" Owen demanded, his voice low.

"The woman who wrote the letter is Anna. She wants retribution against your family. If she discovers you're here, she won't hesitate to kill you."

"You're saying I've been set up?" Owen asked.

"We all have. This is one big plot concocted by Anna."

"What are we going to do about her?"

"We're going to kill her," Ackley said, his voice dark. "The only problem is, she is already ten steps ahead of us."

"We're catching up," Reid insisted.

"We need to do it faster."

"What does this have to do with Idina?" Dexter asked, leaning back in the chair and propping his right foot on his left leg.

"In Anna's letter," Owen said, "she was extremely specific about what she wanted us to do. She said when the young woman was kidnapped, that was the start of the end. The purpose of the kidnapping was to lure Ackley and Gordon out into the open where Anna could eliminate them. Then the fighting would start. At that time, the dukes are meant to die. Afterward, the king and any remaining royal family members are to be eliminated."

"Do we have any hope in getting Idina back before the fighting starts?" Reid asked.

"She is being taken south of Lake Folme to an open area where Anna wants the fighting to take place."

"I doubt the king will travel there with the dukes," Ackley mumbled.

"When the fighting starts, a group of men is to head to the palace to make the remaining kills."

"Out of curiosity, why did Melenia agree to this?" Dexter asked.

"For a few reasons. One, my mother wanted to help if the innocent people in your kingdom truly were suffering. Two, we desperately needed the money. And three, my mother sent me without telling Anna because she feared there was something we were missing. They tasked me with figuring out what it is. Now I know."

Reid's eyes filled with tears. This was her mother they were talking about. *Her mother.* How could Anna be so cruel and heartless?

"Are you okay?" Dexter asked.

She nodded. "I need a moment alone." She exited the office, leaning against the wall in the hallway. It felt like the walls were spinning around her.

"Is she okay?" Owen asked.

"Anna is her mother," Dexter explained.

"Whom she didn't know was alive until a few weeks ago," Ackley pointed out.

"You know Anna better than anyone else," Dexter said, the chair legs scraping against the floor. "Why did she take Idina instead of killing her in the castle?"

There was a long pause before Ackley answered, "I think she intended for her men to kidnap Reid. That's what was supposed to set everything into motion. Only, Reid wasn't here. So the lackeys she sent took Idina instead."

Dexter's slow footsteps echoed in the room. "Is that why you left with Reid?" His voice sent a chill down Reid's spine.

"I didn't know for sure."

"You saved Reid at the expense of your own sister," Owen mused. "Interesting."

"Yes," Ackley mumbled. "And now I need to get my sister back."

"Then let's get to it. The faster we end this, the sooner I can return to Melenia."

CHAPTER SEVENTEEN

The following days were excruciating. More than once, Reid wished she were a bird and could fly over the kingdom to see what was going on. Had Ackley and Owen managed to find Idina? Had the king sent his and the Melenia soldiers north to make a stand? Where were the Axian soldiers? Were Colbert and Markis okay?

All counties north of the Gast River—with the exception of Lyndr—had their soldiers camped outside the City of Buckley. Duchess Lyndr had taken her soldiers south into Axian. Gordon spent his days organizing the counties' armies into one single unit marching under the Marsden banner. He told Reid he needed to stay busy, so he didn't go crazy worrying about his sister.

Leigh remained locked in her room. The only one she let in was Nara. Nara told Reid that Leigh was devastated and felt as if she'd lost not one, but two, children.

Dexter continued to hold meetings with the duchesses in order to make sure they felt included on the invasion south to oust the king and save their husbands.

"I miss Axian," Dexter said as he came into the bedchamber he shared with Reid. "I miss my father, my brother, and even the damn dog, Finn."

She laughed as she removed her tunic. "Has there been any word from Colbert?"

"No, but I've sent him several messages."

"He always struck me as the bookish type."

"What does that have to do with anything?"

"I don't picture him commanding the Axian army." Granted, he had a lot of help. Markis was with him, along with countless other officers.

"Sometimes, I forget how little you know about my family."

Curious, she turned toward him, even though she only had her shift on.

"Colbert is an excellent swordsman," he explained as he went over to the fireplace, tossing another log on the fire.

Reid recalled how Colbert had thrown himself in front of the dagger to save Dexter's life, which meant he had to be brave as well. Opening the armoire, she withdrew her nightdress. On her way to the bathing chamber, she caught a glimpse of Dexter as he removed his tunic and undershirt, revealing his muscled torso.

She froze, heat creeping up her neck and onto her face. He was beautiful.

"Need something?" he asked, his voice husky, matching the dim lighting cast by the fire.

Standing there like a fool, unable to speak, she shook her head and ducked into the bathing chamber. Tossing her nightdress on the floor, she realized she'd grabbed the wrong one. Silently cursing, she picked up the dress and went back into the bedchamber. Stretched out on the bed, shirtless, Dexter wore only loose pants that hugged his hips.

Reid's eyes widened at the sight. Being sure to keep her mouth shut so she didn't drool like a damned fool, she forced herself to walk slowly to the armoire so she wouldn't do something stupid like trip.

"What's the matter?" Dexter asked. "You seem flustered." The corners of his lips rose as he fought a smile.

She wanted to punch him. He knew he was making her uncomfortable being half naked. Instead of putting clothes on, he was laughing. Well, two could play that game. At the armoire, with her back to Dexter, she shoved the wrong nightdress back into the armoire. Taking a slow breath, she steeled her resolve and removed her shift, letting it fall to the floor like water. She heard him suck in a breath. Good, now he knew what it felt like. Ever so slowly, she removed her pants. With her back still facing Dexter, she leaned forward and withdrew the correct nightdress. She put it over her head and pulled it down her torso, shimmying so the fabric slid the rest of the way.

She felt ridiculous acting like a harlot. However, she wanted to show Dexter what it felt like to be around someone who was half naked. Turning to face him, she hoped she'd flustered him as much as he did her.

Dexter was still as a statue, his eyes wide as the moon. She smirked. From where she stood, she could see him swallow.

"What are you doing?" he asked, his voice hoarse.

She raised a single eyebrow. "What? You think you're the only one who can waltz around here showing that much skin?"

"If I would have known that's all I had to do to get you half naked, I would have done it a long time ago." He jumped off the bed. "What will you do if I remove the rest of my clothing?"

Now he was teasing her. She grabbed a pillow from the bed, then hurled it.

He deftly caught it. "You shouldn't have done that." He smirked, dropping the pillow. With a devious glint in his eyes, he untied his pants. They slid straight to the floor. He stood there in only his underwear. "Now what are you going to do?"

She was two seconds from throwing herself at him. As calmly as possible, she replied, "I'm going to go to bed." She quickly climbed under the sheets, pulling them up to her chin. Maybe if she didn't look at Dexter, the image of him in nothing but his underwear wouldn't stay seared into her mind.

Chuckling, Dexter crawled under the blankets next to her. "Funny you should say that. I'm going to bed, too." He reached over, brushing a stray strand of hair out of her face. "You're beautiful." He propped his head on his hand, watching her. "What are you afraid of? Or are you just not ready?"

She pinched her eyes closed, not knowing the answer.

He pressed his lips to her forehead. "I love you, Reid Winston. Let me show you—my wife—how much." He kissed her right cheek, then her left cheek.

She could feel his body heat next to her. "I have a better idea," she said, opening her eyes. "How about I show you how much I love you?" Her voice shook slightly.

"Why don't we show each other?"

She rolled onto her side, facing him. "Okay."

He blinked. "Okay?"

She nodded, ready to spend the night with her husband.

His lips devoured hers.

The following morning, Reid woke up in Dexter's arms, the

sheets tangled around their twined legs. Stretching, she was surprised she'd slept at all. They'd spent most the night kissing and being together.

Someone knocked gently on their door.

Since Dexter was still asleep, Reid slipped out of bed. Grabbing a discarded blanket from the floor, she pulled it around her naked body before going over to the door, opening it an inch.

Nara stood in the hallway. "I need to speak with you two immediately. Lord Victor and Lord Robert are here."

Reid blinked. "My second cousin Victor and Lord Robert from Axian?" While she understood how Victor had caught up to them, she had no idea what he was doing with Lord Robert.

"Yes. They're both in the castle's private sitting room." Forehead creased with worry, she tightened her eyes.

"We'll be right there, Mum," Dexter said groggily.

Reid glanced over her shoulder at Dexter. He sat up in bed, rubbing his eyes. Even in the morning with his hair tousled, he was still handsome.

"We'll get dressed and meet you there," Reid said to Nara.

Nara's face softened as she gave Reid a knowing smile before leaving.

Reid closed the door. Dexter waved her over to him. When she neared the bed, he yanked her closer. After tugging the blanket off her body, he leaned back on the bed, pulling her on top of him. His lips found hers.

"Your mother is expecting us," Reid said around kisses. If they didn't stop this soon, the likelihood of making it to the sitting room this morning diminished greatly.

"Minor details." He flipped her so his body was now on top of hers. "But we do need to go and see why those two are here.

We'll have to finish this later." He playfully bit her shoulder before getting up and pulling on his pants.

Sighing, Reid did the same. One of these days, they'd be able to be lazy and lounge around their room all day. Today was not that day.

***

Reid and Dexter entered the private sitting room. Lord Victor and Lord Robert sat on one of the sofas, each with a teacup in hand. Nara and Leigh sat across from them. Since Leigh was present, she must think the lords' presence had something to do with Idina.

Taking one of the chairs, Reid sat and addressed them. "Where is she?"

"If you're referring to Princess Idina," Lord Robert said, setting his cup down, "word is the Melenia army has captured her as a prisoner of war."

Leigh's face paled. Nara reached over, rubbing her back.

"Why are you two here?" Dexter asked, coming up behind Reid and placing his hands protectively on the back of her chair.

Robert chuckled. "Are you two playing king and queen?"

Reid was about to inform him that they were married, but she kept that to herself. Dexter knew Robert and what kind of man he was. She needed to let him deal with the lord.

Instead of responding, Dexter waited for Robert to answer.

He rolled his shoulders back. "King Eldon sent Marsden soldiers to eliminate the Axian ruling families."

Reid's heart pounded—did that include her grandparents?

"Clearly he wasn't successful in his endeavor since you're here," Dexter murmured.

"The Marsden soldiers encountered Axian soldiers at every manor they visited." Robert leaned back against the sofa, crossing his legs. "It seems you managed to organize and control your men even from so far away."

Relief washed through Reid. Her grandparents were unharmed.

Since Dexter and Colbert had several plans in place before Eldon arrived at the palace, they were able to organize their soldiers quickly and prevent the attacks on the ruling families.

Instead of acknowledging his own military genius, Dexter asked again, "What are you doing here?"

Robert cleared his throat, shifting on the sofa. "You know what my position has been all these years."

"Yes," Dexter replied. "You want Axian to be its own independent kingdom. You've made yourself perfectly clear on the matter."

"I've changed my mind."

Although Reid couldn't see Dexter, she felt him tense behind her.

"Explain."

Robert took a deep breath. "I see now Axian being its own kingdom won't work. I understand Marsden will always be a threat." He uncrossed his legs and then crossed them again, seemingly irritated at having to explain himself. "Fine. I'll say it since that's what you want. I support your bid for the throne."

The room seemed unnaturally quiet. Reid wondered why Robert felt compelled to come all the way to the City of Buckley to convey his position on the matter. She pinched her lips, letting Dexter handle this one. He pushed off the chair, moving to sit on the arm of it, next to Reid.

"So, Lord Robert, you're here to show your support for me." Dexter's eyes sliced over to Victor. "Why are you here?"

Victor scooted toward the edge of the sofa. "I'm here on behalf of Duke Gregor Axian."

"My grandfather sent you?" Reid asked. She'd thought he was here per Anna's instructions.

"After…uh…losing you in northern Axian, I returned to the manor to check on Duke Axian. Since he has no legally living children, I've been appointed as his caregiver and am responsible for his well-being. The king did try to take his land. Thankfully, the Axian soldiers held the king's men back."

So Victor's loyalties were tied. "Does Anna know you're here?"

"She does. She asked for me to report back on the nature of your relationship with Dexter. She wants to know if it has changed." He looked from Reid to Dexter and then back again, silently questioning them.

"You will tell her it is the same." Reid clasped her hands together. Anna couldn't discover the depth of Reid's feelings for Dexter. If Anna did, it would compromise everything, and she'd probably end up adding Reid to her list of people to kill.

"Why did Duke Axian send you?" Dexter inquired.

"Like Lord Robert, Duke Axian is indebted to you for what you have done. He asked I check on Reid. I am doing so under the guise that I am here on Anna's orders."

"The time to strike is now," Robert insisted. "We can't give Eldon time to regroup."

"Is that so?" Dexter stood and wandered over to the window, gazing outside. "To be clear, you want me to remove the unlawful king, get the Melenia army out of our kingdom, you want your land and title retained, and you would like peace restored to the land?"

"Yes," Robert said, tugging the collar of his tunic away from his neck.

Reid supposed Robert was afraid of things changing and only supported Dexter because Dexter would maintain a sense of familiarity. What Reid didn't like was the fact Robert felt no loyalty to Dexter. His desire to support Dexter stemmed from need and what was best for himself—nothing more.

Dexter faced Robert. "In that case, I want a few things in return."

Sitting on the window seat with the curtain closed, concealing her from sight, Reid gazed outside at the dark clouds rolling in. With so many soldiers sleeping in tents just outside the city wall, a storm was not a welcome sight right now. She sighed. All this sitting around, waiting, was starting to get to her. She just wanted this finished so she could start moving the kingdom forward.

The door to the sitting room creaked open. "Reid?" Harlan said.

"I'm in here."

A moment later, her friend pushed the curtain aside, peering into her private space. "What are you doing?"

"I wanted some time alone to think." She'd been hiding there for over an hour.

Harlan crawled onto the window seat with her. "I know what you mean. I'm not used to living with so many opinionated people." He let his head rest against the wall.

For Reid, that was part of it. She was used to being by herself for hours. Yet, now she was rarely alone. She enjoyed the silence—it made her feel calm and tranquil. But she'd hid in here today for a different reason. Thoughts of her mother were inundating her. She kept thinking about Anna's end goal, everything she'd learned about her, and ways they could beat her. So far, Reid hadn't been able to come up with any viable plans. Every time she thought of something, Anna managed to outsmart them. Now, all Reid felt was incredible anxiety.

"Looks nasty out there," Harlan commented.

Reid nodded, staring out the window. "And it hasn't even started raining." Thunder boomed through the sky, rattling the glass.

"Are you okay?" Harlan asked, his voice soft and barely audible.

"Yes." She looked at her friend, wondering why he'd asked her that.

"Dexter sought me out. He asked if I'd speak to you."

That surprised Reid. "About what?"

He shrugged. "He said he thought you could use a friend."

Having Harlan nearby did offer a level of comfort and familiarity. It was like having a piece of home with her. The second she thought about home, tears filled her eyes. Her home had been destroyed.

As if sensing her discomfort, Harlan hurried and said, "I met Lord Robert and your second cousin Victor. They're interesting."

"They're staying here in the castle." She rolled her eyes. Dexter should have made them stay at a local inn.

Harlan fidgeted with the seam of his pants near his knee. "Did you hear a messenger arrived?"

She shook her head—she hadn't heard a thing.

"Word came that when Duchess Lyndr arrived at the City of Radella, the king had her arrested, and he took control of her soldiers."

"Serves her right. We told her not to go."

"The irony is that he arrested her for raising an army against him."

Reid snorted. "I bet she had a fit screaming he's the one who told her to come with an army."

They sat in companionable silence for several minutes. A light rain started falling outside.

"Dexter told me the soldiers are ready to march," Harlan said. "He plans to leave in two days. He wants me to come."

"You should." He could help if someone got injured or if Anna tried poisoning any of the soldiers.

"Umm," Harlan murmured, shifting on the window seat.

"What is it?" She knew her friend well enough to tell when he needed to discuss something with her.

"Nara spoke with me."

Reid narrowed her eyes. Nara wouldn't dare.

"Here." He handed a bag of herbs to her.

Reid's face flamed red. She refused to take the bag. How could Nara have spoken to Harlan about Reid needing something to prevent a pregnancy? She wanted to crawl into the window seat and hide.

"I wish you would have felt comfortable coming to me yourself," Harlan said. "Reid? What's wrong?"

"I can't believe she did that." Reid couldn't decide if she was angry or on the verge of tears. Maybe both.

"If you and Dexter aren't ready to have a child, you need to be taking these."

Reid snatched the bag from his hand.

"There's nothing to be embarrassed about," he insisted. "Lots of women take them. My own wife does."

She could not believe they were discussing something so intimate with one another.

"Why do you always shy away from anything personal like this?" he asked. "Don't you trust me?"

She glanced at her friend. "It's not that. I trust you implicitly." After all, she'd taken him to Axian with her. He was one of the only people she ever confided in.

"Then why don't you talk to me?"

"I do."

"Not about anything personal."

She sighed, leaning her head back against the wall. "How long did it take you to tell me you were engaged?"

"The only reason I didn't tell you right away was because you don't like to talk about that sort of thing!"

"Fine. What do you want to know?"

"Nothing." He shook his head. "All I want is for you to come to me if you need something or want to talk." Pointedly, he looked at the bag clutched in Reid's hand.

"I'm sorry, Harlan. I didn't mean to offend you." The rain picked up, pinging against the window. "I just got so used to keeping everything inside, so I didn't slip and make a mistake." But now everyone knew she was a woman, so she didn't have to be so guarded. However, she didn't know how to change who she was or how she acted.

He took her free hand. "I know. I'm worried now that you're married, our friendship will change. You'll go live in the City of Radella, and I won't get to see you very often."

"We'll have to make a point of spending time together." She squeezed his hand, hoping he understood how much she valued his friendship.

A bell tolled in the distance.

"What's that?" Harlan asked.

The last time Reid had heard that bell was when the princes arrived. "Someone of importance must be here." She jumped off the window seat. "Let's go." She took off running through the castle, Harlan at her heels.

She headed to the front doors, where she met Nara and Leigh. Neither knew what was going on. Throwing the doors open, Reid stepped onto the front steps. Gordon emerged from the barracks, joining them.

"What flag has been raised?" Leigh asked. Her red-rimmed eyes were bloodshot as if she had been crying and hadn't slept in days.

"It's hard to see in the rain," Gordon said, squinting. "I think it's Ackley's flag."

"Does Idina have one?" Reid demanded.

"No," Leigh responded.

"What does this mean?" Harlan asked.

"I don't know." She had no idea if Ackley returned on his own or with the princess.

A stable hand brought a saddled horse over to Gordon, handing him the reins.

"I'll go see." Gordon mounted, then steered his horse toward the city.

Dexter joined them on the steps. "Do we know who arrived?"

"We think it's Ackley." They stood there, no one talking, as they waited to see if Ackley was alone or not. What if Idina had been killed? What if Ackley couldn't find her? The wait was excruciating.

After what felt like forever, the castle gates swung open to reveal four riders. Gordon and Ackley were in front, Owen and Idina behind them. Leigh let out an odd noise, then swayed. Nara wrapped her arm around Leigh, steadying her. Gordon and Ackley were conversing back and forth. Ackley appeared to be fine, no obvious injuries in sight. When they neared the castle, Reid noticed Idina riding with her back straight and head held high. Like Ackley, Idina didn't have any visible injuries. Owen said something to Idina. The princess's eyes widened, and she glared.

They dismounted at the front steps. Leigh threw her arms around her daughter.

Owen came before Dexter. "One princess delivered safe and sound. I've fulfilled my end. Now it's your turn."

Leigh released her daughter. "I'm so glad you're home."

"It's good to be home. The journey was trying."

"Everyone inside out of the rain," Leigh ordered. "I'll have a feast prepared for supper to celebrate my daughter's return."

Idina twisted to address Owen. "Thank you for your services," she said, her voice formal and haughty. "You may return to your men." She gave a curt nod before gliding inside the castle.

Ackley chuckled. "At some point, Owen, you'll need to tell her you're staying with us."

"Oh, it's much more fun this way. I can't wait for supper to see the shock on that beautiful face of hers." Smiling, he sauntered into the castle with Ackley.

"Well, that was unexpected," Nara said.

"I'm glad she's back," Dexter said. "I didn't think they'd find her so quickly."

"I was referring to Owen and Idina fancying one another," his mother replied.

"I don't think she likes him," Reid said.

"She does. Trust me. She has the same look about her that you did when you first came to live with us."

Reid stiffened. She hadn't been in love with Dexter at first. Sure, she might have thought him handsome and admired his dedication, but she hadn't been in love with him.

Dexter kissed Reid's cheek, surprising her.

"What was that for?" she asked.

"No reason." He took her hand. "Let's head inside."

After supper, in which Idina and Owen argued mercilessly, Dexter met with Owen in the study. When Reid went to join them, Dexter blocked the doorway.

"What are you doing?" Reid asked, confused.

"I want to speak with him alone."

"Why?"

"I need you to trust me on this," he mumbled. "I'll be along shortly." He closed the door, effectively dismissing her.

Idina strode along the hallway, coming toward Reid. "I don't know why Owen is still here."

"We told you over supper, he helped rescue you, so we're going to help him reclaim his kingdom."

Idina's face paled. "I still feel awful about that."

Reid joined the princess. They walked side by side. "I'm fairly certain Anna is to blame, not you."

"I don't want to talk about it."

When they reached the princess's bedchamber, Idina invited Reid inside. While the princess changed into her nightclothes, Reid knelt on the hearth, stoking the fire back to life.

Idina crawled into bed. "I'm fine, Reid. Exhausted, but unharmed."

"I didn't ask." Although she wanted to know everything that had happened to the princess.

"Then stop hovering."

Reid sighed, sitting on the edge of the bed. "I'm relieved you're okay. We were all so worried about you."

"It was a trying ordeal to be sure. Those two idiots tied me up so I couldn't fight. I'm going to have Gordon show me how to get out of that situation during our next training session."

"Where were you taken?"

"South. That was not how I envisioned my first adventure into Axian going. I was tossed on a boat, then taken to Axian where we met up with a group of Melenia soldiers. There was some confusion about me being the wrong person. The next thing I know, Prince Owen shows up, demanding they release me. Once they do, he instructs them to tell the army to be prepared to turn on King Eldon and fight with Prince Dexter. Then he and Ackley brought me home." She laid down, pulling the blankets up.

"I see." Reid decided to tease Idina to see if there was any truth to what Nara said earlier. "So Owen rescued you?"

Idina rolled her eyes. "My brother rescued me."

"Prince Owen is handsome to be sure. And he's now the king of Melenia. I can see why you're taken with him."

Idina's eyes narrowed. "Of all people to say something, I didn't expect it to be you."

Reid started laughing. "Admit it. You like him."

"I will do no such thing."

"I saw the way he watched you. He fancies you, too."

"Reid Ellington—"

"It's Reid Winston now," she reminded her.

Idina raised a single eyebrow. "Oh, I see."

Reid stood to go.

"You and Dexter finally did the deed."

It was Reid's turn to be embarrassed.

"I'm right, aren't I?" Idina got on her knees. "Look at you blush! Tell me all about it."

"I will do no such thing." Reid headed to the door.

"Did you enjoy it?"

Reid exited the room without answering, coming face to face with Gytha. "Where have you been?" She hadn't seen the warrior woman all day.

Gytha smiled. "Doing an errand for Prince Dexter."

"Well, Idina is in bed. I'll see you tomorrow." She thought it was a good idea for Gytha to guard Idina in case someone snuck into the castle again.

"I'm here for you, not for her."

Reid groaned. She'd forgotten Gytha had been assigned as her protection.

Once they reached the bedchamber Reid had been staying in, Gytha searched the room before bidding Reid goodnight. Then Gytha leaned against the wall in the hallway next to the door.

"You're not going to remain out there all night, are you?" Reid asked.

"Why?" Gytha smiled wickedly. "Afraid I'll hear something?"

"What is with everyone teasing me?" Reid snapped.

"Sorry," Gytha said, not sounding sorry at all. "I'm only here until Dexter retires for the evening. Then there will be two guards stationed here for the duration of the night. There are also two men outside your window."

Reid supposed she'd have to get used to this if she were going to be crowned queen.

"Are you okay?" Gytha asked. "You seem off. Considering the princess is home, I thought you'd be happier."

"Until Eldon and my mother are dealt with, I will continue to worry."

"I understand. But know I will do everything in my power to keep you safe."

Reid stood there, staring at Gytha. What had she done to earn such loyalty? Or was Gytha simply extending her loyalty to Reid out of respect for Dexter? Reid wasn't sure. However, she appreciated having Gytha on her side. They'd come a long way since the first time they'd met.

"Thank you."

"For what?" Gytha asked.

"For being you. And for being my friend."

"Friend is a strong word, Lady Reid." Gytha chuckled. "But I do consider you my friend."

CHAPTER EIGHTEEN

Reid peeled her eyelids open, blinking at the bright morning sun shining between the curtains.

"You're awake," Dexter murmured, curled beside her.

She hadn't even heard him come in last night. She stretched, and he slid his hand over her stomach. "What did you talk to Owen about?"

He propped himself up on his elbow, then kissed the tip of her nose. "Plans for the future." He kissed her cheek.

"Are you trying to distract me?" If so, it was certainly working.

"I'm not the distracting one." He kissed her other cheek.

"Dexter, I'm serious." She wanted to know what he'd discussed with Owen.

Sighing, he laid on his back. "We talked about how to eliminate Eldon. I also wanted his thoughts on how to best handle our armies."

"Why couldn't I be there for that?"

"Because I also asked him about Idina."

"What about?"

"I needed to make sure no harm came to her. She is my cousin."

Reid had forgotten about that.

"I also wanted to make sure the Melenia ships off our northern coast won't pose a threat."

"How so?"

"I can't move our entire army south knowing there are war ships up north—even if not many soldiers are on board."

"What did he agree to?"

"Owen dispatched men to each port in order to communicate with the ships. The ships are to sail east, then dock at one of the larger ports in Axian." He sat up. "We also discussed ways of uniting our kingdoms." Standing, he raised his arms in the air, stretching his torso.

Reid yawned. "It must be too early because I'm not following you." Why did they have to bother uniting their kingdoms? Couldn't Owen just take his soldiers and return home? Once he regained control of Melenia, then the Marsden soldiers who accompanied him would come back to Marsden. Then, they'd leave each other the hell alone.

Dexter pushed the curtains aside, staring outside. "Owen wants to marry Idina."

Sitting upright, Reid blinked. "Really?" While she thought there was some sort of attraction between the pair, she hadn't suspected Owen would want to marry Idina.

"Strategically, it makes sense. For both kingdoms." He came over, then sat on the edge of the bed, next to Reid.

"Did you talk to Idina about it?"

He rubbed the side of his jaw. "Not yet."

Relief filled Reid. She would have been furious if Dexter had made the union without speaking to Idina about it first.

"Do you think she'll agree?" he asked.

"I have no idea." Reid didn't know how the princess would feel about leaving Marsden. "Do you want me to speak to her about it?"

Dexter chuckled. "No, definitely not."

"Why is that funny?"

"Because it is." He shook his head. "I'll discuss the matter with Ackley to see how he thinks we should handle it." Reaching out, Dexter tucked a stray strand of hair behind Reid's ear. "You're adorable when you're mad."

"I'm not mad." And she most certainly wasn't adorable. Her eyes narrowed. No one had ever accused her of being adorable before.

Dexter chuckled. "Want to get a round of sparring in before breakfast?"

Was that even a question? "Of course."

Dexter stood on the front steps of the castle. Dressed in a black tunic with the Winston family crest embroidered on the front —compliments of Gordon—he appeared commanding and regal. They all agreed ahead of time Dexter would remain on the top step alone while the rest of the royal family stood on the lower steps, facing him and offering their support. At the end of his speech, they would join him.

Reid stood next to Idina and Nara. She'd decided to wear a dress, not wanting to alienate the citizens of Marsden. Change would come slowly. The duchesses stood behind the royal family. Then behind them were the soldiers and people of the city. They'd opened the gates in the wall surrounding the castle, allowing everyone in to hear the announcement. Dexter had insisted the castle not be cordoned off.

After briefly introducing himself, Dexter thanked everyone for coming. He outlined his plan, and Prince Gordon, Prince Ackley, and all the duchesses publicly supported it. Dexter explained Eldon was not the rightful heir since he was not Hudson's son. Since Hudson didn't declare Gordon his heir, the line shifted back to Henrick. Upon Henrick's death, the title passed to Dexter, Henrick's declared heir. At this point, the royal family, along with the duchesses, came up behind Dexter, emphasizing their full support. Dexter then went on to say Eldon was in Axian holding the dukes hostage in an attempt to lure the Marsden army there. Eldon intended to execute the dukes to take complete and total control of Marsden.

"I promise not to let this happen," Dexter bellowed. "Marsden was founded hundreds of years ago by eleven families. They divided this land into ten counties, one family in charge of each. The last family was declared sovereign and without land. That will not change! I will take up the crown as your king with my wife, Lady Reid Ellington-Winston, at my side. Together, we will uphold the rules and traditions of this great kingdom!"

Everyone burst into applause. Reid stepped forward so she stood next to Dexter. She wondered about these antiquated rules and traditions he'd just promised to uphold that she wanted to change.

"Eldon brought a foreign kingdom here promising them control of our mines in exchange for their help. I have renegotiated the terms, and Melenia has ceased all control of the mines. The mines have been rightly restored to the Bridger family. Melenia will be returning to the mainland,

and we will move forward with peace between our kingdoms."

Again, cheering erupted.

"My fellow Marsdens," Dexter said, immediately reclaiming everyone's attention. "It is time to go into Axian to right the wrongs. Together, we will insist Eldon step down, and I will take his place." Dexter clutched Reid's fingers, raising their clasped hands in the air. "For Marsden!"

The soldiers started chanting, "Marsden!"

Dexter and Reid went into the castle, the duchesses and royal family following. Inside, Dexter thanked everyone for being there. "I also want to say how proud I am that each of you has been brave enough to use your ring to ensure we remain a great kingdom."

"The duchesses and I have been talking," Duchess Tucker said. "We want to join you as you march south into Axian."

"There may be fighting," he informed them.

"We understand. And we will make sure to stay out of the way. However, we want to see the City of Radella, we want to see the false king removed, and we are eager to be reunited with our loved ones."

"Very well," Dexter said. "Ready yourselves. We leave within the hour."

Reid couldn't help but think about when she and Harlan had traveled into Axian on their own. It had been much simpler than this. Dressed in thick leather armor, sitting atop her horse with Dexter at her side, she headed south toward Lake Folme. Owen, Gordon, and Ackley were riding toward the front of the procession, Dexter and Reid were with Leigh, Nara, and Idina in the middle, and the duchesses were riding toward the back with Harlan and Gytha.

With only a hundred or so men remaining behind at the castle, the rest of the army, which consisted of five thousand men from the combined counties, now marched under the Marsden banner. Word had been sent to Colbert to send the Axian soldiers north. Dexter hoped to box Eldon in, forcing him to surrender.

Traveling with so many soldiers proved to be a lengthy process, especially since most were walking. Reid hadn't considered the logistics of getting that many men across the Gast River. Thankfully, Gordon had already thought of it. He'd been sending supplies along with men across Lake Folme over the past week.

Around midday, the majority of the soldiers veered east, heading toward the pass-through in the Modig Mountains. Owen, Gordon, and Ackley accompanied them.

A small contingent of fifty now traveled with the duchesses and royal family members to Lake Folme, where they would cross in small boats. Both groups would reconvene in three days.

When they reached the lake, Reid patiently waited her turn. When Dexter ordered her on a boat, she climbed in and sat. Gytha jumped in beside her.

"It takes forever to travel with so many people," Reid complained.

"You're bored because you don't have a job to do," Gytha pointed out.

Reid blinked, realization sinking in. "Why don't I have a job?"

She shrugged. "That is a question for your husband, not me."

As they made their way across the lake, Reid couldn't help but think about the last time she'd made this trip. She'd been about to meet her fiancé, whom she'd wanted nothing to do with. She'd also thought she was on an exciting mission for the Knights. She remembered clutching the bag holding her next assignment. So much had changed since then.

When they reached the dock, Gytha disembarked. "It is good to be on familiar land."

Reid climbed out of the boat, following Gytha to the gathering place of those who had already crossed.

An odd sensation filled Reid. She glanced around, looking for someone or something out of place. She didn't see anything. "Gytha," she said to her friend. "Why didn't we go with the other soldiers?" Why had they split the group in two? She understood they all couldn't cross via the lake since there weren't many boats. But why couldn't they have all gone through the mountain pass?

"Someone pointed out the trek up the steps would be too difficult for the duchesses." Gytha tilted her head, assessing Reid. "Is everything all right?"

Reid nodded.

Once everyone had crossed, they traveled a bit farther until they reached the spot where they were to meet up with the rest of the army. After they set up camp, Reid crawled into her tent, snuggling under the blankets. A few minutes later, Dexter joined her.

"I feel like I haven't seen you all day," he said as he nuzzled her neck. The temperature had dropped, making the air frigid.

His cold nose tickled her skin. Twisting toward him, she was about to place a kiss on his cheek when the odd sensation she'd had earlier returned. What could be making her feel off-kilter?

"What is it?" Dexter asked.

"I don't know."

"Always trust your instinct." He propped his head on his hand, waiting for her to explain.

She realized what was bothering her. "Is the way we're traveling expected?"

"What do you mean?"

"Assuming Eldon knows we're coming for him and he wants to plan a counterattack, would he be able to figure out the route we're taking?" Since they'd arrived in Axian, she feared they were walking into a trap. After all, that was what they'd done to the king during his journey to the palace when they'd tried to assassinate him.

"There are only so many ways to travel with this large of an army. That's why it's important to be vigilant."

"I understand." However, they'd split the army into two groups, and she was currently with the smaller one. If there was going to be an attack, striking the group she was with would be most effective.

"I always worry before a fight or a battle." He rubbed her arm. "I'm always afraid I missed something. It's normal to second guess yourself."

"How do you feel right now?" she asked. "Are you nervous?"

"Of course. I'm worried something will happen to you, my mother, my brother, my men. I'm responsible for everyone here. If something goes wrong, that's on me."

In the darkness, she could just make out the outline of his face. "Being in a leadership role is tough."

"Yes, it is." He kissed her shoulder. Then his lips trailed up her neck to her own lips.

Rolling her onto her back, Dexter slid his leg over her thigh.

Her hands roamed over his shoulders. Something hard poked her back. "Hang on."

"That's not what I want to hear right now," he murmured between kisses.

"Something is under my bedroll." She reached below her bedding, searching for the stick or whatever it was digging into her back. Her fingers came across metal. "Did you seriously put a dagger under my pillow for me?" She withdrew her hand, half amused he'd left her a gift like that.

Dexter went unnaturally still. "No. I have one beside me, but I didn't put one over by you."

"Maybe Gytha put it there?" When she went to reach back under to withdraw the weapon, Dexter grabbed her wrist.

"Wait." He lit a candle.

Reid moved off her bedding, kneeling on Dexter's while he examined the area around them. He pulled back the blankets, revealing the dagger. When he placed the candle closer, Reid hissed. Thorns were carved onto the hilt, a rose etched on the crossguard, and an intricate pattern covered the blade.

"What is it?" Dexter demanded.

Yanking up her sleeve, she revealed her tattoo. "It's the exact same," she whispered. "What do you think it means?"

Grabbing a discarded sock, he used it to lift the dagger from the ground. "There's a piece of paper." He set the dagger down. "Do you want it?"

Reid wasn't sure.

Dexter gingerly lifted the paper, unfolding it. "It says, *Don't forget your oath. When the time comes, I expect you to do your job.*"

"Where's Victor?" she asked.

"He's with Ackley. Why?"

"Do you think she did this?"

"Anna?"

Reid nodded.

"I don't know."

If Anna could sneak in, plant the dagger in Reid's own tent, and slip away unnoticed, Reid had no hope of ever being safe with Anna alive.

"Do you think she intends for you to kill me?"

"Yes." Anna wouldn't stop until she eliminated the entire Winston family. The problem was that now Reid had married Dexter, she was a Winston as well. Did Anna intend to kill Reid, too?

Dexter snuffed out the candle, then poked his head outside the tent. Reid heard him talking with the two posted guards. When he came back inside, he informed her that he'd requested two additional guards so there was someone on each side of the tent. He then wrapped the dagger in his sock, placing it in Reid's bag.

He laid down. "Do you remember the night we announced our engagement to the City of Radella?"

When Reid stretched out next to him, he wrapped his arm around her body, her back resting against his chest. "I do."

"I told you I didn't want to fall in love because then I would be a slave."

Reid remembered him saying something along those lines.

"I feared if I loved a woman, she could be used against me."

Now that Reid was in her current predicament, she realized he had a valid point.

"What I never understood is how the opposite can be true as well."

"What do you mean?" she asked.

"As scared as I am of something happening to you, I feel more empowered because I have you by my side. You make me stronger. You make me a better man."

Reid had no idea what to say to that.

"I promise that once Eldon is dealt with, we'll face your mother together."

She squeezed his hand, feeling a sense of comfort, peace, and happiness she'd never felt before.

The following day, the duchesses each expressed a desire to learn the art of weaponry. Dexter jumped at the chance to teach the women some basic moves with a sword and dagger. That evening, after the sun set, most people turned in early. Reid and Dexter crawled into their tent, eager for a few minutes alone.

"Who's there?" Dexter demanded as he shoved Reid behind him while simultaneously withdrawing his sword.

"Keep your voice down," Gordon hissed. "No one can know we're here."

Reid's heart skipped a beat—she hadn't expected anyone to be in there—especially Gordon since he was supposed to be traveling with the army. After quickly lighting a candle, she scanned the tent, seeing Ackley and Owen were there as well, the three of them crouched alongside the back wall.

Dexter put his sword down. "What's going on?" His whispered voice revealed a hint of panic.

"The bridge at the pass-through was gone," Ackley revealed. "We can't cross the Modig Mountains that way."

Which meant someone destroyed it on purpose. Reid had been there not long ago with Harlan, and the bridge had been in impeccable condition.

"I sent the army west while we came here to see what you

wanted to do. The soldiers can cross the Gast River at the bridge in Ellington."

"I'm not certain the bridge could withstand so many crossing it," Reid said.

"I agree," Gordon replied. "The only other option is the lake, but that will take far too long to get that many across with our limited number of boats."

Reid rubbed her temple, wondering who would have done this. Eldon or Anna?

"Continue to have the soldiers proceed west," Dexter ordered. "Pretend as if they're going to cross the bridge in Ellington. As your men travel along the Gast River, I want a unit of men stationed every mile or so. I don't want to be taken by surprise if Eldon is planning something."

"I think that's a wise move," Gordon replied.

"While the soldiers are making a big production of going west," Ackley said, "what do you really intend to do?"

Dexter smiled. "We're going to sneak into the palace and catch Eldon off guard."

"Do not forget, my soldiers can help," Owen stated.

"Or provide the cover we need to sneak in," Reid suggested.

"We should assume someone is watching this camp, reporting back to the king," Gordon said.

"Our plan will only work if everyone believes we're still here," Ackley pointed out. "Which means we'll have to sneak out of here under the cover of night. We'll need to travel quickly and without being seen."

"The only issue I have is the duchesses," Dexter said.

"I can remain behind to guard them," Gordon offered.

Dexter shook his head. "When we reach the palace, we can only legally remove the king with the duchesses invoking the power the rings give them to make such a choice."

"Then we'll take them with us," Reid said.

Ackley snorted. "We're supposed to do this stealthily."

"Since Duchess Lyndr isn't here, that leaves only seven women besides me." Reid held up her ring, indicating she could speak on her father's behalf. "There are four of you. I think we can do it." The only thing would be if the duchesses believed they could.

"I don't know," Gordon said, shaking his head.

"You don't give them enough credit." Reid folded her arms. "Why don't we at least consult them and go from there?"

"I think that's wise," Dexter replied.

"I'll speak with them," Ackley said, getting to his feet. "Once I'm done, I'll come back here." Donning a black cape, he slid out of the tent, blending in with the night.

"Do you know where your men are stationed?" Dexter asked Owen.

"Most are just outside the City of Radella. However, Eldon has about a hundred on the palace lawn. I think that's all we'll need."

"When are we going to leave?" Reid asked.

"Tonight," Gordon stated. "We don't have any time to waste."

"Do you think Princess Idina will be safe here?" Owen inquired.

"There are over fifty soldiers at this camp," Gordon said. "My sister will be fine."

Reid chuckled. "If anything, she'll be running this camp."

Owen smiled.

"Idina will remain here with my mother and Princess Nara," Gordon said.

"We'll take Gytha and Harlan with us," Dexter added. He knelt, then started shoving supplies in his traveling bag.

"Harlan?" Reid asked, surprised Dexter wanted to take him along. Granted, Harlan knew how to fight, but he wasn't a soldier.

"After what happened with the Ellington soldiers and the sleep tonic," Dexter replied, "I like having Harlan close by."

It turned out all the duchesses wanted to accompany them to the City of Radella. Not a single one balked at the idea of traveling at night. Dexter insisted the women wear armor, so Ackley rounded up seven soldiers who happily donated their clothing and armor to the women. Then Dexter asked those same men to reside in the duchesses' tents, pretending to be the duchesses, ill from something they ate. He wanted them to remain in the tents, out of sight, for as long as possible. His hope was if someone were watching the camp, they'd assume the duchesses were ill, not gone.

Once everyone was ready, Dexter paired them up, one proficient fighter with one duchess. He placed Reid with Duchess Tucker. Then, each pair left the tent ten minutes apart, pretending to be soldiers on patrol, heading directly south. Once all fourteen regrouped, they began their trek to the City of Radella.

They traveled for the rest of the night, stopping only when the sun started to rise. After finding what Dexter deemed a secure location, they slept until sunset. Then they woke and headed out, traveling as fast as they could under the cover of darkness while avoiding all towns and farms.

After five nights, they reached the outskirts of the City of Radella. Dexter led them to an abandoned shed. When he opened the door, a familiar person awaited them.

"It's about time you showed up."

CHAPTER NINETEEN

Reid couldn't believe Seb was there.

"The men are in place," Seb said, tossing a sword to Dexter, who deftly caught it.

"Excellent." He removed the sword strapped to his waist, sheathing the new one in its place. "Get everyone here loaded up."

"Gladly." Seb turned, revealing a shed stocked with hundreds of weapons. He started distributing knives to the duchesses.

"You knew Seb would be here?" Reid asked Dexter.

"I sent him ahead of us," he said as if that explained everything.

"What men does he refer to?"

"The men and women you met at the meeting."

The revolutionaries as Reid had called them.

Once everyone had been supplied with more than enough weapons, the group continued toward the city, Owen leading the way. At the first set of buildings, a low whistle rang out. Owen answered it with a higher-pitched one.

A Melenia soldier stepped out of the shadows. "Prince Owen?"

"Yes, along with some others. See that we're not followed. I need to speak with Commander Beck."

The man nodded. "I'll escort you to the commander myself."

Even though it was night, the duchesses examined their surroundings with wide eyes. Unlike home, the roads were paved, and the city had a clean and orderly feel to it. Most buildings were anywhere from two to five stories tall, and they were made from smooth stones in an assortment of colors and textures.

After the Melenia soldier whistled, a dozen soldiers joined them. He quickly repeated Owen's instructions. Half moved back into the shadows, presumably watching the roads to ensure no one followed. The other half escorted their group. They took the smaller roads instead of the main ones cutting through the city. When the palace came into sight, they stopped, pressing against one of the buildings.

Reid couldn't believe what she saw. Instead of the beautiful, green lawn surrounding the palace, tents covered the entire area and soldiers milled about. At least a dozen campfires lit the sky.

One of the soldiers whistled, and another soldier joined them, briefing Owen on the situation. When he finished, Owen addressed the group.

"The camp is comprised of soldiers from Melenia, Lyndr, and Marsden," he explained. "We're going to split into three groups, so we don't attract unwanted attention. One of my men will lead each group to the commander's tent. Be on guard."

They all agreed. Reid was grouped with Dexter, Harlan, Gytha, and Duchess Tucker.

"Lead the way," Dexter said to the soldier who approached them.

He gestured for them to follow. They stepped out of the shadows, heading for the east end of the camp.

Reid made a point to keep her head down and to walk quickly, like she had somewhere to be. As she made her way through the camp, she clutched a dagger in the palm of her hand, just in case. The soldier led their group through a maze of tents, around soldiers, and past men cooking at campfires.

When they reached one of the larger tents, the soldier had them wait on the side of it until the other two groups arrived. When they did, Owen and Dexter ducked inside while everyone else remained outside the tent, waiting in the shadows. Thankfully, the Melenia soldiers who guarded the area studiously ignored them.

Angry voices came from within the tent. Reid looked at the soldiers, wondering if they planned to see what was going on. The men eyed one another, but they made no move to intervene.

"Dexter is a strong fighter," Gytha murmured beside Reid. "You don't need to worry about him."

Reid nodded, knowing he could fend for himself, but still anxious. After another five minutes passed, she started pacing to prevent herself from storming in there to check on her husband.

Dexter exited the tent, cleared his throat, and straightened his tunic. He waved them inside.

Reid quickly ducked into the tent, the others following. The tent contained a large, round table with papers strewn about it. Behind that, there was a desk, a cot, and another table. Off to the side, Owen stood over a tied-up Commander Beck, his foot on the man's chest.

The duchesses convened around the table, examining everything.

"You and you," Owen said, pointing at two Melenia soldiers. "Commander Beck has been relieved of his position. Take him to the officer's tent next to here. I want you to watch over him."

The two soldiers agreed. Then they each grabbed an arm, dragging the commander from the tent.

"Is everything okay?" Reid asked.

Owen sheathed his sword as he approached the table. "When I told the commander my father had been killed and I would be ascending the throne, he didn't take the news well. Then I proceeded to explain we would be aiding Dexter to remove Eldon. That's when he lost it and tried to punch me." Owen shook his head.

"I subdued him," Dexter added, also coming to stand at the table alongside Reid.

"You sent for us?" a soldier asked as he ducked into the tent.

"Yes," Owen replied. "Are all twelve of my officers here?"

"We are."

Owen waved them over to the table. They crammed around it, examining a crude map of the palace.

Owen shifted a candle closer to the map, illuminating it a bit more. "Word is that Eldon got rid of all the servants, fearful they weren't loyal to him."

Before Eldon had arrived at the palace, they'd replaced the servants with soldiers. Since Eldon had relieved them of duty, Reid wondered if the soldiers were around here somewhere or if they'd gone to Camp Lival, where the army was supposed to go to regroup and organize.

"Eldon is staying on the fourth floor in this room." Owen pointed to the fifth door from the staircase.

Reid didn't think that room belonged to anyone in the royal family.

"The queen is staying in the adjacent room," Owen continued. "Guards are posted here and here." He pointed outside the door and at the top of the staircase.

"We'll enter the palace from the side door," Dexter said. "Then we'll take the most direct route to the fourth floor." His finger trailed along the map, tracing the route he intended to take. "Owen will choose six of his most proficient men to accompany us. I have a dozen people I want to come as well."

Reid assumed he referred to his revolutionaries. Since he didn't know if any of his Axian soldiers were still in the palace somewhere, it made sense he'd take Seb and some of the citizens he'd been working with and training for years.

"When we reach Eldon's room, the soldiers and my men will storm inside first, taking the king into custody. Once completed, the duchesses and I will enter. Together, we will officially strip him of his title, and I will take up the crown." He clenched and unclenched his hand.

"I know my brother," Ackley said. "I doubt he will go easily. Surprised or not."

That was what Reid had been thinking. While she knew Dexter had said they'd take him into custody, they all knew they'd most likely have to kill Eldon. He would rather die than lose his position.

"I suggest a few utilize the hidden passageways," Ackley said. "Just in case something goes wrong."

Reid thought that wise, especially since the king didn't

know about them. Well, unless Harlow had told him.

"Captain Gytha," Dexter said. "How well do you know the passageways?"

"Not very."

"I know them," Reid said. "Nara made me memorize them before the king came."

Dexter studied Reid for a long minute. "Lady Reid will lead a group of soldiers in through the passageways. Captain Gytha will accompany her." He rubbed his face. "Anyone have any other suggestions before we begin?"

"What about our husbands?" Duchess Bridger asked.

"As soon as the king is removed from power, we'll find your husbands. I promise."

"Then let's go take the kingdom," Duchess Tucker said.

After Dexter briefed everyone on their positions, what they were in charge of accomplishing, and what each person was responsible for, he asked for a moment alone with his wife. Everyone filed out of the cramped tent, leaving the couple alone. Reid's heartbeat sped up as she faced her husband, knowing the enormous and risky task before them.

"I don't want to say goodbye," Dexter said.

"Then don't."

He grinned, wrapping his arms around her and pulling her close. "But I do need to tell you to be careful. We don't know what Eldon has planned."

"I know." She slid her hands behind his neck, shoving the fear for what lie ahead out of her mind. All she wanted to do right now was focus on her husband.

"Eldon might not know we're coming for him tonight, but

that doesn't mean he won't have certain precautions in place."

"I'll be careful," she promised, "on one condition. You need to be careful as well. Let your men handle the situation. Don't try to do it all on your own."

He chuckled, his eyes softening as he regarded her.

"Promise me," she insisted.

"I promise." He kissed her forehead. "Once you've gotten Gytha and the soldiers into position at the king's suite, I want you out of the way." He kissed her right cheek. "If fighting breaks out, I don't want you injured or killed in the chaos." He kissed her left cheek.

She couldn't insist on helping since she'd made him promise the same thing. "Okay." She tilted her head up, and his lips devoured hers. Going onto her tiptoes, she deepened the kiss. His fingers dug into her sides.

Ackley cleared his throat. "Sorry to interrupt, but your men are here and everyone is ready."

Dexter placed his hands on either side of Reid's face. "Be safe," he whispered. "I love you." He kissed the tip of her nose before letting go and striding out of the tent, already barking orders.

Gytha entered. "Are you ready?" She scanned Reid from head to toe.

Reid nodded. She'd been going over the layout of the passageways in her head, trying to make sure she remembered the path she needed to take. They couldn't afford to get lost or make a wrong turn.

After exiting the tent, Reid led Gytha, along with six Melenia soldiers, toward the palace. When they reached the side entrance—the same one she'd gone in through with Harlan the first time she'd visited the place—she found the door locked. Gytha withdrew her dagger, breaking the lock off and popping the door open. In the hallway, Reid counted her steps until she hit one hundred. Then she pressed on the bottom stone with her foot. The lock clicked, and a hidden door swung open. She waved everyone in, closing the door behind her.

A wave of dizziness overcame her. Everything was happening so quickly she hadn't had time to think.

"Lady Reid?" Gytha whispered.

In complete darkness, mild panic set in. What if she led these people the wrong way? What if she led them to their deaths?

"Dexter is counting on you," Gytha reminded her.

Stifling her fear, Reid put her hand to the wall just as Nara had shown her all those weeks ago. She could do this. "Everyone, press against the wall to the left," she whispered. From here on out, they couldn't talk since they'd be walking alongside interior hallways and guests' bedchambers. Going to the front of the line, she whispered, "Place your hand on the shoulder in front of you." Standing in front of Gytha, she waited for the woman to put her hand on Reid. "What's wrong?"

"I have a dagger in one hand and a sword in the other. I don't have a third hand to put on your shoulder."

"Put the sword away," Reid hissed. The secret passageways were narrow and the space too confined to have a sword in hand.

Gytha huffed but complied. Once she sheathed the weapon, she put her free hand on Reid's shoulder.

Taking a deep breath, Reid led the way, keeping her left hand on the wall. It was a trick Nara had shown her in order to not get turned around in the darkness, as well as to help with her balance.

She made turn after turn until she came to the stairwell. It was so narrow some of the soldiers had to turn sideways in order to fit. Reid led them up to the fourth floor. Once there, she took a second to pause and listen for any signs of fighting that could be going on in the palace.

The only sound she heard was an eerie silence that somehow matched the dark passageways.

With her heart pounding, she led the way toward the king's suite. There should be an offshoot of the passageway that would lead directly to his room. She just had to make sure she chose the right one. As she went along, she carefully counted the offshoots until she reached the fifth one. Then she turned, leading everyone down the narrow corridor that came to an abrupt dead end.

Reid stopped, then twisted to her right, knowing the door was somewhere in front of her. Not wanting to accidentally push it open, she leaned away from it. Gytha remained next to her, their shoulders brushing.

The king should be asleep in his bed. The soldiers, along with Dexter, Gordon, Ackley, and Owen, were supposed to enter the castle five minutes after Reid and her group had. She'd expected them to be outside the king's suite by now, about to storm in. The soldiers and Dexter's revolutionaries would go first. Once the king was subdued, Gordon and Ackley would enter, confirming it was safe before Dexter and Owen went in. Then, one of the soldiers would fetch the duchesses.

Reid and her group were there in case something went wrong. They could prevent the king from escaping in the event he'd discovered the passageways, or they could guide soldiers out of the king's room if the king managed to get reinforcements, blocking Dexter's men inside.

But, if everything went according to plan, Ackley would

knock on the wall giving the all-clear signal, allowing them to exit the passageways. They would join Dexter in the bedchamber, allowing Reid to use her ring to strip Eldon of his title and pass it to Dexter.

So what was taking so long? No noises came from within the king's suite. She was sure they'd be able to hear voices or the clashing of steel. Something. Anything.

Gytha shifted beside her, letting out an irritated sigh.

Grabbing Gytha's hand, Reid squeezed it as panic wormed its way in. Something was wrong. She was sure of it. Too much time had passed.

Unversed in battle strategy, what to do if the plan went awry eluded her. Her gut told her to abort the mission. However, she wanted a second opinion. Leaning closer to Gytha, she whispered in the warrior woman's ear, asking her opinion on the matter.

A moment later, Gytha replied, "Retreat."

Reid wove her way to the end of their human chain, then led the way to the first floor. Fear took hold, and her hands began shaking. Had any harm come to Dexter? What about Ackley and Gordon? Needing to find out the state of things, she stopped at what should be a sitting room near the front of the palace. Pressing her ear against the door, she listened. Not hearing anything, she pried the door open. Moonlight spilled into the room, providing enough light to see. She exited the passageways and paused, listening. Not hearing any commotion coming from within, she rushed over to the window, peering outside.

Several of the soldiers had gathered near the front door, facing it. Reid angled her head, trying to see what they were looking at.

Her knees almost gave out when she saw Eldon on the

front steps, Commander Beck at his side. How had Beck managed to escape? He'd been tied up with two soldiers watching over him.

Gytha peered outside, then cursed.

"What do you want us to do?" one of the soldiers accompanying Reid asked.

About to turn to address the soldier, something caught her eye. The front door opened, and soldiers donning Melenia battle gear shoved Dexter, Gordon, Owen, and Duke Ellington out of the palace, forcing them to their knees. Reid started shaking.

"Come," Gytha said. "We must act quickly before it's too late."

Reid had no idea what her father was doing here. Unable to even consider that at the moment, she scanned the area, searching for the duchesses, Harlan, or Ackley. Not seeing them anywhere, she prayed they were safely hiding somewhere.

"Eldon is going to kill them," Gytha snapped. "We must stop him."

"If you can get out there," Reid said as she sprinted alongside Gytha, exiting the sitting room "can you kill Eldon?"

"Yes."

Fear took hold of Reid as she ran toward the front of the palace. What if someone stopped them? What if Eldon killed everyone before Gytha could get there? What if they failed?

Movement came from the right, and Reid glanced that way. Skidding to a halt, her mouth dropped open as Colbert, Markis, and Ackley exited the library.

Reid didn't even know what question to ask first.

"The six of you," Ackley barked, indicating the soldiers, "go to the back room of the library and guard the duchesses."

The soldiers did as instructed.

"Let's go," Colbert said, leading the way to the staircase. "We don't have much time."

"The Axian army is approaching," Ackley said. "We just need to hold Eldon off until they arrive."

"We may not have that long," Colbert replied.

"What's the plan?" Reid asked, trying to keep up as they took the stairs two at a time.

Markis patted his bow. "We're going to take the king out."

At the third floor, the group sprinted down the hallway. Colbert burst into one of the rooms, running straight to the window. "One more room to the east."

They ran to the adjacent room. Ackley kicked a chair out of the way as Markis readied his bow, nocking an arrow. Colbert slowly opened the window, trying not to make a sound.

"Reid Ellington," Eldon's voice boomed over the front lawn. "Reveal yourself!"

Four soldiers stepped forward, withdrawing their swords.

"Why does he want me?" she wondered.

"Stop this at once," Owen demanded. "Commander Beck, I hereby declare you a traitor to the crown."

"The prince is mistaken," Commander Beck stated. "It is he who is a traitor. He tried declaring himself the king of Melenia, overthrowing his own father!"

"Lady Ellington," Eldon bellowed. "I will start with your father. Reveal yourself or he dies."

"Should I go down there?" Reid asked. "It'll buy us some time."

"I don't need time," Markis said. "I just need permission."

"Reid?" Ackley said. "Do you give permission to take out the false king?"

She wanted to vomit. How could she give the order to kill

someone? "He's your brother." Would he hate her for giving the order? Or did he need her to do it so he didn't blame himself?

"You will be our queen."

She couldn't make these sorts of decisions. "Markis, can you injure his leg instead of killing him?"

"I can. However, if I do that, he can still order your father's death."

Four soldiers, one king, one commander. No time. Her entire body shook. "Injure them all."

"As you wish." Markis released the bowstring, his first arrow sailing straight toward the king, embedding in his thigh. The king went down. Then the four soldiers started screaming, an arrow protruding from each's sword arm. Commander Beck was last, the arrow striking his thigh.

Reid ran, Gytha right behind her. She went as fast as she could, knowing complete chaos ensued on the front steps. Reid had to get out there as soon as possible. Down the stairs she went, through corridor after corridor until she reached the front doors, throwing them open.

Blood pooled over the steps. Dexter, Gordon, Owen, and Duke Ellington all stood with swords in hand. Owen ordered the Melenia soldiers to stand down while Gordon bound Eldon's wrists. In the distance, Reid saw the Axian army approaching.

Her eyes locked with Dexter's.

"Are you all right?" he demanded.

"I am."

He nodded once, his face relieved.

Colbert, Ackley, and Markis joined them on the front steps. Owen was still trying to gain control of his army as many of the soldiers turned to face the oncoming Axian army.

Dexter took off running with Gytha and Markis at his side. He screamed orders as he ran, trying to prevent the Axian army from slaughtering the Melenians.

Commander Beck stretched out his arm. Reid caught sight of a small dagger in his palm. He fingered the weapon, positioning it to strike Owen.

Without thinking, Reid yelled, "No!" while stepping on Beck's wrist, forcing him to release the weapon. As Owen turned toward Reid to see what the commotion was, Beck reached up, grabbing Reid and slamming her to the ground. Reid rolled onto her side, trying to catch her breath. Ackley turned, then hurled a dagger at Beck. She squeezed her eyes shut, hearing the sickening sound of the dagger embedding in flesh. When she opened her eyes, she glanced to the side, spotting a knife sticking out of Beck's chest. He was sprawled on the steps, lifeless.

Owen crouched beside her. "Are you okay?"

Reid nodded.

"You saved my life."

"Of course," she wheezed.

He helped her to her feet.

Duke Ellington ran over to Reid, wrapping her in a hug.

"What are you doing here?" she asked.

"I don't know. I went to bed one night. When I woke up, I found myself here in the palace. I think someone drugged me, then brought me here."

But who would do such a thing? And why?

Gordon turned when his wife exited the palace, a small bump rounding her stomach. He ran to her, throwing his arms around her.

The Axian army stopped advancing. It appeared Dexter was

at the frontline with Gytha and Markis, ordering everyone to stand down.

"I'm going to make sure my men comply," Owen said, sprinting down the steps toward Dexter.

"Why don't the rest of us go inside?" Duke Ellington suggested.

Ackley pulled Eldon to his feet, dragging him into the palace. Reid followed them to the sitting room. After lighting a few candles, Ackley knelt beside Eldon, snapping the arrow shaft off before wrapping a strip of fabric around the wound.

After helping his wife sit, Gordon asked if anyone knew where the duchesses were.

"They're in the library," Reid replied, standing alongside her father, across from Eldon.

Gordon went into the hallway, ordering two soldiers to retrieve the duchesses. "What about the dukes?" he asked when he came back into the sitting room.

"They're in the dungeon," Colbert answered.

"If you'll show me where it is," Ackley said, "I'll fetch them."

Colbert nodded, and they exited the room.

A few minutes later, a soldier led the duchesses into the room. Eldon started laughing when he saw them dressed in pants with leather vests for armor.

While they waited, Reid explained to the duchesses what had transpired on the front steps of the palace.

Colbert and Ackley returned with the dukes, along with Duchess Lyndr. The dukes went to their wives, many hugging one another despite the rancid smell from being locked in the dungeon for so long.

Once the reunion was complete, the dukes glared at Eldon with hatred. A few even spat curses.

"Dexter hasn't arrived yet?" Colbert asked.

"No. He's still outside with the army," Reid answered.

"I'll let him know we're ready for him." Colbert left the room.

"This is a coup," Eldon snarled. "You have no right to do this. I'm trying to protect this kingdom. You're dooming us all!"

Dexter entered the room with his brother at his side.

Relieved to see him, Reid stepped forward, gaining everyone's attention. Even though her body tingled with nervousness, she forced herself to be the leader the kingdom needed right now. "As you are aware, Eldon Winston is not the son of the late King Hudson Winston. I believe the line should revert to the late king's brother, Prince Henrick. However, Prince Henrick died several weeks ago, murdered by his own son, Eldon. Prince Dexter Winston is the legal and declared heir of Henrick. Therefore, I vote to remove the false king, bestowing the title upon the true heir, Prince Dexter Winston. This can only be completed with a vote by our founding families—those in possession of the duke's ring. All those in favor of stripping Eldon of the crown, raise your hand."

Every single duke and duchess raised his or her hand.

"All those in favor of declaring Dexter Winston the new king, raise your hand."

Again, every single person complied.

Gordon stepped forward. "Since the late King Hudson was my father, I will do the honor. Eldon Winston, my half-brother, I hereby strip you of the crown. I willingly give the title to my cousin, the rightful heir, Dexter Winston."

Eldon's face turned red with anger as he said a few choice words, which everyone ignored.

"Prince Dexter," Gordon said. "When we get a binder, we

will have you crowned before our court. However, for all intents and purposes," he withdrew his sword, placing it on Dexter's head, "I hereby declare you the rightful King of Marsden."

Everyone in the room dropped to one knee in subjugation.

As Reid knelt there, pride swelled within her. She'd helped put the rightful heir on the throne.

"I take this title very seriously," Dexter said. "I promise to uphold Marsden's laws and to work with *all* the dukes and duchesses."

Everyone stood, applauding and congratulating Dexter.

"If you'll excuse me, we have a lot of soldiers converging on the palace lawn. I need to announce myself as king to ensure we don't have any skirmishes." He bowed his head before exiting the room, Gordon hurrying after him.

"What about Eldon?" Duke Ellington asked.

"I suggest we throw him in the dungeon," Duke Tucker said. Everyone whole-heartedly agreed.

"I'll escort him there," Ackley offered. He came up behind his brother, forcing him to stand and walk in front of him.

"I'll go with you," Reid said, not wanting Ackley to have to do this alone. "Colbert, if you could please see the dukes and duchesses receive the appropriate accommodations?"

"Of course."

Ackley and Reid took Eldon out of the sitting room. Ackley ordered a handful of soldiers to accompany them. The group made their way through the hallways until they came to a lone door.

"Does this lead to the dungeon?" she asked.

"It does."

The door looked like any other door. She never would have guessed it led to cells for holding prisoners.

Ackley ordered the soldiers to remain there. Stepping around Eldon, he opened the door, revealing a steep stairwell.

Eldon went first, limping as he made his way down. Ackley followed his brother. Reid went last, being careful not to slip on the slick stone steps. Torches lined the narrow path, providing enough light to see. At the bottom, a single corridor extended before them with a dozen doors on either side. The thick air smelled of human excrement, making Reid gag.

"I'm surprised it's so small." Reid thought it would be larger, especially given the size of the palace and surrounding city.

"From what I understand," Ackley replied, "this is supposed to be a temporary facility. Prisoners are housed elsewhere."

Reid would have to ask Dexter. Maybe the military compound had a larger dungeon below it.

Ackley reached around Eldon, swinging a door open and shoving his brother inside.

Eldon laughed as he stumbled over to the flimsy cot. His wound had bled through the makeshift bandage, soaking it with blood. Shaking his head, he said, "You're no better than Henrick."

Ackley simply shrugged.

"He betrayed his own brother," Eldon spat. "And now you betray me."

"You're alive," Ackley said. "Just remember that." He closed the door, locking it.

CHAPTER TWENTY

The last time Reid stood in her suite had been on her first wedding day. Little had she known at the time Eldon was about to declare Henrick dead, stop Reid and Dexter from marrying, and order Ackley's execution. So much had changed since then.

Gytha knocked on the open door, gaining Reid's attention. "King Dexter asked me to check on you."

Reid waved her into the room.

"Is everything okay?" Gytha asked, joining Reid at the window overlooking the palace lawn.

"Everything is fine." She just wished she could crawl into bed for a few hours. However, too much had to be done. She'd only ducked in here to change and freshen up. "Any word on when Idina, Nara, and Leigh will be here?"

"King Dexter sent a messenger north to their camp. The soldiers with them are to accompany them here immediately."

The sun had just crested the land in the distance, casting the area in a soft glow. Melenia soldiers camped on the front lawn. Owen wanted his soldiers to pack up in the next day or two, reconvening east of the city, where the rest of his forces were currently stationed. Then, once everyone had been accounted for, they would travel together to the port where the war ships were supposed to dock.

"Has Dexter decided how many men will be accompanying Owen?"

"There are only so many ships. I think he said about seven hundred can be transported to Melenia. He's asking for volunteers."

"I assume you're staying?" She couldn't imagine not having Gytha nearby.

"Axian is my home. I don't intend to leave." The warrior woman nudged Reid's shoulder.

"I'm glad."

A dog bounded into the room, jumping on Reid. She knelt on the floor, allowing Finn to assault her with his kisses. She laughed while scratching him behind his ears.

Colbert stuck his head in the room. "I see some things never change." He absently played with the door handle.

She stood. "Is everything all right?"

"Dex wants you to join him downstairs. He's going to speak with the ruling families in thirty minutes."

"Do you know what it's about?"

"We're just trying to make sure everyone is accounted for and adequate security is in place. We don't know what all Eldon has done since we've been gone."

Reid assumed Dexter would want every room, corridor, and passageway checked. He wouldn't be able to rest until he knew —without a doubt—he had total and complete control of the palace again.

"I'll be right there." She still needed to change out of her traveling clothes. Not only did she smell, but she also didn't present the image of a queen. Even though she hadn't been crowned yet—her coronation would take place directly after her public wedding ceremony to Dexter—she needed to start presenting the appropriate persona now.

After Reid quickly bathed and put on a dress, Gytha escorted her to the great hall located on the first floor. Dozens of people already filled the room. Reid recognized the dukes and duchesses, who'd all managed to bathe and change since they'd last parted, along with a few other people she assumed to be the ruling families from Axian. She suddenly felt like an incompetent child. How could she go before these powerful people and speak? How could she presume to know what was best for this kingdom when she'd experienced so little of it?

"Breathe in and out," Gytha mumbled. "Otherwise, you will faint."

Dexter entered the room, his commanding presence drawing Reid's attention. He strode over to her, offering her his arm. Taking hold, she clutched it as he led her to the dais at the front of the room.

"Ready?" Dexter whispered.

"I'm as ready as I'll ever be."

"We're doing this together." He squeezed her hand as they turned to face everyone. "Thank you for joining me," he said, his loud voice garnering everyone's rapt attention.

Off to the side, Reid noticed Dana and Harlow standing side by side.

"As many of you may have heard by now, I struck a deal with Melenia's new king, Owen. He is a good man who is going to peacefully leave Marsden, taking his soldiers home with him. His kingdom has been overrun by a neighboring one, and I have agreed to send some of our soldiers to aid him in retaking his kingdom. I will not force anyone to go. Instead, I am seeking volunteers."

"I, for one," Duke Bridger said, "am pleased you managed to get them to relinquish control of our mines."

"And, I," Ackley said, raising his hand, "have volunteered to accompany King Owen. I will oversee our Marsden soldiers."

Shock jolted through Reid. Ackley had decided to leave? What if something happened to him? Why hadn't he said anything to her ahead of time?

"Since the ruling families are all here," Dexter said, "I want everyone to discuss our kingdom, the future, and any changes you want made to trade, taxes, or anything else. I invite you each to stay here in my home while we tackle these issues over the upcoming weeks. Lady Reid and I had a small, private wedding ceremony at her home in Ellington. However, I plan to hold a public ceremony for all to witness, along with our joint coronations immediately following our vows. I invite you all to stay for these important ceremonies."

The doors banged open. A guard entered, a sheen of sweat on his forehead. "Your Highness," he said, sprinting down the aisle toward Dexter. "Eldon Winston is dead."

A wave of dizziness washed through Reid. The last time she'd been in this room, they'd announced Prince Henrick's death.

"Are you certain he's dead?" Dexter asked, mirroring Reid's own question. "His leg wound wasn't serious—I had a healer treat it."

The guard nodded. "I went into the dungeon to deliver some bread for his breakfast. When I slid it in, I noticed his head hanging off the side of the cot, so I examined him closer. A white substance dripped from the corner of his mouth, and he wasn't breathing."

Although he didn't say it, the implication was clear—someone had poisoned Eldon.

"Who went to see him in the dungeon?" Reid demanded.

"This guard and I accompanied the healer," Dexter said.

"Besides that," the guard replied, "no one."

Reid cringed. Everyone in this room expected Dexter to lead them through this trying time. If he couldn't even keep a prisoner safe in his own dungeon, how would he effectively rule the kingdom?

Ackley stepped forward. "Did you say a white substance dripped from his mouth?"

"Yes."

"What about his eyes? Anything unusual?"

"They were open," the guard answered. "And a little red. Come to think of it, his skin had a few red blotches too."

"Thank you," Ackley said. "See that the cell remains secure. Don't move the body until I examine it."

"Yes, Your Highness." With a nod, he pivoted and hurried from the room.

"Harlan?" Ackley said.

Harlan pushed away from the wall. "Yes?"

"I need your help." Ackley stepped closer to Reid and Dexter. "My father and grandfather were found in a similar fashion. Be on guard."

"Do you think Anna poisoned him?" Reid whispered.

"Someone did." He strode from the room, Harlan following.

"Thank you for your time," Dexter said. "I will be available tomorrow if anyone needs to speak with me." He and Reid exited the side door leading to the antechamber.

"What are we going to do with Harlow?" Reid asked. With Harlow no longer the queen, what would her position and title be?

He rubbed his face. "I haven't had a chance to speak with her." He put his hands on his hips. "Come to think of it, I haven't even seen her."

"She was in the great hall listening to you speak."

"She shouldn't have learned about her husband's death that way." Dexter wrapped Reid in a hug, placing his chin on her head. "We need to talk to her to make sure she's okay."

Gytha entered the antechamber. "Markis wants to go over a few security measures with you."

Dexter sighed, moving his lips to Reid's right ear and whispering, "Tonight, I don't care how much needs to be done, you're mine."

A smile spread across her face. "Deal."

After Dexter left, Gytha eyed Reid. "You look like you're about to fall over. You haven't slept since yesterday. Why don't you lie down for a few hours?"

"There's so much to be done."

"And you need to be coherent to do everything."

Reid yawned, exhaustion consuming her. "Okay. But I only want to rest for a little bit."

Now that the Axian army had returned to the City of Radella, Dexter had stationed soldiers throughout the palace. As Reid passed them, she asked if anyone had seen Harlow. No one recalled seeing her.

When Reid entered her suite, she went straight to her bed and sprawled across it, not even bothering to remove her shoes.

"I want it done tonight," a voice whispered. "Sneak into Owen's tent and kill him. Make sure you use an Axian weapon

—that way, his soldiers will attack. I want as many dead as possible."

"Consider it done," another voice murmured.

Reid blinked. Darkness filled her room, and she couldn't see anything.

"Nice job with Eldon."

"That one was fun."

"It's time to eliminate the rest of the Winston family. When the fighting breaks out, make sure to take care of Ackley and Gordon. I'll see to Dexter myself. I already sent someone to deal with Idina, Leigh, and Nara. Come this time tomorrow, I'll finally have my revenge."

"You can count on me."

A shuffling noise came from the corner of the room, then it went quiet. Afraid to move, Reid remained there, going over everything she'd heard. Had the person whispering been her mother? Maybe it had simply been a dream.

Reid's bed dipped as someone sat next to her. The silence became deafening. She couldn't move. Squeezing her eyes shut, she pretended to be asleep, all the while praying her mother didn't stab her in the back, killing her. Anna had said she wanted the Winston family dead. Reid was now married to one, so did that include her? Her name hadn't been on the list of people to assassinate. But maybe that was the purpose for her mother's visit.

"I'm sorry I wasn't there for you growing up," Anna said, her voice low and soothing.

Not knowing what to do, Reid forced herself to take slow, even breaths.

"But I'm here now. We can finally get to know one another. I can be a mother to you." Anna gently stroked Reid's head. "When the time comes, I know you won't disappoint me.

You're my daughter. You are strong, fierce, and loyal. You will do what needs to be done to right the wrongs of the past." The bed shifted as Anna stood.

Why had Anna said all that to Reid now when Reid didn't want to hear it? It was too late. Or had Anna done it knowing Reid was awake?

Reid remained frozen. She had no idea what time of day it was. But one thing she knew for certain—she had to stop whomever Anna had been talking to from killing Owen, subsequently starting a war between Melenia and Marsden.

It felt like an hour had passed, but it had probably only been a couple of minutes. She needed to find Dexter to tell him what she'd overheard.

The door to her bedchamber creaked open. "Reid?" Gytha said. "It's time to wake up. Commander, I mean, King Dexter needs you." She marched forward, pushing the curtains open.

A dull light filtered into the room, revealing the sun setting in the distance. It had to be close to supper. "You let me sleep longer than I wanted."

"I lost track of time. I was busy trying to find Harlow, then I had to run a few errands for the king."

"Did you find her?"

"I did. She was in her room, packing her things. She said she wanted to return to Bridger with her parents."

Reid absently nodded as she stood and stretched. "Are there guards outside my room?"

"Of course. Now that you are about to be the queen, you will be guarded at all times. Why?"

Reid didn't want to say anything in case Anna lurked nearby. "Come with me." She exited her suite, absently noticing the two posted guards. A lot of good they did with the secret passageways compromised. Out in the hallway, she started running. Down a flight of stairs and along a corridor before entering a room at random.

"What is the matter?" Gytha asked, sword in hand.

Reid grabbed the warrior woman, pulling her head lower. She whispered, "Someone was in my bedchamber while I was sleeping."

"The two posted guards told me you hadn't been disturbed."

"We both know there's more than one way in and out of my room." After she spoke to Harlow that one day, the woman had left through a hidden door Reid had no prior knowledge of.

Gytha sheathed her sword, then started pacing. "That means it was someone with knowledge of the passageways."

Few people knew the labyrinth of tunnels that existed in and below the palace. "I think it was Anna. She was talking to another person, although I don't know who. Anna wants Owen killed tonight, hoping it starts a fight between Melenia and Marsden. Then, in the chaos, she wants the royal family assassinated."

"We have to stop it."

"I agree. But we have to be smart. Anna can't know we're trying to foil her plans."

"You're right," Gytha said, still pacing back and forth. "I have an idea. Come with me."

Reid marched beside Gytha. The warrior woman had managed to steal two Melenia uniforms. The pants were a little long, so Reid had folded them up. "Dexter is going to be livid," she mumbled as they wound their way through soldiers and past tents, pretending as if they belonged there.

"Next one on the left," Gytha muttered under her breath.

When Reid came to the correct tent, she cleared her throat. "Commander?" she said, using her best male voice.

"Enter," Seb replied.

Reid ducked inside while Gytha stood watch.

"I was wondering who it was," he said. "No one calls me that these days."

"I need your help."

"Figured as much." He sat on his bed, papers in hand.

"An assassin has been sent after Idina, Nara, and Leigh."

"Why haven't you told your husband?" he asked.

"I think he's being watched. In order to stop the assassinations, someone outside the royal family and army must intervene."

"When did the assassin leave?"

"I don't know."

"Then I best get to work."

"Should I tell anyone else?"

"No. I have Dexter's men if I need them." He placed his hands on Reid's shoulders. "I'll do my best to stop the assassin." With that promise, he exited the tent.

Reid waited a minute before joining Gytha outside. The warrior woman tilted her head to the left, so Reid went that way.

"Owen's tent is to the right of the command tent," Gytha whispered.

Walking through the camp, Reid made sure to extend her stride in order to mimic a man's. She easily fell into the role she'd played her entire life. Gytha, on the other hand, appeared stiff and rigid. While the woman normally wore pants and felt at home around an army, she'd never had to pretend to be a man before. Since Melenia only employed men and the two women needed to blend in, this seemed the easiest solution.

Reid pulled out the piece of paper she'd stashed in her pocket. "I have a message for Prince Owen," she said to the guard outside the command tent.

"He's changing for supper," the soldier replied.

Reid dipped her head, then went directly to Owen's tent. "Permission to enter," she said, hoping that wasn't out of line.

Owen pulled the flap back. His eyes locked with Reid's. After a minute, he waved her in. Again, Gytha remained outside keeping watch.

"What's the matter?" he asked.

Quickly, Reid explained how she woke up and overheard someone giving the order to assassinate Owen to try to start a war between their kingdoms.

"Any idea who it is?" he asked.

"I believe I know who gave the order, but I don't know who will be executing it."

"And you're here to warn me?"

"I am. It's supposed to happen tonight while you're sleeping."

He sat on the edge of his cot. "I'll be on guard, and I'll have extra soldiers stationed around my tent."

"I fear that won't be enough." All the assassin had to do was give the nearby soldiers a sleeping tonic, then enter and kill Owen.

"What do you suggest?"

"I think I should be in here with you." Since it appeared Reid's mother wouldn't allow any harm to come to her.

"In order for me to cooperate, I want the entire story."

"It's long."

"It appears we have the time."

So Reid told him everything about her life growing up—her forced engagement to Dexter, the Knights, her mother, and why Melenia was sucked into Anna's twisted plan. It took hours to get everything out. Owen patiently listened, asking only a few questions here and there.

When Reid finished, she guessed it had to be close to midnight. It sounded as if the activity had died down outside the tent, indicating most soldiers had retired for the night.

Owen nodded off. Since Reid had taken a nap earlier, she felt refreshed and able to stay awake. She sat in the middle of the tent, diligently keeping watch. Gytha had said she would remain outside with the tent in view at all times.

As the night wore on, it became harder and harder for Reid to keep her eyes open. The candle died out, so she lit another one, wanting to be able to see all corners of the tent. When the guard passed by every ten minutes or so, Reid counted his steps—usually thirteen—until she no longer heard his boots brushing the grass. Voices would laugh from some far-off part of the camp, a dog would bark in the distance, or a whistle would ring out as guards changed positions or communicated with one another. She'd gotten so used to hearing these sounds that when they faded, an eerie silence descended over the camp causing the hairs on the nape of her neck to rise.

Things were quiet. *Too* quiet.

Crouching, she went over to Owen, gently shaking him awake. When he opened his eyes, she put her finger to her lips. He nodded and withdrew a knife, alert and ready to fight. They sat back to back in the middle of the tent, each watching. Waiting. Not the hoot of an owl or even the chirp of crickets could be heard. The only sound came from Reid and Owen breathing.

"Where's Lady Reid?" a delicate female voice asked, cutting

through the silent night. "I must speak with her at once. There's an emergency at the palace, and no one can find her."

Reid recognized the voice as Harlow's.

Someone mumbled a reply, too low for Reid to hear.

"No, you don't understand," Harlow said, her voice filled with urgency. "King Dexter is injured. I must find Lady Reid at once."

Reid jumped to her feet. Dexter was hurt? If Anna had done anything to harm him, Reid would kill the woman herself. She lifted the tent flap. "Harlow?"

"Oh, Reid!" Harlow exclaimed, rushing toward her. She pushed the hood of her cape back. "You must come at once. Dexter is asking for you." She reached her hand forward.

Reid was about to take Harlow's extended hand when an eerie sensation filled her. If something had happened to Dexter, wouldn't Ackley or Colbert have come for Reid? Deciding to trust her gut, she took Harlow's hand, yanking Harlow toward her. She twisted, wrapping her arms around Harlow and pinning the woman against her body. As she shoved her inside the tent, Reid covered Harlow's mouth.

Owen's brows drew together as he stood there, knife in hand. Slowly, he turned to face the back of the tent. The bottom lifted up, and someone slid inside. When the person stood, Reid looked into the cold and furious eyes of her mother.

Reid removed her shaking hand from Harlow's mouth and reached into her sleeve, pulling out a dagger and placing the tip at Harlow's throat. Reid made sure to keep Harlow's body in front of her own, trying to protect herself as much as possible.

"Reid," Anna said, her voice firm and commanding. "Take Queen Harlow and get out of here. Now."

"What's going on?" Harlow demanded. "Are you the one who tried to kill King Dexter?"

"That's none of your concern," Anna snapped. Then, to Reid, she said, "Get out of here." She palmed a small blade in her right hand.

The tent flap opened, and Ackley entered. "I thought I saw you go by," he said to Anna.

Reid stepped to the side with Harlow still in her arms. Owen moved to the other side, allowing Ackley to have a clear line of sight to Anna.

"At least I can take care of you both at once," Anna hissed. She whipped out a dagger with her left hand, throwing it at Owen.

He deftly blocked it. "That all you got?"

She unsheathed a small sword.

Owen ran at her, knocking her to the ground.

"She has a blade in her right hand," Reid yelled, hoping Owen heard her.

Ackley lunged for Anna, grabbing her right arm and forcing her to drop the blade.

Reid released Harlow. "You better get out of here."

Breathing fast, Harlow ran from the tent.

Anna managed to wrap her legs around Owen's arms, pinning them down. Ackley picked up the discarded blade, tossing it farther away. Anna raised her small sword, about to plunge it into Owen's side.

The tent collapsed.

Reid couldn't see.

She tried to regain her footing, but there was too much fabric weighing her down, making it hard to breathe. Something ripped above her. Reaching up, she pushed on the material until her hands found air. Someone grabbed her fingers, pulling her upright and out of the heavy canvas.

Ackley had been the one to yank her to her feet. "Are you okay?" he demanded.

Gasping for air, she nodded.

A dagger sliced through the fabric behind them. They turned in time to see Anna's head pop through the collapsed tent. Then she slowly stood, the cloth now at her feet.

Reid searched for Owen, not seeing any movement under the collapsed tent. Was he still alive?

"Why do you have to be so difficult?" Anna sneered at Reid. "Not only am I your superior, but I am also your mother. You should obey me without question." She shoved her hair out of her face, her shoulders heaving. "I thought you were loyal. I thought you took your oath seriously."

Reid glanced around. The guards who'd been on patrol were on the ground, not moving. No snores or any other sign of life came from the eerily quiet camp. "What did you do?"

"What needed to be done."

Out of the shadows, Dexter emerged behind Anna, a sword in hand. His eyes had a deadly glint as they remained focused on his prey. Slowly raising his arm, he prepared to make a killing blow.

Even though Reid shook from the adrenaline coursing through her, she tried to remain calm so Anna wouldn't know someone lurked only inches behind her.

Ackley's eyes widened. "No!" He stepped forward, ramming his sword toward Dexter. Only, the sword slid past Dexter's right side, striking Harlow, who stood behind him. Harlow's eyes widened. She dropped the knife she'd been about to kill Dexter with, grabbing Ackley's sword and trying to remove it. As she tumbled to the ground, blood pooled around her body.

Furious, Anna whirled, stabbing her knife straight at Dexter. Ackley hurled himself sideways to shield Dexter, the knife embedding into him instead.

Shocked, Reid threw her own dagger, missing Anna's chest. Instead, it sliced into her arm.

Anna whipped around. Her eyes narrowed as she stalked toward her daughter. "I planned to give you everything. But you're not worth it. You're as useless as your father." She swung a tight fist, punching Reid in the stomach. "You should've been born a man. You're just as worthless."

Hunching over, Reid tried to breathe as pain pierced through her.

Anna rammed a knee into Reid's face, striking her forehead and flipping her onto the ground. Stars exploded across her vision. She wanted to roll over and cower, but, if she hesitated for even a second, Anna would strike her again, gaining the upper hand. When Anna's foot came into view, Reid's mother hovering over her with a knife, she summoned every ounce of strength she had. Praying it worked, she shot her hand out, grabbing Anna's ankle and yanking as hard as she could.

Anna fell to the ground, the knife knocked from her hand.

"I am not useless," Reid gritted out as she twisted, putting a leg on Anna's body and pinning her in place. "I am *not* worthless."

Anna reached forward, clawing at Reid.

Reid grabbed Anna's arm, wrenching it. "What's truly useless is a mother who abandons her daughters." Her voice cracked with pain and fury as she spat the words.

Screams rang out. Several people approached, looming over

them. Reid recognized several of the faces—a combination of Ackley's Knights and Dexter's mercenaries.

Two of the Knights reached for Anna. Not sure what to do, Reid released her.

"What are you doing?" Anna demanded. "Let go."

"You are hereby stripped of your title," the one Knight said, restraining her.

"You're taking my title? I gave you your title!" She ducked, then twisted, breaking the Knights' hold on her. She darted toward Reid, her eyes wild.

One of the Knights tossed a sword at Reid. She deftly caught it, barely having enough time to bring the sword up and ram it into her mother's stomach.

"What have you…done?" Anna asked, her voice fading as blood oozed from the wound.

Reid didn't let go of the sword. "What needed to be done."

Anna dropped to her knees, gazing at Reid with a mixture of anger, hurt, and love.

The life faded from her mother's eyes.

Refusing to feel anything for the mother she never knew, Reid stepped back from the body. Wiping her brow, she observed the scene before her. Dexter and Gordon were kneeling on the ground beside someone. Reid ran over. Sprawled between them, Ackley sucked in short, raspy breaths. "What happened?" Panic and fear rose within her, making it hard to focus.

"When Anna tried to kill Dexter, Ackley stepped in front of him," Gordon explained. "Anna struck Ackley instead."

"Has a healer been sent for?" Reid demanded.

"Yes."

Dropping to her knees, Reid reached forward, clutching

Ackley's hand. He couldn't die. Especially not for doing something so selfless and brave.

He tilted his head. "I'm sorry I didn't stop Anna for you," he wheezed.

"Everything will be fine." Reid pushed his hair off his brow. "You should have used your sword to deflect the blow, not your body."

The corners of his lips pulled up ever so slightly. "Couldn't let Dexter die. Besides, I used my sword on Harlow."

Harlan ran toward them, a bag in hand. When he reached Ackley, he knelt, pulling out various jars. "How deep?"

"He has leather armor on," Gordon replied, "so the knife didn't go too far in. The problem is the blade Anna used had poison on it."

"That's what I feared. Let me see it."

Dexter stood, then pulled Reid away. "Let Harlan work."

She nodded, unable to believe everything that had happened. "How's Owen?"

"He was knocked unconscious. I think he's going to be okay, though." He held Reid at arm's length, examining her from head to toe. "Are you injured? Did Anna cut you with her knife at all?"

It felt as if a boulder had struck her stomach, and her head throbbed with pain. However, she didn't have any nicks from Anna's knife. "I'm fine." Knights and mercenaries ran about, making Reid dizzy. "I'm glad you showed up in time." If he hadn't, the outcome might have been quite different.

"Ackley had a feeling something like this would happen, so we've been monitoring the situation. When I saw you dressed as a man in a Melenia soldier's uniform, I knew it was time to act. We followed you, watching from the shadows. Ackley said there had to be one Knight he wasn't aware of. When Harlow showed up, we realized it had to be her. When she started to drug the camp, we had confirmation. I can't believe she almost killed me."

"Harlow's a Knight?"

"Apparently Anna recruited her years ago. They've been working together for quite some time." Dexter wrapped his arms around Reid, pulling her closer. "I don't know what I would have done if something had happened to you tonight. It was hard to sit back and wait until just the right time to attack."

Thankfully, nothing had happened. To her, anyway.

"Are you all right?" he asked.

"Yes. Just sore. And tired."

"I'm referring to you having to kill your mother."

"Oh." Reid hadn't had time to fully process everything. "I don't know. But I do know you're here if I need anything."

"Always."

"Where's Gytha?" Reid asked, scanning the area.

"She's one of the soldiers who received the sleep tonic."

"She'll wake up from it, won't she?" Harlan had managed to wake up all her father's soldiers before. Surely, he could do it again.

"Reid," Harlan called.

She ran over to where he sat next to Ackley. "Is he all right?" Ackley's eyes were closed, but his chest moved up and down. His tunic and leather armor had been removed and his undershirt torn open, revealing the wound near his ribs.

"I've treated the wound and stitched it together. His breathing is getting stronger. I think he'll be all right."

Relief filled her.

"I need you to stay with him to monitor his progress. If he's not awake and coherent within the hour, come and get me."

"Where are you going?"

He glanced around. "I have hundreds of soldiers to rouse."

She nodded. "Gordon, help me get Ackley inside."

Gordon lifted his brother, carrying him inside the palace. He took him up to an empty bedchamber, carefully placing him on the bed. "I need to get back outside and help."

Reid nodded. "I won't leave Ackley's side until I know he's okay."

"Thank you." He left the room.

Sitting beside Ackley on the bed, she picked up his hand, stroking it. His eyes remained closed. He looked so different like this. Younger. Innocent. His chest continued to rise and fall, the only indication he still lived.

After fifteen minutes, his eyes fluttered open. "Am I dreaming?" he croaked out.

"Thank goodness you're awake. How do you feel?"

"Terrible." He winced. "But I guess pain is good. That means I'm alive." He squeezed her hand. "Is there any word on my mother and sister?"

"No, not yet." They wouldn't know if Seb foiled the assassination attempt for a couple of days. "I can't believe you stepped in front of that blade for Dexter."

"I didn't do it for him."

She rolled her eyes. "For your king then."

Adamantly, he shook his head. "I did it for you, Reid."

Her brows drew together in confusion. "What do you mean —for me?"

"I'm sorry." He averted his gaze. "I didn't mean to confess anything or make you uncomfortable."

She shook her head. "But you've never thought of me that way." They were like brother and sister, weren't they?

"I didn't realize I loved you until you were kidnapped. By

then, it was too late. You'd just married Dexter that day." He sighed. "That's why I volunteered to go to Melenia. I can't stay here and watch you with Dexter. It's too painful. Besides, I told Idina she should marry Owen. It's a smart match she'll benefit from. Now I can keep an eye on her, too. I'm sorry. I don't know what Harlan gave me. He had me drink some tonic that apparently makes me pour out my deepest secrets."

She squeezed his hand. "Your secrets are safe with me."

Someone knocked on the door. "Can I come in?" Gytha asked.

"Of course." Wiping the tears from her eyes, Reid stood.

"How's he doing?"

"He'll live."

"Do you mind if I sit with him?" Gytha asked.

"Not at all. I'll go help outside since I know Ackley is in good hands." Forcing a smile, Reid walked out of the bedchamber, not looking back. She didn't want to see the expression on Ackley's face.

Out in the hallway, she slid to the floor, burying her face in her hands. So much had happened tonight. She didn't know what to think or feel.

A wet nose nudged her arm, and she looked into Finn's excited eyes. He licked her face, making her laugh.

"One of these days, Reid," Colbert said as he strolled down the hallway toward her, "you'll need to take my advice."

"And what advice would that be?" she asked, wiping her eyes yet again.

"All of it." Colbert reached down, placing his hand on Reid's head. "I told you about Ackley a long time ago."

She didn't want to talk about it.

"Are you okay?"

She shrugged.

"Dex had all the dukes and duchesses locked in the great hall as a precautionary measure tonight. I was in there with them. Your father has been worried sick about you. I think you should go see him."

She nodded, then stood. The pair headed along the hallway, Finn running in circles around them.

CHAPTER TWENTY-ONE

R eid stood in front of the mirror, observing her dress. The ivory fabric hugged her chest and arms, flowing freely to the floor. When she turned, it swished like water. A simple necklace her father had given her accentuated the scooped neck.

"You look beautiful," Kamden said.

Reid turned to face her sisters. Ainsley, Bailey, Emerson, and Kamden, all together in Axian for Reid's public wedding and official coronation.

"I can't believe you're going to be the queen of Marsden in a couple of hours," Kamden said, sighing. "It's so romantic."

"I don't know about that," Reid replied.

"Only Kamden would think it romantic," Ainsley said. "Being the queen won't be an easy task. You're going to have your hands full with people wanting something from you. It will be hard to maintain your sense of self and make time for your family."

Reid rolled her eyes. Ainsley always had to be overly practical.

"Since no one else is bringing it up," Bailey said, "I will. Do you have any questions about what's expected of you on your wedding night?"

"She's already married," Kamden reminded her.

"But they've been in separate bedchambers," Emerson pointed out.

"Only to make this day more special," Reid explained. Originally, Nara had designed a suite where they'd each have a private room connected by a joined room. However, Reid and Dexter decided they no longer wanted that arrangement. A new suite had to be made—one containing a single bed for them to share. Their new suite hadn't been ready until today.

Seeming scandalized, Bailey's eyes went wide. "Do you mean you've already had *relations* with your husband?"

Kamden snorted. "Have you seen her husband? Of course she's shared his bed. She'd be stupid not to."

Ainsley stepped forward, putting her hands on Reid's shoulders. "Now that you've been with a man, is there anything you'd like to talk about?"

Shocked her sisters wanted to discuss something so personal, Reid shook her head.

Ainsley sighed. "Try not to look so horrified at the prospect of sharing something with us."

"I'm sorry," Reid muttered. "It's just…"

"We know," Emerson said. "You hate to talk about anything personal."

Kamden laughed. "Oh, Reid, we love you dearly. But you should try to lighten up. If you can't talk with us about these things, who are you going to talk to?"

Someone knocked on the door. "Come in," Reid called, glad this conversation was at an end.

Gytha entered. "Are you ready?" She wore her captain's uniform.

"I am."

"I've been sent to escort you all to the great hall where the ceremony will take place."

The five sisters followed Gytha from the suite to the first floor of the palace. They stopped outside the great hall where Duke Ellington waited.

"Look at my beautiful daughters." He smiled, taking them all in.

"Come," Gytha said. "The four of you are sitting in the first row." She led Reid's sisters into the hall.

Alone with her father, Reid said, "Thank you for raising me with love and compassion. Thank you for teaching me to not only read and write, but also to be a good person. Thank you for trusting me to be your heir. Most of all, I want to thank you for being my father."

"I'm so proud of the person you've become." His eyes filled with tears. "You'll make an excellent queen."

The doors opened wide, revealing a packed room. Reid took her father's arm, allowing him to escort her down the aisle. Walking tall and proud, she welcomed the responsibility about to be bestowed upon her. She smiled as she passed so many familiar faces. Joce, her lady's maid. Rick and Ava, the couple who aided Reid and Dexter when assassins ambushed them. All the dukes and duchesses, including Reid's grandparents. Lord Robert and Reid's second cousin, Victor. Seb, Markis, and Harlan. Her sisters, along with their families. Nara, Leigh, Colbert, and Ackley. Dana clutched Gordon's arm, her stomach showing she was indeed with child. Idina sat next to Owen. The pair had spent the past couple of weeks getting to know one another.

So many familiar faces, so many people Reid had come to know and care for, all there to support her and Dexter.

Duke Ellington stopped in front of Dexter, handing his daughter over to him. Reid slid her hand into Dexter's, a smile lighting her face. He wore a dashing uniform befitting of a commander and a king.

The binder started the ceremony with a speech about love, commitment, family, and duty. Then he moved on to their vows. Reid and Dexter faced one another, reaffirming their marriage vows. When the binder pronounced Reid and Dexter husband and wife—*again*—Dexter leaned down and gently but firmly kissed Reid's lips. His eyes twinkled, promising more later. Reid couldn't help but smile. It seemed as if she did that a lot lately.

"And now," the binder announced, "it is time to crown Marsden's new king and queen."

Cushions were placed on the floor for Dexter and Reid to kneel upon.

The binder briefly discussed the formation of Marsden hundreds of years ago. Then he proceeded to talk about how the founding families divided the land, each family ruling a county, with one family overseeing it all. He explained the importance of this balance of power, and the duty Dexter and Reid had to maintain it.

Crowns were placed on their heads. After, they each repeated the words the binder said, swearing to watch over their subjects, work in conjunction with the dukes, and to put Marsden's interests above their own.

"Please stand."

Dexter and Reid stood, joining hands.

"Face your subjects."

They turned toward those present in the great hall.

"I now present to you King Dexter Winston and Queen Reid Winston."

A thunderous applause erupted in the hall. Bells started tolling, indicating the end of the ceremonies.

Dexter led Reid down the aisle, past their family and friends, through the palace, and to the front doors. Hundreds of people had crammed together on the front lawn. When the couple exited the palace, the crowd started cheering.

Dexter and Reid raised their joined hands. Those present started chanting for their new monarchs. Leaning down, Dexter kissed Reid.

The happy couple went back inside for their reception. There was food to be eaten, toasts to be made, and dancing to be done. When Reid was too exhausted to remain on her feet, Dexter gladly swooped her into his arms, carrying her to their room.

The following day, Dexter and Reid went to their private sitting room to bid Owen, Idina, and Ackley farewell. The Melenia army had already left for the Axian port, where the ships docked to transport them and several hundred of Marsden's soldiers across the Wendan Ocean to Melenia. Earlier that morning, Gytha had requested permission to accompany Idina as her personal guard. Dexter had granted it. Reid suspected Gytha wanted to make sure Ackley had an ally in the foreign kingdom.

While Dexter went over last-minute details with Owen, Reid hugged Idina. "Are you sure you want to do this?" Reid asked.

"My answer is the same as the last twenty times you asked," Idina replied.

Reid released her. "I just want to make sure." She'd feel awful if Idina married Owen out of obligation and not desire.

"Don't worry," Idina said. "I'm sure. I've always wanted to travel and see the world. This will allow me to experience more than I ever could staying here."

"It's time to get going," Ackley announced.

"My men will remain in Melenia until the Russek army has withdrawn and you've regained control," Dexter said. "If there's anything else we can do to help, send word."

"I will," Owen replied. "Once I've reestablished control, the Russek king will pay for slaughtering my family."

Reid turned to Gytha. "I'm going to miss you." That was something she never would have thought possible the first time she'd met the warrior woman.

"And I will miss you, Queen Reid." Gytha chuckled. "That still doesn't sound right to me. You will always be Lady Reid to me."

"I hope to see you again."

"You're not getting rid of me forever," Gytha assured her. "Just for a little bit."

Sucking in a breath, Reid faced Ackley. "I was hoping you'd stay to head up the Knights." Now that Anna was dead, the organization needed a new leader.

"There's already someone in charge," he replied.

"Who?" It was probably one of the twelve Knights who'd worked with him as a unit in Gordon's army.

"I can't tell you," he said. "And don't even try to figure it out. The Knights must be independent of the monarchy."

While Reid agreed, she couldn't help but be curious.

"Now that you're married," he reminded her, "you're no

longer a Knight. So you are not privy to that information." He nudged her with his shoulder. "Stop trying to figure it out."

Dexter chuckled. "It's going to drive her mad not knowing."

"I know." Ackley smiled, though it seemed tinged with sadness. "And that makes it all the sweeter."

Dexter wrapped his arm around Reid, and they watched their friends exit the room.

"I'm going to miss them," Reid said.

"So am I."

Kamden entered. "Father is ready to leave."

The duke had chosen to return to Ellington with his four daughters and their families today.

"Why is everyone leaving all at once?" Reid complained.

Kamden chuckled. "Because you two need some time alone. The kingdom eagerly awaits a new heir."

Reid's face flushed with embarrassment. "I'll see you to the stables," she mumbled, wanting to change the topic of conversation. "I hope you'll come back to visit me."

"Of course. Especially now I know I have grandparents here in Axian."

At the stables, there was a flurry of activity as Duke Ellington prepared to depart. Reid bid each of her sisters farewell, begging them to visit when they had a chance.

Duke Ellington wrapped Reid in a hug. "I'm going to miss you."

"I'm going to miss you, too." She removed the ring her father had given her all those months ago. "Now that I'm queen, I can't be your heir as well. Make sure you give this to one of my sisters."

He took the ring, sliding it back on his finger. "I will." After kissing her, he mounted his horse.

"Don't worry about Father," Kamden said. "I'll keep an eye on him."

Kamden took the reins to her horse, about to mount. Reid reached out, grabbing her sister's forearm. Kamden hissed.

"Are you okay?" Reid asked.

"I'm fine," Kamden said. "I just have a small cut on my arm. Nothing to concern yourself with." She mounted. "I'll write to you once we're home!" She steered her horse out of the stables, Duke Ellington following. The rest of Reid's family was situated in horse-drawn carriages. The carriages lurched forward, following the duke.

"What's the matter?" Dexter asked.

Reid touched her forearm—the location of her Knight's tattoo. Her eyes widened.

"Do I even want to know?"

She shook her head.

Markis and Colbert strolled into the stables, Finn with them. "We're headed over to the military compound," Markis said. "Do you two want to join us for a friendly sparring match?"

"As fun as that sounds," Dexter replied, "you two go on without us. Reid and I are going to take the rest of the day off."

Colbert snorted before shaking his head and exiting the stables.

"What are we going to do for the rest of the day?" Reid asked, dozens of possibilities coming to mind.

Dexter took her hand, pulling her from the stables and into the palace. "I have something to show you."

She had no idea what it could be.

He stopped before a door. "Ready?"

"For what?"

"We're going to play a game."

"A game?"

"Yes."

"I'm very competitive."

"I know." He smirked. "And I am demanding a rematch." He opened the door, revealing a pub.

It looked exactly like the pub near her grandparents' manor. It even had the same dartboard hanging on the wall.

"Shall we?" Dexter sat at one of the tables.

Reid took a seat across from him. Two mugs had been placed on the table, along with a handful of coins. She burst out laughing. "Once wasn't enough?" Picking up a coin, she positioned it under her finger and flicked it, hitting Dexter's forehead.

"With you, once is never enough." He winked.

THE END

ABOUT THE AUTHOR

Jennifer Anne Davis graduated from the University of San Diego with a degree in English and a teaching credential. She is currently a full-time writer and mother of three kids. She is happily married to her high school sweetheart and lives in the San Diego area.

Jennifer is the recipient of the San Diego Book Awards Best Published Young Adult Novel (2013), winner of the Kindle Book Awards (2018), a finalist in the USA Best Book Awards (2014), and a finalist in the Next Generation Indie Book Awards (2014).

Visit Jennifer at:
www.JenniferAnneDavis.com

facebook.com/AuthorJenniferAnneDavis

twitter.com/authorjennifer

instagram.com/authorjennifer

bookbub.com/authors/jennifer-anne-davis

goodreads.com/jenniferannedavis

pinterest.com/authorjennifer